SNAKEHEAD

ANN HALAM

Orion
Children's Books

Many thanks to Dana Facaros, whose excellent guide book to the Greek Islands has been a good companion on all my trips to the Cyclades, for allowing me to use the quotations from a classic hymn to Charon, as my 'Dark Water' song (page 42). And to Gilly and Robin Cameron-Cooper, who rented us their beautiful house on Naxos; my writing retreat for the summer of 2005.

First published in Great Britain in 2007
by Orion Children's Books
a division of the Orion Publishing Group Ltd
Orion House
5 Upper St Martin's Lane
London WC2H 9EA

A catalogue record for this book is
available from the British Library.

Typeset by Input Data Services Ltd,
Frome

Printed in Great Britain by
Clays Ltd, St Ives plc

ISBN 978 1 84255 269 8

The Orion Publishing Group's policy is to use papers that
are natural, renewable and recyclable products and made
from wood grown in sustainable forests. The logging and
manufacturing processes are expected to conform to the
environmental regulations of the country of origin.

www.orionbooks.co.uk

For Philip Sinclair-Jones

My mother and I emerged from the tumult of rich smells; the dark narrow alleys of Naxos market, into bright sunlight. We saw the crowd of refugees and recoiled in horror. Just for a moment both of us were convinced that half the population of Serifos had arrived, destitute, while we were trading (and spying a little, on the side). We'd only been away four days, but war had broken out. These were the survivors, which meant that everyone we loved was dead or enslaved, it was all over—

A second look reassured us. The people clogging up the busy waterfront had come a long way; they didn't even look like islanders. We grinned at each other ruefully, sharing the shock and the guilty relief. Oh, good, not us this time. Some other poor victims of hateful injustice, divine displeasure or a pirate raid.

Moumi and I had been making this trip together, twice a

shipping season, since I was a little boy. I had loved the whole thing, in those days. The market stalls where I got spoiled rotten. The quiet times when I would sit under a tree or by a fountain, and think; while Moumi talked to merchants, and other, shifty-looking people. Everything was different now that I was almost a man. I understood what was going on at home, and that knowledge had opened my eyes to the state my whole world was in.

'The trouble is,' said Moumi, 'too many refugees have been dumped on the Naxians, and it's mostly the worst off. The ones who have nothing: no relatives who will take them in, no trades. Oh, I hope the town doesn't turn the soldiers on them.'

Naxos isn't the richest of the islands we call the 'Turning Islands'; which is 'Kyklades' in Greek. It isn't the one with most sea-route connections, either, that's Paros; but it's the biggest. Penniless refugees tended to end up here as a last resort, on the grounds there was always room for a few more.

We were blocking the alley. We led the mules along the colonnade and stopped by a drinking fountain to regroup. We had laden animals: one of them – dear Brainy – liable to panic in a noisy crowd. We shifted Music to the back and Brainy to the middle place (which he usually didn't like), beside a group of men who were muttering about Trojans and Achaeans.

Troy ruled the far-distant east end of the Middle Sea. The Achaeans had taken over on the Greek Mainland, which lay to the north of us; a little too close for comfort. These two Great Powers (or bully gangs, depending on your point of view) were in a continual state of undeclared war, always picking on each others' so-called allies. The men thought one or other of them was responsible for the new influx, but they couldn't decide which. I asked a Naxian matriarch, who was standing there frowning darkly at the scene; accompanied by servant boys and a heavy hand-cart full of oil jars.

'Excuse me, ma'am. Do *you* know who they are?'

The lady looked us over, noting our colouring: Moumi's hair, coming out from under her scarf in ringlets of pure gold. Her eyes narrowed suspiciously, between the lines of Egyptian-style kohl. 'You're Achaeans, aren't you?'

'Not any more,' said my mother, without taking offence. 'We were invited to leave, by the king of our former country, shortly after my son was born. We were castaways ourselves once, that's why we feel sympathy for the refugees' plight.'

My mother looks like a teenager, strangers often take her for my sister. But when she feels like it she can take on the hauteur of an Argolide princess; because that's what she used to be. Also, we had three fine-looking mules in tow: which made us respectable even if we weren't Naxians. The lady changed her tone. 'They're not from the Turning Islands, madam. No one can understand the language they speak. The sailors say they're from the south, Libya or somewhere like that. Apparently there's been a quake and tidal wave, it wiped out a whole coast.'

A shiver went through me. A big quake is a fearful portent – but it wasn't fear I felt, not exactly fear. 'Was there a Supernatural involved?' I blurted. 'Who was it?'

The woman took a second look, her eyes widened and I suspected she'd recognised us. Our story was old news, but it had been spread all over the place by tale-tellers, and people tend to remember gossip about the god-touched. We still got that spooked reaction occasionally. I didn't like it, but sometimes – I have to admit – it was my own fault. At moments of stress I tend to forget that normal people don't talk about the Achaean Divinities as if they're disreputable family connections—

'It's none of my business,' the Naxian lady muttered, fearful and wary. 'Excuse me, my lady, er, young sir. I must get to the

3

dock.' She hustled her boys and her cart away.

'Don't *do* that, Perseus,' said my mother.

(... whose name was Danae, of the shower of gold: the famous imprisoned princess who had once been visited by the chief of the Achaean Gods, my father.)

'Sorry. I didn't think.'

I saw that the nymph of the fountain, barely visible in the sunlight, was watching me. I wondered what that fragile creature made of our tragedies and disasters, and all the human bustle that had grown up around her timeless little world—

Meanwhile my mortal mother, who could not see the spirit of the water, had forged off on her own with the mules, into the churning crowd. I hurried to catch up.

The lady with the cart of oil was heading for the Paros jetty, where the regular ferry was already in dock. Our ship, the mighty Blue Star *Afroditi*, was still far out on the dark sea. Port Authority tugs could be seen guiding her in, their smart oars flashing in the sunlight.

The Naxos Militia were in amongst the crowd, trying to get the refugees to move on. They had a right, I suppose, but the refugees had nowhere to go. Some of them had set up little camps, oblivious of people trying to get by: as if they thought they could settle down and live on the waterfront. It was a mess. Scuffles were breaking out. Armoured men were grappling with unarmed men and women, pathetic belongings were flying about, children were screaming.

The Holy Sisters had arrived, I could see their grey robes moving towards the trouble: but how much good could they do? The militia disgusted me, they made me think of the so-called king of Serifos and his brutal followers. Yet I could understand their frustration, and I had no answers. Me, I just wanted to fling everything I possessed at the miserable folk, and run away—

I got up front and grabbed Dolly's bridle. Moumi dropped

4

back to keep the rearguard, by Music's glossy dark rump. Brainy pressed close to Dolly, our sensible old grey, his ears back and his big teeth bared. We reached the gates of the splendid harbour mole. We were allowed to pass through, and got waved over to the mule line. Everything was suddenly quiet and ordered again: but I was ready to spit, between fury and shame at my own helplessness.

Moumi started unloading. I began to help, not sure why she was doing this. Bundles of vegetables, wax-sealed jars of honey and kitron liqueur, sacks of pulses, speciality oils and spices—

'Coin would be better,' she said. 'But we haven't enough.'

We tried to avoid taking coin for our trade-goods. With all due respect, if you ask for an assay on the spot it can cause offence. And even if the coin is pure, and weighs what it's supposed to weigh, the metals market changes so fast. You can never be sure what silver or copper is going to be worth, a shipping season down the line. If we were paid in money we spent it, at once, on the kind of fancy sundries a taverna can always use: napkins, scented soap, exotic produce.

'Better for what?'

'I'm going to give half a mule-load to the Holy Sisters,' said Moumi, refastening Brainy's pack strap with a brisk tug. 'They can trade it for food, shelter, whatever those people need. I've been running over the figures in my head. We can afford it.'

That's one of the reasons why I love my mother. She never puts on airs about it, like some smug charitable ladies: but she makes up her mind fast, and she does the right thing while I'm floundering. 'What'll Dicty say?'

Moumi grinned at me. We both knew that the boss wouldn't say a thing, except to wonder if she should have given more. 'Generosity is good advertising,' she quoted.

'It impresses people,' I agreed, also quoting the boss. 'An

open hand makes you look successful, and that's always good for business.'

'I'll get a receipt. The nuns will tell the refugees who we are, and where we live. They'll know where to come if they can ever pay us back.'

We sorted out half a load of easily tradeable goods, and Moumi set off. She took Dolly, who could be trusted. Brainy looked after them in disbelief, and looked at me with a horrified expression in his big eyes, like *we're never going to see them again!* He's a scaredy cat, poor Brainy. I never knew a brighter mule, but he has too much imagination.

So there I was alone on the dock with the mules, two laden pack-saddles and a half-load that would be Dolly's when she came back. Music let out two or three of his cracking great honks, (it's not for nothing he's called Music), tipped up his nearside back hoof and drifted off into a trance on three legs. Brainy calmed down and relaxed, with his chin on Music's backside. I had some preserved figs in my wallet, and a couple of olive-bread rolls. I propped myself against a pack-saddle, chewing, and checked out the action.

Like her sister ship the *Dimitra*, the ship that had brought us to Naxos, *Afroditi* plied the whole western line. She was coming back from Fira now – the island which had once been the queen of the Kyklades, a fabulous city-state, but was now a ruined stump of land where nobody could live. She'd touched at Milos, the obsidian island, where the cutting-edge black glass comes from. She'd be going all the way to the Mainland after she dropped us at Serifos. She had plenty of custom: islanders and foreigners, couriers and merchants; maybe from as far away as Kriti or Eygpt.

The drivers and foot-passengers were in the covered arcade. The sun was going down behind Great Mother's sanctuary isle across the harbour channel, but it was still hot enough to bother people. The Port Authority police, in their spruce white uniforms, were watching the tugs or else had taken shelter in the big open customs shed. Only muleboys and teamsters' lads were hanging around the vehicle lines. Among them I could see a gang I didn't care to meet, and I had a feeling they were talking about me.

I decided to go for a stroll. There was a girl walking on her own along the edge of the dock. She'd caught my eye, so I headed in that direction. She was tall and slim, and had a distinguished look. I thought she might be a Phoenician, for the highly intellectual reason that she was wearing a red dress. The word for Phoenician in our language means 'the Red People'. No one really knows why. It's not as if they're *red*, as if they'd been painted; they're more a baked brick-colour. But this girl's skin was dark, a clear, vivid darkness like polished obsidian.

She didn't notice me, so I kept on looking. She had very good hair. It fell down her back in closely curling black ringlets, not tied or braided but held off her face with combs. Under her red dress she was wearing trousers gathered at the ankle, a style we call 'Skythian', though nobody I know has ever *seen* a Skythian. The dress was fastened on both shoulders; which I liked. The girls on our island leave one shoulder and breast bare, unless they're doing heavy work. They think this is stylish, to me it looks half-cooked. The two brooches gave her a nice cleavage. She stopped and stared into the clear water of the harbour, pushing a pair of yellow bracelets up and down her arms; lost in thought.

I stopped at a polite distance, just close enough for conversation. 'There's supposed to be big octopus in there, they come out hunting about now; d'you see any?'

'No.'

'Are you waiting for the *Afroditi*?'

'Yes.'

'Are you going far? Is the rest of your party in the arcade?'

She looked up, at last. She looked at me very directly, with sombre eyes: letting me know she had too much on her mind to care about my lame chat-up lines.

'I'm travelling alone. Thank you.'

I was startled. Every shipping season well-off young people travelled for fun around the Middle Sea, looking for adventure: girls as well as boys. I envied them, and knew that could never be me. But she didn't look like one of those carefree kids, and who travels *alone*? It isn't healthy these days, no matter who you are.

The next thing she said surprised me even more.

'I've been watching you. The lady you were with: I saw her taking a mule-load to the Holy Sisters. What was that for?'

'It's for the refugees,' I said. 'The victims of the Libyan earthquake.'

'That's what I thought.' Her eyes were black and very sad. Was she travelling to a funeral, maybe? 'It was good of you and the lady, is she your sister?'

'She's my mother. We're in the taverna business, we were over here picking up supplies.' I was embarrassed, I didn't want us to sound like do-gooders. 'Generosity is great advertising, an open hand makes you look successful.'

Not a smile. I wanted to say I *was not* trying to pick her up ... Don't be stupid, I told myself. Back off, make your retreat. But while my attention had been on this beautiful girl, the layabouts I didn't want to meet had followed me.

'Hey, Perseus. Hey, Big Boy!'

The chief miscreant was right there, strutting, fists in his belt. The rest of them, brainless muleboys and shiftless ox-cart juniors, were bunched behind him.

'Tell your pretty new girlfriend, let's hear it. Is the yeller-haired "lady" your mother, or your sister—' He smacked his lips. 'Or *what*—?'

8

It is my fate to be unusually big and strong for my age – well, for any age, to be honest. I was hardly shaving, but I looked like a challenge to the muscle-worshipping idiots of this world. This one was a prize specimen. I'd met him before, but managed to get away without having to thump him. He wasn't a Serifiote, or he'd have known better. He was from Paros. Leather straps round his biceps, his bullet head shaved nearly to the skin, Trojan style, a sick, scared and greedy look on his pasty face … He was too old for his company, nothing like my equal, and just *dying* to take on the god-touched.

'Blah, blah,' I said, 'Yackity-yack. Go ahead and talk, it doesn't bother me.'

Then he said something else about Moumi, involving our so-called king, that I could not ignore as childish filth. The rest of them sniggered. I glanced around, to make sure the stranger had made herself scarce. She was still there, her black eyes snapping.

'I'll hold your tunic,' she said. 'Take it off.'

She was right, it was a good tunic and it would get wrecked. So I stripped, and went for the foul-mouthed toad. All the fury and shame in me, over those poor people on the waterfront, came boiling to my fists. I used it coldly. A couple of his friends decided to pitch in; which was *their* mistake. They talk about me, but they never learn.

The hangers-on picked the losers up and hauled them away. I dressed again and sat on a bollard, mopping the light sweat I'd worked up. 'Will they be back?' said the girl in the red dress. 'Shall I fetch the port police?'

'No, it's all right. I'm sorry you had to see that, but now at least they won't bother me on the ship. Guys I've knocked down tend to avoid me for a while.' I looked at her, mugging apology. 'I'm not proud of it—'

She laughed, really laughed, and it was like the sun coming

out. Her clear-cut face was suddenly *radiant*. 'Yes you are,' she said.

I fell in love, at that moment. Was it because she laughed at me, because she saw through me? I don't know. It was like lightning, and it had struck us both. I saw the same jolt in her eyes, it blazed in the air between us.

'What's your name?' I demanded, urgently, as if I had a right.

'Oh.' She stared, and shook her head. 'Just call me Kore.'

Now *Kore* is a Greek word, and it just means girl. It wouldn't have been so strange, but she was obviously a foreigner so I'd assumed she didn't know our language. We were *speaking* Greek. I saw her blush, and I felt like an oaf. She didn't want to know me, I was wrong about that lightning. It was time to quit. I tried to do it gracefully.

'All right, er, Girl. I'm Perseus, as you may have gathered. I'm from Serifos, from Dicty's taverna. If you're ever passing—'

There was a sudden frantic blowing of conches and shrilling of whistles. *Afroditi* was at the dock, the Port Authority police were marshalling the heavy vehicles. Huge ox cars, managed with daring and style, drawn by four and six pairs of massive, fiery beasts (you may think an ox is placid, but not these animals), came thundering down the mole and crashed up the great gangplank. It was a sight I loved, this mad, dangerous, and totally unneccessary race: but the noise was tremendous, the rush of their passing overwhelming. When I looked around, when I could speak, she was gone.

The sun had gone down, the stars began to glow. My mother was talking to friends. Something remarkable had happened. Our pal Taki the shipping magnate, owner of the Blue Star line, was on board. He'd taken pity on the most hopeless of the refugees, the ones the Naxians refused to keep. Taki was not known for his kind heart! People were saying that the Holy Sisters must have threatened him with divine vengeance: like all sailors he was terribly superstitious. I was on the upper deck, on my own. I listened to the boom-swish, boom-swish of the oars, the crack of canvas in the breeze. I felt the timbers beneath me taking life; from the ocean that gave the Goddess Afroditi herself birth. The girl who had changed *my* life for ever was on board this ship, but I was a tongue-tied fool: I didn't dare to look for her. A little wooden crate went bobbing by, far below on the choppy dark waves. I shuddered and backed away, stumbling—

'Not got your sealegs yet, Perseus?'

It was the girl in the red dress, holding a shawl around her head and shoulders against the cool of the evening. I noticed she wasn't wearing her bracelets any more.

'It's nothing. Just something I saw in the water.' I knew I was looking sick. I leaned on the side again, and she came to stand beside me, her elbow almost touching mine. Her nearness made my throat close up, my head started to spin.

She looked down. 'A wooden box?'

'Anything small, floating, makes me queasy if I'm not expecting it. I don't really remember why. It's because of something a long time ago.'

She looked at me, I looked at her. The feeling between us was so real I could hardly breathe.

'I've been talking to your mother.'

'Oh.'

'I need a job, I need somewhere to stay, in the islands. She thinks I can work at your taverna. I'm very grateful for the chance.'

'That's good,' I croaked.

'I was *S'bw'r* . . . ' she said, abruptly, in our language. Something that hardly sounded like a word, that I couldn't try to pronounce. 'It's my temple name. I can't use it. I can't use my

11

real Greek name either, at the moment. Will "Kore" do, on the islands?'

I felt incredibly privileged. I knew what a 'temple name' meant in Eygpt and the East, it was a special thing, rarely shared with anyone. I knew what she was trying to say: that she trusted me, that she felt the fire too, but she had her secrets ... As I had mine.

I nodded, choked by the fire in my blood. '*Kore* will be fine.'

And she left me.

My mother and I slept in our blankets under the stars, with the rest of the commercial travellers and deck passengers. The cabin class slept below in airless dens. The staterooms, usually reserved for the filthy rich, were given over to refugees. I didn't know where Kore was. By dawn we'd cleared Paros; where we wouldn't be stopping on this trip. I went to check the mules. Dolly and Music were good travellers, they were bored but comfortable. Brainy was convinced he was going to feed the fishes this time, but I managed to cheer him up.

When I came back Moumi was talking to Taki, and the *Afroditi*'s first officer. I joined them in time to hear that it was a wealthy cabin passenger who'd convinced him to get all charitable. 'As the young lady said, it's good to be known as generous,' explained Taki. 'It's excellent advertising.'

Nobody was talking about the earthquake itself: that would have been a very ill-omened topic. Moumi and I winked at each other, the first officer gave a cough he hid behind his hand. '*How* did she persuade you?' said my mother. 'Come on, fess up.'

Taki looked smug 'Well, gold did come into it. My personal generosity, *plus* a fair weight of well-worked gold, extremely pure.'

I remembered Kore's bracelets. They'd struck me as very

Egyptian, very flash, maybe gold leaf on wood. *Solid gold* on her arms? And looking for work in our taverna? What kind of mystery was this? Moumi shook her head at me, fractionally. I understood I should keep my mouth shut; but I didn't need to be told that.

'Oh, Taki,' sighed my mother. She glanced wryly at the Blue Star Marines, in full armour, who were sharing the foredeck with us. They were necessary. Every ship that put to sea these days had to be ready to meet pirates, or worse. 'Do you really need more treasure? You should have got her to pay you in water.'

The old people, the few who remembered, said our world would *never* recover from the Great Disaster. The winds were not the same, the wells had dried. That was the real reason why there was no more peace or plenty for the islands of the Middle Sea.

Taki laughed. Very rich people, I've noticed, are often great optimists. The fat of their wealth cushions them from rational fear. 'Don't be silly, Danae. How can we run out of water?' He spread his muscular arms, and his fine copper armlets glinted ruddy as flame in the sun. 'The sea is all around, the fountain of life and joy! The mighty sun draws up the salt water and it falls again as sweet rain, for ever and ever. The Great Disaster was a long time ago. Probably it wasn't so bad, and soon there'll be no one alive to moan about "all the changes", which will be a good thing! Life is what you make it! If there's really a drought, you landlubbers just have to figure out which Supernatural you've annoyed. Sacrifice a few pretty young people; that'll fix it.'

Nice. Human sacrifice was Taki's idea of an efficient, modern solution.

2

To Andromeda's dismay, the earthquake victims all chose to disembark at Serifos. She understood a few words of their language, she'd heard them talking about it. Either their hearts failed them, at the thought of a longer journey to nowhere; or they were afraid to stay on board when their benefactors were leaving the ship. They knew about the generous offering that had been made on Naxos waterfront. She hoped they didn't know how their fares had been paid; she'd asked for discretion. *Afroditi* was too big for the island's harbour.

Flat-bottomed lighters came out to collect passengers, animals and freight. She drew her shawl over her face as she descended into the crowded boat – although she did not think she could be recognised.

The waterfront was very small, quiet and strange to her eyes. Naxos had been familiar compared with this. She asked the lady with the golden hair where the refugees would go. She was angry with herself because she'd given all her treasure to the shipping magnate, which had surely been unnecessary; and now she had nothing more to give. She did not know how to haggle, she was so ignorant of real life.

'The sisters will look after them, for now. I'll get someone to take them to the Enclosure.' The noble lady saw that Andromeda didn't understand. 'The Great Mother's Enclosure is our temple,' she explained, in a friendly tone. 'Our only temple, we don't worship the Achaean Divinities in Seatown.'

'Sanctuary,' said Andromeda, carefully.

The lady smiled. 'You speak our language, Kore?'

'Yes. A little—'

The waterfront was lined with shady tamarisks and planes. Under the sweeping plumes of one great tamarisk a boy took the laden mules and led them off. Andromeda followed lady Danae and her tall son through a wicket gate. At the back of a terrace set with tables and chairs, more tables stood in a well-proportioned room; decorated with faded murals. There was a counter down one side and stone hearth in the centre, where a red fire glowed on this summer's day. Meat was roasting on spits turned by an urchin: who leapt up crying, 'Papa Dicty, Papa Dicty! Here they are!'

A small, spare man with a seamed face like a walnut came out of the recesses beyond the hearth, wiping his hands on a white linen apron. He had a fringe of grey hair around his bald head, but he did not move like an old man. He embraced the lady, calling her, *my daughter*. Perseus did not kneel, which shocked Andromeda a little – because in spite of the apron Papa Dicty was obviously the master. But he bowed very low; and then he too was embraced. She heard a murmur pass between the three of them: the lady and her son, and the older man ... *all well enough? All well enough* ... It sounded strangely, in this quiet haven, like the password of an armed camp.

'And who is this young lady?' asked Papa Dicty: looking at her with great attention, and speaking Greek. She knelt, pushing the shawl back, and faced him unflinching: though she felt as if he knew *exactly* who she was, and what she'd done.

'This is "Kore",' said the lady. 'We met in Naxos. She's travelling to see the world, but she would like to earn her keep. We need someone else for the dining room, since Nika left. I'm hoping she'll stay with us for the season.'

'Good,' said the master. 'Very good. On your feet, my dear. Come back into the kitchen, we'll do the interview there, I'm at work that can't be left.'

The kitchen was another *old* room, though the thatch and the beamed roof were new. Hams and bundles of herbs dangled, sunlight poured in from a yard where chickens scratched and another huge tamarisk stood. There were stovetops and ovens. The scrubbed counters were laden with fresh greens, pumpkins, cheeses, roots, vivid-coloured fruits.

In the midst of the room stood a marble-topped table. Papa Dicty returned to this and plunged his hands into a pillow of soft white dough, which he flung about as he spoke, in the most remarkable way. A girl with her hair tied in a linen cloth, who wore a yellow, one-shouldered tunic with great smudges of flour all over it, was pushing clouts of the same dough into a metal device.

'We're making wheat ribbons,' said the master. 'One of our specialities, and my own invention. Only our hard grain, for which Serifos is famous, will do. The flour must be milled extra fine, then we add eggs and oil. The proportions are secret, of course. Anthe, please keep turning steadily! This is a *kitchen,* not a theatre show.'

'All right, all right,' said the girl with the device, frankly staring at Andromeda.

She was afraid that the questions must start now, and how could she lie to decent people? She had not prepared herself for this, she had no idea what story to tell them. But instead they started talking, in a mixture of Greek and the island language, about the offering lady Danae had made to the Holy Sisters of Naxos.

The master approved. 'You have a receipt?'

'Of course,' said the lady, and showed him a tablet. 'Sealed and dated, by the Holy Mother herself. The Africans will all know our name.'

'Well that's nice,' said Anthe, rolling her eyes. 'You could hang it up in the dining room.'

Andromeda was amazed at the girl's insolence, yet there was something attractive about her. She was small and stocky, with strong eyebrows and a wide mouth. She kept on turning the handle as she spoke, without looking at the device, which was spilling sheaves of slim, dough-ribbons into a metal hopper.

'We could use something humorous to lighten up those murky old wall-pictures.'

'Anthe, I've told you a hundred times, I *will not* have my establishment cluttered with stuffed puffer fish, smoked mermaids, dirty old net weights, sea urchin shells, rude pictures, and worthless foreign money—'

'Oh, excuse me! Of course, the valuable receipt must be buried in Great Mother's Enclosure. Maybe we can use it to ransom ourselves, next time pirates come—'

Andromeda stared at the painted walls. She saw the dim shapes of court ladies in tiered gowns, bull-dancing maidens; a pleasure-boat parade, lifelike flights of swallows, a frieze of crocuses: all mouldering softly, patches of bare plaster showing where the paint had fallen away. They must date from before the Disaster. Was this once a palace? she wondered. Was life here once as stern and formal as at home? A side of meat lay wrapped in muslin on a cold slab, the scent of pungent cooking herbs filled the air. A red hen trotted in from the yard: gave a squawk and ran out.

'Well now, can you wait at table, my dear? Have you been trained at home?'

She started. Papa Dicty had divided his dough into smooth batons, ready for that ribbon-making device. His penetrating gaze was fixed on her again.

'No, but I can learn. And I have been trained in other domestic arts. I can clean, sweep, dye cloth, spin and dye yarn, do laundry.'

'That's the spirit. Any special skills?'

'I weave, a little.'

The master looked thoughtful. 'You can't sing, by any chance?'

'N-no.'

'Play a musical instrument? Regular music gives a place ambience.'

Anthe snorted. Her elbow jogged a bowl, which went crashing to the spotless stone-flagged floor, spilling a trickle of gooey yellow. '*Anthe!* Pay attention!' Papa Dicty swooped on the broken pot, and smacked the girl gently on the head with it. 'Don't you know, every single time you break a pot, I have to buy a new one. The potter has to make a new one, and we add between us to this island's mountainous, appalling burden of shattered crocks? We are drowning our Mother in rubbish! She will bite back, you know! There'll be another Great Disaster, here on Serifos, and you'll be the entire cause!'

'It's *clay*!' protested Anthe. 'It'll just melt into the earth!'

'Oh, certainly. In a few thousand years, for sure, maybe, when your bones and mine are dust. And now see! Those ribbons are crooked!'

'And now I have egg on my headcloth, Sir! I didn't deserve that!'

'I'll show you to your room,' said Perseus. Andromeda realised that he had been watching her, and her cheeks grew hot. She looked for the lady: but lady Danae was talking to a handsome young man who'd come in from the dining room.

'Don't mind them,' said Perseus, as she followed him into the yard. 'The boss is training Anthe to be a cook, he says she's very talented. But he has to put egg in her hair sometimes, to keep her in order.' He led her up a flight of stone steps to a gallery lined with doors. 'Guest rooms,' he said. Another stair, wooden this time, took them to a flat roof, with an extra room standing in one corner like an upturned white box. He lifted the door-latch: she saw a small, clean and bare space. The walls were whitewashed, there was a bedframe, a window that looked towards terraced hills, shutters to keep out wind and rain; a niche for a lamp.

'This was Nika's,' he said. 'Our head waitress, she left to get married.'

Andromeda nodded. She was wondering about the refugees. What kind of shelter did they have? What about all the other people who had fled? It struck her, horribly, that she was going to be ashamed and guilty now, for ever.

'I'll bring you a mattress,' said Perseus. 'Bedlinen, a water pitcher, oh, and a lamp. Is there anything else I can do?'

She wanted to cry out, *I don't deserve this!* She set down her bundle and stared at this immeasurable gift. A room of her own, no attendants, no staring eyes, a place where she could be herself—

'It's not much, I know,' said the tall boy with the chestnut hair, a little stiffly. 'I'm only glad the cat hasn't left any fish-entrails up here, to add to the glory of the scene.'

Down in the yard someone was singing and crashing things

about. A woman's voice could be heard, loud and furious, she seemed to be berating a kitchenmaid.

Andromeda remembered that she was *Kore*, travelling to see the world. Ordinary hired-girls probably had rooms of their own all the time. She tried to recover. 'The master is your grandfather? He called the lady Danae, "daughter".'

'Not by birth. It's a long story. My mother was on her own, with a baby, in … in bad circumstances. Dicty took us in. We've been with him ever since.'

'I'm sorry. I apologise for touching on a painful subject.'

He smiled. 'You speak our language very beautifully. Don't be sorry, we've been very happy. Serifos is a good place, we have a happy life.'

'I'm sure I'll be happy here too.'

She was lying. They were *both* lying, as it happened, though Andromeda would not understand that until later. But they were brave lies, and brave lies, strangely enough, have a habit of becoming the truth.

The taverna had a busy night, and it started early. I took a quick bathe in the wellhouse and went straight to work, in my usual place at the front of the house – seating people, explaining specials, pointing out the delights of the regular dishes (depicted in full colour on the menu board above the bar). Anthe and the boss were in the kitchen, making their under-cooks fly. Palikari, our dashing cocktail waiter and my best friend, ran the bar and the waiting staff. Moumi was everywhere, making sure there were fresh towels and scented water to wash people's feet and hands, supervising the juniors, chatting easily with our customers; both the friends and those who were not our friends at all.

The tale-tellers had arrived in force, eager to get the latest from Naxos, and the big world beyond. They'd spotted the refugees on their way to the Enclosure: they wanted to know all about the 'Libyan earthquake'. The reports we gave them would be carried to every street corner in Seatown, and every village on the island. We were happy to provide this service, because it put us in charge of the news (though Pali sometimes muttered that information is gold, and we should make them pay). I hardly had time to think about my beautiful stranger, though I had to duck and dive to avoid gossiping about her. Anything's an event to tale-tellers. I told them they'd meet our stylish new waitress tomorrow, and they'd better not harrass her.

Very late, when the crowd thinned out, Moumi took over the front desk and I went out for a breath of air. It was early summer, the night was cool. Our fine, sheltered harbour was calm as a bowl of dark milk. Stars shimmered through the quiet ripples, a breeze whispered. Sailors sat on the decks of the boats at their moorings, playing dice by lamplight. Voices called to me, *Hey, Perseus, all's well?* and I called back, *All's well.* But all was not well. The lights of the High Place (the king's fortress never slept) glittered like wicked jewelled eyes, peering over the shoulder of the hill above Seatown.

I must have been about seven years old when I first found out that Papa Dicty was the king's older brother. I don't remember if someone told me. Maybe I just realised the truth, the way children do: suddenly *hearing* what they've often been told, *seeing* what's always been in front of them. But I remember how shocked and bewildered I felt. It wasn't as if Polydectes was a good king. For an older brother to step down and let the better man rule was just what a true prince ought to do. But Polydectes kidnapped little boys hardly older than me, and made them work in his metal mines. He forced bigger boys to be his soldiers, and never let them come home. The soldiers took anything the king wanted from the farms and villages, without giving anything in return . . .

I thought about it, by myself, then I asked the boss what

was going on. Maybe he had *thought* Polydectes would be a better king, but it had turned out to be a mistake? So why didn't he take the kingship back, by force if he had to? I would fight for you! I said. Everyone loves you, except the king's bad men. We would *all* fight for you, and then everything would be all right!

The boss said nothing. He took me down to the seashore, and built a little Serifos of sand right by the rising tide. He took his time, marking the harbours and the villages with shells, and building the hills in the middle. Beside it he laid a stem of dry grass, and a much bigger stick. 'Now, Perseus,' he said. 'In our islands, women have always ruled in everything except war. Do you know why that is?'

'Because the things women do, cooking and farming and buying and selling, dancing and singing, and making things, are what people do all the time? So they know best? And war is rare, but men are naturally good at it, so they should be in charge?'

This wasn't purely my own reasoning, I was only a kid. But it made sense to me.

He nodded. 'That's the way we have always seen it. But times have changed, and the rule of women is passing away. Now, watch this.' He took the stem of grass, and used the end of it to make gentle strokes across his model of Serifos. 'Did I do much damage?'

I shook my head. I didn't see what he was getting at.

'When women ruled, and war was a *small* part of life, it was safe to settle disputes by force of arms. But now war is a big part of life, throughout the Middle Sea.'

'I know,' I said, proud of myself. 'The Achaeans and the Trojans!'

'And others,' said Dicty, as if talking to himself. 'Smaller fry, but no less dangerous. It's the disease of our times.' Then he gave me the grass stem, took up the stick and drew deep jagged grooves through the island made of sand. At once the sea came swooping in along the wounds he had carved. Swiftly, the grooves became chasms, the island started to fall apart—

'I stepped down from the kingship because my brother challenged me, Perseus. I knew he had friends on the Mainland, and they would come to his support. Then I would be beaten, and my supporters killed or enslaved; or I would have to seek for powerful allies of my own. Either way, *Serifos would be destroyed.* Do you understand that?'

'I think so.'

'My brother is not a good king, Perseus, but a civil war would be worse. Our matriarchs understand that, and so do I. That's why I will keep the truce I have agreed with my brother as long as I possibly, possibly can. I shall not leave, I shall look after my people, and my beloved Serifos: but I won't fight him.'

We squatted there on the beach, just a grandfather playing with a child, and watched the fragile island of sand disappear. Maybe I only understood his lesson the way a child understands, but I would never forget that swift, deadly onrush of darkness—

I picked a stem of dry grass and sat on the dock with my legs dangling, swishing my harmless weapon through the air. Papa Dicty was still keeping the truce. Polydectes was still up there in the High Place, lording it over us. But something had changed.

Our so-called king had been unpleasantly interested in my mother, ever since he'd found out that the castaway with the baby was actually a princess. Dicty had never regarded that threat as serious. The king treated his own people brutally, but he wouldn't risk taking Danae as his 'wife' against her will. That might not have gone down well with his Mainland friends. But now I was nearly a man and Papa Dicty's adopted grandson, and that was different. Polydectes had a right to see me as his direct rival for the throne.

The calm of the night was an illusion. Serifos was full of turmoil under the surface; and so was I. Things I didn't understand about myself (what does it mean to be *the son of a Supernatural*?) churned and swirled in my head, along with the threat of war, the portent of a great earthquake, and – above all – the beautiful stranger who called herself 'Girl'. I relived the dreadful embarrassment of showing that poky little room to the girl who wore solid gold, I wanted to die of shame because our kitchen yard smelled of fish. I was a rebellious seven year old again. I felt the whole world was against me, I wanted to yell out SHE'S MINE! YOU CAN'T TAKE HER! Who was I shouting at? I didn't know. I wanted to know what 'Kore' was thinking. What did she think of me? I wanted to touch her, I wanted to fight battles for her, be a hero for her: make her a queen. But she was cold and proud, she had let me know I was not wanted. I would NEVER, NEVER dare to let her know how I felt—

Back at Dicty's the yard geese gargled and muttered, as the kitchen gate opened: but they knew me. The restaurant was empty except for a couple of quietly incapable sailors, and a lingering party of swells from the High Place (we were the enemy, but we were also the best taverna on the island). Dicty and my mother were sitting at our family table with Anthe; and the local resident Egyptian, a friend of ours. They were showing him the Egyptian 'red carrots' that Moumi and I had brought back from Naxos.

Our local Egyptian was a strange man, who claimed he came from a country nobody had heard of, on the other side of an ocean that was not the River Ocean beyond the Pillars Of The West, and not the fabled Eastern Ocean either. He said he'd been shipwrecked on the southern tip of Africa on a giant raft, as a young boy. His companions had stayed down there, but he had made his way north, through many adventures and many strange nations, to the Middle Sea.

His personal name was unpronounceable. We called him Aten: because he was blatantly an Egyptian, in spite of the tall stories (which we enjoyed). He had that hairless, brown skin, same colour all year; and the slick black hair. Also, a clinching point, he never wore a cloak or a tunic, but always just a white linen kilt. Which everyone knows is the way Egyptians dress.

He was married to a Naxian woman, who'd moved here after some political trouble at home. They had a farm in the valley behind Seatown, and were famous as growers of the exotic yellow-fleshed tubers called *opotatos*: which Aten had brought (he claimed) all the way from the land where he was born. Opotatos are poisonous. The green part of the plant, even when carefully prepared, makes some people very sick. At Dicty's we served the roots soaked, sliced and fried, with salt and sharp wine, and the High Town swells loved it. They got a kick out of the risk – and the staggering price.

'I have no idea,' Aten was saying, as I joined them. 'I am *not* an Egyptian. I am Peruvian. They're a strange colour, so I expect the flavour is poor. Carrots are supposed to be greenish yellow, Dicty.'

'*Our* carrots are greenish yellow,' agreed Dicty, patiently. 'I just told you, these red fellows are from Egypt. When you meet a new foodstuff it's like welcoming a guest, you have to get acquainted with the thing's spirit, treat it as it wants to be treated. They're very sweet, perhaps they should only be used for desserts. Go on, try one.'

'Hm. That is actually *tasty*. What are the growing conditions—?'

At last the High Place party left. Palikari and Anthe turfed out the drunken sailors, and we stopped talking about vegetables.

25

Papa Dicty had told Anthe his kitchen was not a theatre show: but sometimes we were like actors, changing masks as the drama unfolded. Aten and his wife were our allies. As resident foreigners they had less to fear from the king, and Moni the Naxian was a woman who believed fiercely in the old ways, the way of life Papa Dicty was fighting to preserve. Aten was in town to consult with Papa Dicty about the state of affairs inland, in the villages; and to hear the news Moumi and I had picked up on Naxos. When we went across to the Big Island we met other Serifiotes, secretly: people who would not dare to talk to us at home ...

There wasn't much to report this time, only more of the bad tidings we knew already. The truce was wearing thin, Polydectes was plotting something. But there was an unexpected new factor. A mysterious and wealthy young lady, somehow connected with the earthquake victims: who was travelling under a false name, and clearly looking for a place to hide. Could we afford to give her our protection?

'She gave Taki gold. I wonder what else she has hidden in that bundle of hers,' mused Dicty. 'A queen's diadem?'

'But the refugees didn't show any sign of knowing her,' protested Anthe.

'None at all,' agreed my mother.

'So she can't be *their* queen. Maybe she's just noble and generous. She saw those earthquake victims, her heart opened and she couldn't help it. Gold might be common as clay where she comes from. Aten says there are places like that in Africa.'

'True,' admitted our Egyptian. 'But Anthe, she may be everything you say, and still have powerful enemies who may descend upon us. My lord, if you protect her, the king could use that against you—'

(By 'my lord' he meant Papa Dicty.)

'If she's of high enough rank,' put in my mother, reluctantly, 'her people might never have seen her face. How many

26

Achaean princesses run around in the street? But when she had to risk being discovered, or else abandon them, she didn't hesitate.'

'What about you, Perseus?' asked Palikari. 'The women are on Kore's side. You're being unusually quiet, what do *you* think?'

'Dunno,' I muttered, glowering at my best friend for no reason at all.

'Hm . . .' The boss was making up his mind. 'She's a young woman of few words, and proud deeds, and I watched her in my kitchen this afternoon. She's well-trained, she can hold her tongue.' Dicty passed a hand over his bald head, a habit of his when puzzled. 'I see the danger, Aten, and it should be discussed, but I won't call a Town Meeting. I'll take advice, quietly: see what our matriarchs think.'

We didn't hold Town Meetings often. People hadn't much heart for discussing minor problems, when the real problem was the king, and we'd all agreed there was nothing to be done about him . . . Silence fell. There was something about Kore that nobody wanted to bring up: not even the boss, who was never superstitious. Somewhere far away, on the coast of Africa, there had been a major earthquake. A fearful portent, an ominous sign of Supernatural meddling in human affairs . . . She had come to us like smoke blown from a distant fire. What could she tell us, if she dared?

The last lamp was guttering, we decided to spare the oil and go to bed.

Whatever she was hiding, our new waitress had told the truth about her skills. She didn't know a thing about cooking, serving food, or attending to guests. But she was a thorough housemaid, and a speedy learner. The only half-truth was when she'd said she could weave 'a little'. Her weaving was superb. She'd brought a frame loom dismantled in her pack, along with a finely carved shuttle, hanks of dyed yarn and some outlandish loom weights of carved stone (not solid gold!). Word quickly got about. Over the next few days, a procession of the finest weavers in Seatown came to visit the little room on the flat roof. Our matriarchs were impressed by the quality of her work, her knowledge of dyes and yarns; her daring use of colour. They also liked her respectful manners; and they liked her silence. 'The more a young woman thinks, the less she speaks,' said the great Balba (our chief weaver) to Papa Dicty. 'She seems to me a sensible girl. Let her stay.'

She tried not to show her interest in the refugees. But we noticed that when someone raised the subject in the taverna (and of course people were talking about them), our new waitress would drift over, trying to make it casual, and listen to the conversation. We made up errands for her so she could go out and explore; and check up on her people on the quiet. This trick – it was Anthe's idea – didn't work. Kore didn't say no, but she always found some reason why she couldn't go out just then.

We introduced her to our household gods, Mémé the cat and Brébé the ferret (that's 'gods' with a small 'g', in our language it means 'pets'); and she was approved. We introduced her to the poultry. Our yard geese grudgingly agreed not to yell blue murder at her, after a few days ... I showed her the forge and the little furnace yard, where Dicty worked on gadgets like his wheat-ribbon press. 'In my country,' she said, giving me a thoughtful look, 'metal-working is a craft reserved for princes' ... I didn't comment on that.

When we realised that our fugitive *would not* leave the house alone, Papa Dicty arranged things so that the four of us young people had time off together – and Pali and Anthe and I pretended this happened all the time, which it certainly did not!

We showed her the glories of Seatown; which was a short tour. The only place worth seeing was the Enclosure, and we knew she didn't want to go there. We took her up into the hills west of the town: so that she could see, across the ripening terraces of hard wheat, the forest-clothed 'mountains' (rather small mountains) of our island's heart. In hard winters we have snow and ice up there. We go and cut the ice and bury it in a deep cave, and bring it down in summer – so we can have iced desserts and fresh meat at Dicty's through the hottest weather. Just the way people did before the Disaster, when our taverna was a seaside mansion. Pali and I said we'd show her the cave one day. She said *thank you*, in her quiet way; but her eyes shone. (Anthe hated the idea of being underground!) We took her sea-bathing in our favourite cove, north of the harbour. She could swim; but she'd never been in the sea before. We took her to visit Aten and his wife.

Moni the Naxian was a skilled herbalist. She showed Kore the leaves and flowers of the opotato, and they were soon deep in conversation about the curious qualities of that rare plant. They went off for a study-walk around Moni's garden, while we stayed with Aten and played with the children. It was the same story as with the matriarchs of Seatown: Moni was impressed, and mystified.

'This girl is *extremely* learned,' she said. 'And so young. Who *can* she be?'

I'd been afraid 'Kore' wouldn't get on with Anthe and Palikari. She was so proud and reserved, I'd thought she'd look down on my friends. I was wrong about that. In a few days she was best mates with Anthe, our impulsive, sarcastic wildcat. She had Pali confiding in her as if she was his big sister, about the painful state of his heart. He had no prospects, nothing but his place at Dicty's. How could he convince Anthe to accept him as a serious marriage suitor? I'd see the two girls with their heads together. I'd see Kore listening to Pali's

29

troubles, while she helped him clean up behind the bar, and I was terribly jealous. But we didn't talk about our *real* troubles. Whatever she heard about the truce between Papa Dicty in Seatown and his brother in the High Place, she didn't hear it from us. And she didn't tell us her secrets, either.

The feeling that everything had come to a crisis slipped away from me. Yet the tension was still there: in her sombre eyes, in the burden she would not share. She was playing a part – trying to be this other girl, 'Kore', travelling to see the world, our new best friend. But you'd look around and she'd be gone. She'd be back in that poky little room: alone, silent, working at her loom.

I went up to the roof one night, with the feeble excuse that I was bringing her a better lamp. The door was half open, I could see her at work. Mémé was curled up on some hanks of green yarn, Seatown yarn: a gift from Balba. Everyone could get close to 'Kore' except me. I even envied the cat. I knocked on the wood. She looked round, and didn't say a word. At least she didn't say, *go away*. I propped myself on the doorjamb.

'You'll ruin your eyes.'

But it was impossible to 'make conversation' with this girl. She'd look you dead in the eye, and your pointless phrases crumbled.

'Am I using too much oil? I'm sorry, I forget myself. I'll stop.'

'Oh no!' Panicked by her nearness, I heard my voice come out as a strangled yelp. 'I, uh, brought you a better lamp ... Kore, don't you *ever* sleep?'

It was easier to call her *Kore* now that we weren't speaking Greek. A lot of islanders have Greek names, after all; including myself. They're fashionable.

'Of course I do.'

'I just wondered, because I hear your loom going, through the night.'

She counted threads with her shuttle. 'I'm sorry if I keep you awake. Sometimes I just don't get sleepy.'

'Nor me, sometimes. What are you working on, I can't make it out?'

'It'll make sense when it's done.' Then she turned and smiled, the same look in her eyes as when she'd laughed at me, on Naxos dock, in that moment when I'd *known* that she felt the same shock of fire as I did. 'At least, I hope it will.'

I said *goodnight*. I left her and lay awake with that smile in my arms, like a barbed treasure. How could I feel like this, whenever our eyes met, if she didn't feel it too? I love you but it can't happen, that's what she was telling me.

Adamant, absolute—

My mother, when she'd seen the way Kore behaved, said, *there's a girl who has been watched and kept indoors all her life.* But I felt that my girl (who could not ever be mine) was in a prison of her own making. She was behind bars even now: shackled by chains no one else could see.

3

Kore had been with us ten days, midsummer was upon us. It was the hottest part of the afternoon. I was renewing our whitewash, on the trees, along the coping of the terrace wall and around the flagstones, ready for the festival. The hearth burned low. Mémé the cat and Brébé the ferret were fast asleep on the bench beside it, curled together so you could hardly tell where orange-spotted tabby cat ended, and gingery-furred ferret began. The waterfront was dead quiet, except for the soughing of the summer wind; the taverna was empty. Kore and Anthe, nominally in charge, were sitting by the wall of the dining room in cool shadow, talking about art.

I could have hustled them into helping me, but the whitewashing job was a peaceful, mindless one. Popo the house-painter had been round, trying to persuade us that we wanted a few red shells or blue dolphins to add to our festive finery. We'd politely declined but he'd left his colours, saying

32

he'd be back later, to talk to the boss. Out of the corner of my eye I watched Anthe, who kept touching the pots of yellow, red and blue that Popo carried around with him in a bucket. She was fascinated, she couldn't leave them alone. I was interested to see what would happen.

'I don't like these old *pictures*,' said our wildcat. 'I know they're ancient, and precious. But if you're just going to copy what already exists in life, why bother? Art should be about making something new.'

'The court ladies aren't lifelike,' answered Kore, sleepily. 'They all have the same face. And whoever saw swallows flying in a double row, like that? It's the *patterns* that mattered to the painter, you can tell.'

'All right, but still, why imitate things?' Anthe's small, strong hand had lifted the brush out of the red paint pot, as if she couldn't help it. She looked at the wall beside her. Unluckily there was a bare patch, at a convenient height. 'When you're weaving, don't you often make patterns without pictures? Don't you think that your colours are *enough on their own*? The way the best meat should be served almost raw, and the best salad vegetables barely dressed?'

'But dyes are imitation colours, Anthe, and so is paint. It's not "redness" in that pot. It's ground-up Egyptian beetles. Oh, Anthe, *don't—*'

Too late.

'I know about the beetles,' said Anthe. 'Don't tell me about beetles.' She looked at the bright red splash she had made, and seemed to decide there was no use stopping now. A sweep of blue, a splotch of yellow, a gaudy orange swirl over the place where red and yellow had dripped into each other—

'You see what I mean? Honest colours, and nothing but!'

It had happened so fast. At least, so far, only a gap in one of the precious paintings was affected. I dumped my whitewash brush and came over, moving like a hunter. Anthe

33

was armed and dangerous, we had to get the yellow brush away from her, *carefully*, before worse happened—

I shifted the bucket of paint pots out of reach. 'But what is it meant to be, Anthe dear?' asked Kore, edging to grab the wildcat's wrist.

'Nothing! It's just *colour*.'

Palikari and Papa Dicty came hurrying in from the street.

'You have to come with us!' Pali was out of breath. 'Trouble! We need to move the refugees, right now— '

The boss looked at the daubs of paint on the wall, and then at Anthe, who was standing there red-handed (or yellow-handed). 'Have you changed your trade, child?'

'No—!' Anthe wailed, coming out of her mad fit. 'Oh, no! I've ruined my life! I don't know why I did that! Master! Forgive me!'

'If you haven't changed your trade, then get started in the kitchen. You're on your own. People still want to eat, even in hot weather. Send Koukla out to mind the front desk. Perseus, Kore, come with us: you're both needed at the Enclosure.'

They told us what had happened as we hurried through the streets. The boss had been making his usual rounds with Moumi, talking to people as they rested in the heat of the day: hearing grievances, picking up news. He'd been met by an informant of ours, who brought an ugly rumour. The king had decided that those ill-omened earthquake refugees had been camped in the Great Mother Enclosure for long enough.

'Your king would invade a sanctuary!' Kore cried.

'Oh yes,' said Pali grimly.

'I doubt if Polydectes would really commit such an affront,' said the boss, briskly. 'But our relations with the king are not good, Kore, and he could apply pressure. We should put temptation out of his way, right now.'

We'd reached the Enclosure, which stood at the north end

of the curving waterfront, at the foot of the High Place hill; inland from the jumble of Seatown's houses and alleys. It was an ancient holy place, not walled, just encircled by a fence. The buildings inside were wattle and daub, nothing permanent except for the bathing caves, and the sanctuary itself. The gates were open. Kore stopped, as if brought up short by an invisible barrier. I saw a look of *dread* in her eyes.

'I was hoping you would be able to help us, dear girl,' said Papa Dicty, watching her. 'If you know any words of their language, at all?'

She nodded, and swallowed her terror. 'I'll do what I can.'

Moumi was with Holy Mother and the sisters. There were twenty 'families' of refugees who had not yet been resettled, including an old man in the hospital who seemed to have no family or friends ... Holy Mother, who had no respect for anyone alive, was very annoyed with all of us, including the boss.

'I have no objection to sheltering them, Dicty,' she snapped. 'The victims of an earthquake are sacred. They may stay with us as long as need be, no matter what the king says. But first you send them here, then you tell me I have to make fresh plans for distressed foreigners, using nothing but sign language, in an afternoon. Not one of them speaks a word of Greek. I could have used a modicum of notice!'

The boss apologised humbly, but he'd made up his mind. The next hours passed in a blur. Kore helped the nuns to prepare the refugees. Moumi, Dicty and Holy Mother, who knew every household in Seatown, came up with ideas, and gave us directions. Palikari and I tramped the streets, and the nearby farms. Nobody turned us down, when we explained the need; except for the people on the Koutala path who had sickness in the house. I had a new respect for the decency of ordinary Serifiotes by the end of the day. But it was tough going. We were *beggars* – even if we were begging for others, not for ourselves – and as some wise person once said, there is no harder trade. Nineteen families, with their belongings and babes-in-arms, were moved to private households. The bedridden old man stayed. As Holy Mother said, with any luck he'd be safe home with Great Mother before the king could get down the hill.

Finally we went back to the taverna, to start the evening's work.

That night Kore didn't vanish when the last chores were done. Papa Dicty retired to his room, after congratulating us on a good job well done. The rest of us moved into the back yard, to collapse in coolness and privacy. Anthe was brooding, still scared that the boss was going to send her home in disgrace. Kore'd had a stunned, bewildered look all evening – barely concealed by a waitress's obligatory cheerful smile. She sat on the wellhouse bench, her hands knotted in her lap.

'I thought Serifos was safe!' she cried, suddenly; almost accusingly. 'I thought this was a peaceful haven! Why did you help the refugees, when you have such troubles of your own!'

'We have a king we don't love,' sighed Pali. He was lying flat out on a clean patch of paving, with his eyes closed. 'He keeps trying to pick a fight with the boss, who is his brother: a fight that would ruin us. But don't worry, our boss is cunning as a fox, he's always found a way out. So far . . .'

My friend opened his eyes, and looked at me. I knew what was on his mind.

But I looked away.

'It's true, we have our troubles,' said Moumi. 'Shall I tell you *my* story, Kore? Or perhaps you know it already?'

Kore shook her head. We'd finally seen her with the refugees today, and the mystery only deepened. She didn't know them, they didn't know her, yet they *frightened* her. She was so shaken now that she might tell us the truth at last, but a direct question would be no use, she'd just disappear off to her room.

36

I knew what Moumi was trying to do. Trade one painful story for another—

'I was a princess. I was Danae of Argos, it's a kingdom on the Mainland. My father had been told that his grandson, his rightful heir, would kill him. I was the only legitimate child; his only child born of a noble mother. When I was nine years old he locked me in a tower, and swore I would spend my life there. Never see the sky, never touch the earth. I was allowed one nurse to look after me. I cried a lot at first, but she told me I was lucky to be alive, and I had the sense to know it was true. My father was a hard man. So I learned to be happy in my prison. Unfortunately, tale-tellers spread it about that the princess in the tower was astoundingly beautiful and wise—'

'Absolutely true,' I put in.

Moumi laughed. 'Well, anyway. There was a night, which I remember vivdly, when I had a thrilling, frightening, golden dream, and that's all I've ever known of my son's father. I'm sure the Supernatural Person involved didn't mean any harm—'

No matter what they do to you, it's bad luck to criticise the Supernaturals.

'But of course I was in a lot of trouble. My nurse *knew* that no mortal man had been near me. I was like a child, I didn't understand. I thought it was lovely when she told me I was going to have a baby, because I would have somebody to play with. Well, Perseus was born, and my father found out. He had my nurse killed when she told him the truth. He didn't kill us, just in case she was right. He had us nailed into a wooden crate, and the crate was taken out to sea, and dumped in the ocean. I was about fourteen. Perseus was three months old.'

'Great Mother,' breathed Kore. She flashed a glance at me, and resumed staring at the ground. I knew she was thinking of that time on board the *Afroditi*, when she'd seen me flinch away from the sight of a wooden box bobbing on the sea.

'I *hate* my father,' The words burst out. I couldn't possibly remember, but the fear that baby had felt was part of me, right at the heart of me, and I hated it. 'My grandfather was a cowardly idiot, doesn't he know you *never* do yourself any good trying to fool an oracle? I don't care about him. But my so-called holy immortal father has no excuse. He knew exactly what he was doing to Moumi. I hate him!'

'Luckily *he* does not hate *you*,' said my mother, sharply. 'Not yet, at least. He has left us in peace, for which I thank him. Don't talk like that, Perseus.'

'Sorry.'

Moumi got to the point of the story. 'You see, Kore: Perseus and I were condemned to certain death, but we lived. The crate was found on the shore of this island by a fishing-boat owner called Dicty, who opened it up because he heard sounds from inside. My baby and I were alive. Papa Dicty nursed us back to health, we've been with him ever since. We have lived happily, we have lived well. *That's* why I helped the refugees, if you need a reason. I know that fate can be changed, good can come from evil. I know that there's always hope.'

There was a long silence. We were sure Kore was on the brink of speech. But she didn't say a word, just went on staring at the ground.

'Well, I *do* blame your grandfather, Perseus,' growled Anthe, tugging off her cook's headcloth, and giving her hair a fierce shake. 'Achaeans are all the same. They're convinced every woman born is a messenger from the Great All, and they're afraid of us seeing their wickedness. So they lock girls up like criminals, and invent reasons to kill them—'

Anthe had used the old word *Great All*, from before the Disaster, which people don't use any more. We only speak of the Great Mother. I saw Kore give a start, as if she'd suddenly heard someone speaking her own, lost language, that nobody on Serifos knew. Anthe didn't notice. My mother sighed, and stood up.

'Anthe, you are lowering the tone of the conversation. Achaeans are human too: I'm one, and so is Perseus. I'm going to bed. Don't be too late, children.'

She took the lamp, as a strong hint that we weren't to stay up. Mémé could be heard devouring fishheads by the midden, making very strange noises. Palikari hauled himself off the ground, went to sit by Anthe and rumpled her hair. '*Honest colours?*' he remarked. 'Ooh, what a mess. Were you drunk, or what?'

She shrugged him off. 'It's not funny. The boss might never forgive me.'

We were four young people, trapped in different ways but glad to be together, only hoping we could go on sharing our good life, troubled as it was. '*Nowhere's* safe,' said Anthe, at last. 'Not Serifos, not anywhere. The world could be so beautiful, but it's terrible instead, and cruel things happen all the time.'

I thought of this night often, when things had fallen apart.

Dicty wouldn't let Anthe wash her 'honest colours' off the wall. He said it was much better than a stuffed mermaid. She was crushed for a whole morning, and winced if she had to pass the place. But secretly we all liked the daub. It meant fun, friends; a little craziness. It reminded us that life was supposed to be sweet.

Two days later, at the full moon, the famous singer Mando came to Dicty's taverna. The midsummer festival lasted half a moon, and brought out singers, musicians and dancers all over the island. They didn't go to the High Place: midsummer was an old-fashioned, women's feast and not to the king's taste. But Papa Dicty always invited the greatest artists to perform in the restaurant, and he treated them like royalty.

Mando was a village woman from the north of Serifos. She was supposed to have been a beauty, but for all the mid-summers I remembered she'd been quite an old woman. She was short, squat and heavy, with massive shoulders, a furrowed brow, double chins and a distinct moustache. She was also grasping, quarrelsome, and didn't have a good word to say for any of her rivals – but none of that mattered. It was her art that was revered. She turned up at noon, wrapped in a thick dirty mantle, having walked from her last show at Koutala. She shook off the dust, dumped her bundle, took a bath, ate a huge meal and went to sleep in Dicty's own bed, as all our guest rooms were occupied. She slept until late the next day, took another bath; ordered a very hearty breakfast and stayed in her room.

By moonrise the waterfront terrace and the dining room were packed, and it was standing room only in the kitchen yard. To hear Mando sing at Papa Dicty's was one of the highlights of the year, people had come from miles around. I was at the door of the boss's room, waiting to escort her. When she appeared she was dressed in the same style as the faded court ladies on the wall: bands of red around her tiered skirts, a tight bodice straining round her thick waist. Her breasts and shoulders were bare, rouged and powdered. Her hair was dressed in long, glistening black ringlets (helped out by false extensions, I could see). Her facepaint was a white mask, with black lines around her eyes, and red lips. The grumpy old woman with the moustache had vanished, and it wasn't just the paint. Mando had the power over her appearence that all great performers have. When she was ready to sing she was still beautiful.

People cleared a path as I led her to the hearth: where there was a bright fire in spite of the heat, as tradition demanded.

She took her place. I joined Moumi, Papa Dicty, the matri-archs and their consorts at the high table – an honour I would have been glad to surrender.

Children were getting underfoot. Aten and Moni the Naxian were nearby, with their household. My dear friends were perched up on the bar counter, relatively cool and with a great view of the singer. There were festive lamps hanging in a row above the bar. I could see Kore's profile, and her slender hands clasped around her knees. She was wearing blue, a two-brooched dress with a border worked in silver, like starlight in the midnight sky.

Mando sang for two hours, mostly seated. Sometimes she'd get up and dance a few steps, with sweeping, ancient gestures. If it was a modern song that we all knew, she'd beckon to us, letting us know we were allowed to join in for the chorus—

> *Oh, the red rose madder, oh, the blue hyacinth,*
> *Oh the yellow powder stain of the lilies in my garden!*
> *But there's none so pure as the little white convulvulous,*
> *The little wild white convulvulous, who grows where she*
>   *shouldn't*
>
> *Who grows where she shouldn't!*
> *Who blows where she shouldn't!*
> *All* over our fields!

This is a very naughty song, if you take the words the way we islanders take them. Everyone was laughing, nudging and winking at each other (there'd been plenty of drinks earlier). I saw Kore laughing too, her burden swept away by the power of the music. I wanted to be beside her: but I couldn't leave my place. At last Mando gave us 'Dark Water', the funeral song. She sat down for this: leaning forward, her hands planted on her broad knees; and seeming to look through us, through the hearth's flame-shadows, into a vast, lonely distance.

Why are the mountains dark and why so woe-begone?
Is the wind at war there, or does the rainstorm scourge them?
It is not the wind at war there, it it not the rain that scourges
It is only Charon passing across them with the dead
He drives the youths before him, the old folk drags behind
And he bears the tender little ones in a line at his saddle
*   bow*

The audience was completely silent. Partly that was out of respect for the ritual song for the dead. Partly it was Mando's power over our emotions. Death will not be like that for me, I thought. Not me, because I'm immortal like my father.

I didn't care what being immortal meant, I never thought about it, and I didn't want to think about it now. But the sadness drew me in. I understood, as if for the first time, that Moumi, Dicty, *everyone I loved*, would cross over the dark water, and I would be left alone. I would call after them but they wouldn't know me. I would never see them again. Pain struck me, as real as a twisting knife.

I saw that Kore had slipped down from the bar and was standing behind it, head bent. She can't bear to listen, I thought, she has too many sad thoughts—

The singer let the last, long notes drain out of her and relaxed: reaching for a hefty tot of the finest Naxos Kitron liqueur. The whole room sighed together, tears were wiped, and they all shouted for 'Dark Water' over again. I couldn't understand it, once had been plenty for me. Mando smiled smugly: knocked back her Kitron, scratched herself under the arms, and then she carried us away, once more, into the heart-opening darkness of grief.

But *what was Kore doing?*

I watched as she finished covering one of Palikari's scraped-wood tally-boards, her hand gripping a stylus, and grabbed another: as if she was making out some huge, impossible account for an Achaean millionaire, and it was a speed test. Pali and Anthe were peering over her shoulder, and looking at each other. I managed to catch Anthe's eye, she lifted her hands, helpless and mystified: Kore was oblivious.

I hardly noticed when the song ended, until the applause burst out. I was caught up in the strange little drama going on by the bar, somehow it scared me, and I didn't know why. I quickly rearranged my face, and whooped and cheered and pounded my palms together. Everyone shouted that the singer had surpassed herself. Foreigners threw coin, which is *not* a good idea in a crowded bar. Mando stood, and bowed: sat down again, and called for another drink—

Kore was still working away. Palikari suddenly had the presence of mind to drop down from the counter and stand in front of her. Papa Dicty must have been watching too. Before the applause showed any sign of letting up he stood, and spread his arms. 'How beautiful it is that we remember the dead, in our midsummer festivities. I have always thought that's a very moving Serifiote tradition. Now, the crowd in here is unsafe, please go out to the terrace! We can thank and praise the incomparable Mando more pleasantly outdoors, when she's had a chance to catch her breath!'

The people obeyed without protest, they must have been glad to get some fresh air. We cleared the dining room, and the kitchen yard crowd trooped after them, Palikari and I politely encouraging the stragglers. Dicty took a lamp from the high table to the bar, and looked over Kore's shoulder.

'You can read and write?' said the boss softly.

She barely glanced at him. 'Yes . . . Please excuse me, Papa Dicty, I'm trying to remember the metre, one more line . . .'

'That's a strange kind of script. Who taught you, my dear?'

Her hand was still flying. 'It's a new kind of writing, I worked it out. I use different symbols to mean *sounds*, not things. It's much better. You can use it for poetry, not just accounts. You can use it for any language you like.'

'Great Mother,' said the boss.

He sat down hard on a barstool, as if someone had knocked him on the head.

Kore dropped her stylus and leaned back, wringing her hand: it must have been aching. Moumi, Pali, Anthe crowded close. We looked at the little dancing marks; and then at each other, in blank astonishment.

We kept accounts at Dicty's, with the usual signs for different kinds of goods. We stored our yearly figures on clay tablets: and we thought that was pretty special. We knew of Eygptian writing, of course. But no one, *no one* could read and write in the islands these days: not this way, setting down thoughts and ideas. For us the skill had been utterly lost since the Great Disaster. It was rare beyond price, *anywhere in the Middle Sea*.

The king of Serifos was the first threat that leapt to my mind. If he found out about this! But even then I knew that Polydectes was not the danger—

'Great Mother,' said Dicty again, in a hollow tone.

The tallyboards were rough, flaky scraped wood. They weren't meant to last, we used them for kindling when they were done with . . . I could not make Kore's marks stand still. They seemed to whirl, and melt into each other. It was like a language so foreign it sounds like water running, or the twittering of birds.

Papa Dicty was frowning, thinking hard. He stood up again. 'Could you read what you have written, Kore?'

'Of course.' She began to speak, slowly, her eyes on the board.

It was astonishing, and *eerie*. I felt the hairs rise on the back of my neck. She got through the first, ominous lines of the funeral song: then she looked up and saw us all standing there open-mouthed. I saw the horror dawning on her face—

She had given herself away. She had revealed a secret that

marked her like a shining brand. Was that what made her look so terrified?

'You had to do it.' Anthe took her hand. 'You couldn't help it, *I* know.'

'*Here*, what's this caper—?'

It was Mando. She'd been sitting there on her stool, all along. The singer got up and trod heavily across the room, mopping her dripping mascara with a table napkin. 'What's that on those tallyboards? Some kind 'er spell? What are you all looking at? Has this girl stolen my song? Lemme see. How's she done that?'

The funeral song was not Mando's property, it was older than the ocean. It had different words on every island; even for every singer. But on Serifos nobody was allowed to sing 'Dark Water' the Mando way unless she taught them; and she was very choosy.

'No one can steal your songs!' cried Papa Dicty, sweeping the tallyboards out of sight. 'The girl knows a few lines of the lyric: why not, most people do. It's your glorious art that makes the song! But listen, Mando, dear, I was thinking. I want to make you an extra gift, to celebrate a superb performance. I've decided I will tell you the recipe for my wheat ribbons, *and* I'll give you a ribbon press.'

Mando seemed to expand. Though she dressed like a farmhand, when she wasn't singing, she was said to be extremely rich. She made sure she got paid, but the fame her shows brought meant far more to her. Papa Dicty's wheat ribbons! What news to tell the crowd! She bowed, with dignity: took his hand and kissed it. The harsh, blunt farmhand's accent vanished.

'Papa Dicty, you truly honour me. Well, well. I think I *was* in good tone tonight. May I excuse myself, gentlemen and ladies: I must go to my audience.'

Mando left us, like a court lady's very solid ghost. Kore

came out from behind the bar, and drew a deep breath. 'I can't stay. I'll have to leave. But I *will* explain—' She walked quickly, chin up, out into the yard. Anthe made a move to go after her.

'Don't,' said Moumi. 'She'll tell us the truth. Let it wait until morning.'

'I'd better join the people on the terrace,' sighed Papa Dicty. 'Or it will look strange, and impolite to the singer. There's a good chance that nobody noticed what Kore was doing, or understood what they saw, and a good chance that Mando will only remember the wheat ribbons. Let's hope that's the case.'

'I'll come with you,' said Moumi.

The three of us stayed where we were. Palikari whistled, shook his head, reached for shot-cups, and poured a steadying tot of Kitron all round. Anthe downed hers at a gulp. Her hair, too curly to be tamed for long, was coming out of its stylish ringlets. 'Why did she say, *I can't stay*? Does she think we won't protect her? I don't understand why she's terrified. She can read and write, it's a wonderful thing!'

'It's *too* wonderful,' said Palikari, grimly. 'There were informers in here, there always are, and I bet they were watching our mystery girl. She's given herself away, someone will know who she is, a girl who can read and write: as good as if she'd shouted out her real name (whatever it is). The king is going to demand that we hand her over, like a piece of loot. He'll force us to defy him, and you know what ...?' He stopped, set his teeth, looked at the floor and muttered, 'maybe it's high time!'

'Did she say it's a *new kind* of writing?' I asked.

No answer. The lamps were dying, we could barely see each other's faces. Moonlight from outdoors spread cold white sheaves across the floor. There were eyes in the dark down beside the hearth. The spirit that lived there had curled up into a quivering ball of limbs, like a threatened spider.

My friends wanted me to face up to the king of Serifos, before he could strike the first blow. I couldn't blame them if they thought I was afraid of Polydectes, the way I was reacting to this new crisis. But I wasn't.

It wasn't the king who would take Kore from me.

I could see things other people couldn't, I could see hearth-spirits and water nymphs. Now I knew, like thunder after lightning, why I had felt that strange fear, as I saw her driving away with her stylus. It wasn't because my darling possessed a dangerous, covetable skill. I had seen the finality of doom in her eyes, when she looked up from the tallyboards where she had written the Dark Water song.

She was god-touched. And tonight, in this room, in the flickering lamplight, her fate had tracked her down—

4

Kore did not explain herself.

When I came down at first light she was helping Koukla, our stalwart laundry woman and the maids clear up after the big event. At the household breakfast table, after we'd served our guests, she made an announcement. 'I am sorry for what happened,' she said (as if she'd broken a tray of crockery). 'I regret my outburst. Please forgive me and let's not speak about it.'

'That's all right, my dear,' said the boss. 'Could you pass the honey?'

Papa Dicty didn't speak, either. He spent most of that morning with Mando, teaching her the wheat ribbons recipe. Then he asked me to help him in the furnace yard, and we made a press for the singer as promised. I was bewildered by his calm: he'd seemed so *staggered* by what Kore could do. But it came

48

to me that he'd been strangely quiet since the night she arrived. Or since we'd come back from our last trip to Naxos, I wasn't sure which was more significant. The boss had said nothing, done nothing about the threat we all saw – except that he'd moved the refugees, immediately, just on a rumour.

He was waiting for something. What was he waiting for?

I didn't ask. Part of me didn't want to break the silence—

Palikari was convinced there would be trouble. 'I'm not laying blame,' he said, darkly. 'All right, maybe no informer spotted her last night, but look at the staff who went home, any one of them could have overheard us, and *talked* by now, not meaning any harm, just gossiping. The waitresses, the maids, the undercooks. What about Koukla and Kefi? A runner can reach the High Place in an hour, the king's bullies could be on their way!' Kefi was our timid mule boy. He and Koukla were *family*: the fact that he'd think of distrusting them showed how upset Pali was.

'My dear Palikari,' said Papa Dicty, 'I hear only one person talking carelessly, and it's you. Set your mind at rest. The king, as you rightly say, knows very quickly what's going on in Seatown. If he'd wanted to kidnap our new waitress, he'd have been here long ago.'

Pali was not convinced. Kore was no longer just a mystery fugitive. She was treasure, and the king would snatch her from us. As far as Palikari was concerned, the only question was whether we could expect a sneaking raid, or a full frontal attack.

I knew he was wrong: but he infected me. I was full of itchy alarm.

The singer left us. Seatown's own musicians brought a chariot decked in flowers to fetch her away (really a handcart: no one in Seatown possessed a chariot, or the horse to go with it). They harnessed themselves and hauled her, with more sweat than romance, through cheering crowds, to set her on her way. The festival continued, and two days passed. Then Dicty sent me to check on our caique; which was kept for us by a loyal friend, in a cove up the east coast.

We weren't supposed to maintain a sea-going vessel. That was why Papa Dicty had given up his fishing boats and moved into the taverna business. Polydectes didn't want the boss to have independent means of leaving the island; or of sending for allies. But though we'd made a show of doing everything the king asked, of course we had an arrangement, in case we needed to leave Serifos in a hurry. I set out in the cool of the morning, taking Dolly with me, and using the public mule track. We went to one of the east farms, where I left the mule with our steward and cut across country on foot.

Before noon I'd reached the two-hovel 'fishing village' where our friend Bozic kept the boat for us. He was a Mainlander, but not an Achaean. He came from far to the north east, he was a bit of a smuggler, but trustworthy. We agreed that he would bring her to the coves north of Seatown; where there were plenty of places where a small vessel could lie hidden. We went over the signals, and the plans that had been worked out long ago. Then I ran back to the farm, where I picked up Dolly and a load of fresh peas, soft fruit and leaf vegetables.

We walked home at a mule's pace through the summer evening, me with my shoulders prickling for arrows . . . But it might still be a false alarm. I'd been sent to prepare our escape route before, and the danger had passed—

Not this time.

Koukla met me in the kitchen yard, in tears, with the news that Anthe, and Palikari, and Kore had *all three* disappeared. They'd been gone for hours, they must have been taken by the king, they must be dead!

'Where's the boss?' I demanded. 'Where's my mother?'

'They're indoors, Perseus. The shock, it's been too much

for poor Papa, his head's turned, he's behaving as if nothing's wrong!'

I rushed indoors. The boss was working as usual. He told me at once that Kore was safe. She'd been 'missing' since mid-afternoon, but it turned out she'd gone to visit the Enclosure. Holy Mother had sent word that that's where she was.

'What about Pali and Anthe?'

'Ah,' said the boss. 'Now that may be a problem.'

We were surrounded by the clamour of the busy kitchen. Waitresses hurried from the dining room, shouting for squid, honey-baked mullet, wheat ribbons with lobster sauce, greens in lemon and oil. The spit boy shot up to Papa Dicty's station, sweating and red in the face. Dicty inspected a platter of roast meat slices, approved it with a nod; the boy sped to deliver it to the undercook who was making up orders. 'I'd like you to look for them, Perseus. They've been gone too long, and they told no one where they were going. Take Kefi, so you can send him back with a message if need be. You might go upstairs a little way. But no further than the cemetery.'

Upstairs meant the way to the High Place. That road was forbidden to us. The boss was as good as telling me to break the truce. I felt as if I'd been dunked in ice melt. So this is it, I thought. This is really it. I saw the island of sand, long ago: Serifos gouged by warfare. I thought of the darkness rushing in—

'What if I don't find them? Or if I meet opposition?'

'Then you come back. Before I forget, was all well with our friend?'

He meant Bozic. 'Yes. All's well, no problems.'

The boss smiled at me. 'Off you go. Don't make trouble if you don't find it.'

Moumi had been doing my front of house job. She left it to one of the waitresses and came to see me off. It was dark in the yard by then. The geese and chickens were jabbering, settling for the night; the sounds and lights of the taverna seemed far away. Koukla was trembling as if she'd already seen the three of us carried back dead. I hugged her, and she squeezed me as if I was a recalcitrant piece of washing. My mother held up the lamp. I saw the grim resolve in her eyes: dark blue, like mine.

'Why did she go to the Enclosure, Moumi? She's never left the house alone.'

'I don't know ... Perseus, you're not a child any more. This had to come.'

'I know I'm not a child. We'll find them, don't worry. Maybe they went for a walk in the fields, Pali sprained his ankle and they're limping home. Come on, Kefi.'

It had to come, my day of reckoning with the king of Serifos; I knew that. But right now I was thinking of my friends. This was how it happened to other people. Young men, boys, recently even girls too: they went out one day and they never came home. They'd been kidnapped and forced to join the king's guard, or to work in the mines—

What I found hard to bear was the way the people didn't complain. They mourned as dead the children, brothers, sisters, lovers they would never see again. They were robbed, bullied and beaten by the king's men. We heard of incidents all the time, and we gave the victims what help we could. But they were like Papa Dicty himself, still *waiting* for something, before they would resist. Some of them even praised the king. He was a strong leader, he had made Serifos a name in the world—

I'd had some weapons training. There were old men up in the hills, too old to be of interest to the king, who knew how to use a sword and shield. The boss had made sure I was taught how to fight. But I had no weapons, the truce forbade me to be armed. What if we ran into something right now?

Papa Dicty had an uncanny way of knowing what the king would do, and what he *wouldn't* do. He thought we were safe to go hunting for Pali unarmed, that was all the assurance I had—

We were hurrying through the fields behind Seatown, as I went over these thoughts, heading for the hill of the citadel by a roundabout route. Poor Kefi had to scamper to keep up with me.

'Master, dear master, please let me hold your hand!'

'Kefi,' I said, slowing down, 'you can hold my hand if you like, but don't be scared. There'll be no fighting. We're just looking for Pali and Anthe.'

'I am n-not afraid of the soldiers! I am afraid of the d-dark. Wicked things inhabit the dark. There may be ghosts.'

Mortals have an unfortunate habit of being afraid of *anything* that can't harm them. Show them a sword, a whip, a club, they're placid. Offer to beat them up, tell them a fancy food is poisonous, they don't turn a hair. But they're afraid to be alone, out of the sight of houses. They're afraid of the dark, afraid of meeting a cat or being followed by a dog; afraid of a bubbling spring, or a tree that seems mean-tempered. I knew honourable exceptions to this mad rule, but our mule boy was not one of them.

We were unarmed, and heading for forbidden territory. I was scared that we might be running into a murderous ambush. Kefi was terrified that the dead would jump up and bite him. I held him by the hand, and marched him to the road; which we met on the saddle where it started winding to and fro, like a hank of yarn spilled on the hillside. There was a shorter way to the High Place from here, a flight of stone steps that had once led to a Great Mother temple. It had fallen into ruin and the king had had the ruins cleared; they were spoiling his view. The steps remained, overgrown but still painted in faded whitewash. It was because of them that we called going to the High Place 'going upstairs'.

There was a hollow on the saddle, with a spring where the goatherds brought their flocks. I decided this was where Kefi and I would part company. We'd both be better off.

'Listen,' I said. 'You're going to stay here and wait for me, in the hollow. You can peep out and see the lights of the town, and the stars in the sky, so you won't be scared.'

'Wh-what if you don't come back, dear Perseus? What shall I tell your mother?'

'You can tell the time by the stars, can't you?' He nodded. 'If I don't come back by an hour past midnight go home, and tell my mother and the boss. Or if you hear any fighting, run like a rabbit straight away. But in that case, stay off the road.'

The boy's teeth were chattering. He clung to me like a burr.

'P-perseus, you can't leave me. It feels strange. There's s-something wicked in the goat hollow. I'm sure there is. It will frighten me.'

I pulled a snagged thread from my tunic, spat on it, and tied it round the boy's wrist. 'That's a charm, it will keep you safe. Wait here, I'll go and see.'

I unpicked his fingers from my arm, and stepped down into darkness; the starlight immediately cut off by summer foliage. The spring made a faint plaintive song as it rose from the earth, and fell into an old stone basin. At first I could see nothing, but there was a strong goaty smell. I caught the gleam of hooves, the outline of horns amid curly hair. It watched me, slant-eyed; without moving. My eyes got accustomed, and the almost human face came clear. It licked its lips.

'Hey,' I whispered. 'What are you up to?'

'Ssss.'

'Sss, yourself. You don't mess with me, I don't mess with you. All right?'

'No harm, Perseus.'

'I should hope not. Listen, I want to leave a mortal boy

54

here, and he's afraid. Who will look after him for me, and keep him calm and steady?'

'Why is he afraid?' demanded another, fretful, sighing voice. I saw the dryad of the tree above me, leaning from her boughs; looking sulky. 'We are the shadows of shadows, what does he think we can do to him?'

I had no answer. I *really* didn't understand why people were afraid, when they felt the presence of these harmless things; that I could see and mortals could not. But I was afraid of floating boxes, which was just as senseless. A slim cold hand crept into mine. It was the naiad of the spring, a glimmering, transparent girl-shape. 'I will mind him for you, Perseus. I will sing to him and make him comfortable. Will you kiss me?'

'Of course I will, my dear.'

I knelt and drank, just a mouthful. She was sweet on my lips.

Kefi was hugging himself and hopping like a demented grasshopper. I convinced him there was nothing wicked in the hollow, and reminded him that the spring was a kindly one. Then I went on alone, like a fox through the bushes, close to the steps; hoping he wouldn't bolt for home as soon as I was gone. I wondered if he could really tell the time (when I came to think of it, I'd never seen Kefi out this late), and what the gathering of spirits in the goat-hollow meant. Those creatures didn't usually speak, or show themselves so clearly. Maybe they'd come to see the end of me.

The cemetery, which was perched on the hillside halfway between Seatown and the High Place, was our final boundary. I skirted the walls, then I climbed in and hunted between the graves. There was no one about and no obvious sign of a struggle. It was a small field. We sow the dead one upon the other, they don't disturb each other. Still not a sign of Anthe or Pali. But there at the cemetery gates, caught on a bramble, I spotted a ragged scrap that wasn't a leaf. I crouched to pull it free, sniffed it, and smelled our taverna kitchen. I had tapers, flint and tinder in my pouch. But I didn't need a light to see the colour, I knew. They'd been here. Anthe had torn her yellow dress.

I decided I must go further. If I was caught, then the truce would be over no matter what: but I had to find out what had happened. My mind was on my friends, the king's men had been known to torture prisoners. But I was thinking of myself too, with a horrible crawling in my belly that told me I *was not ready*. I was the threat that Polydectes couldn't endure, and I was just a kid, a great overgrown boy with no beard, no brains, no ideas . . .

What could I do? Challenge him to single combat? Not even if he would accept. A tyrant king is like one of those monsters where you chop off one head and a hundred leap into its place. He had an army, most of them kidnapped villagers once, but they were soldiers now. He had nobles, as bad as himself, ready to fall on each other like a pack of savage dogs. I could kill Polydectes, and war would come anyway, laying waste to everything I loved—

I heard a faint groan, over on the stone stairway.

I dropped to the ground, and listened intently. The groan came again. Uphill, but not far. Then I heard someone whispering, pleading. It was Anthe's voice!

I don't know which of us was more relieved when I crawled out of the undergrowth. She was crouched beside Palikari, who was lying in a heap on the steps. She leapt up, with a fish-gutting knife in her fist, smears of blood all over: saw it was me and we fell into each other's arms. Anthe hadn't been touched, and there were no soldiers around, but Pali was in a bad state. She'd ripped up her dress to bandage him, but he had a head wound that was still bleeding, his left shoulder was a mess and he was barely conscious.

She told me what had happened, while I tried to find out the extent of Palikari's injuries. There was a young man who'd been a childhood friend of Pali's, who was now an officer in the king's army. He was an informant we'd used once or twice, but not someone we trusted. Pali had got word to this officer. The man had agreed to meet him at the cemetery, at sunset; with important news about Kore. Pali had gone to the meeting place. Anthe had stayed in hiding, and hadn't heard a sound. She'd waited and waited, but he hadn't come back. So she'd gone looking.

'I found him further up. I tried to stop the bleeding: I got him this far, then he collapsed, and I couldn't rouse him. He's lost a lot of blood. I didn't dare leave him, Perseus. I didn't know what to do.'

'You shouldn't have gone up there alone!'

'What should I have done? Left Pali to die?'

They shouldn't have been here at all. But Pali was a grown man, he had a right to make his own decisions. So did Anthe.

'You didn't see any soldiers?'

'I've seen nobody. No one comes this way, the High Place swells use the road. But I don't think he got away from them, Perseus. I think they left him for us to find. They s-sent for him, and then roughed him up as a warning.'

'Maybe. Let's see what he can tell us, when—'

When we get him home, I was about to say. The words didn't come. The darkness around us shuddered, and cried out. Something ran past me, sobbing *oooh, oooh*, like a broken-hearted child. Almost-human faces flickered: horns and hooves, limbs like supple branches, hair like rustling leaves. All the spirits of the island were awake and crying, running for shelter. Anthe wailed and grabbed me.

'What is it?' I yelled. 'What's the *matter* with you all? What's *happening*?'

Andromeda had wrapped herself in a long dark shawl, but the disguise only made her conspicuous. It was midsummer, she should have covered herself in flowers if she wanted to go unseen on the streets of Seatown. The other girls, and even grown women, were in flimsy one-shouldered dresses; some with the skirts kilted up for wild dancing. But she reached the Enclosure without being stopped or questioned.

She was glad that the refugees had gone, though they had not known her. She'd been very ashamed the day they'd had to get out of here, and she'd had to talk to them. When you start to lie, you think it'll be one lie, severing you from your past, *no I'm not her*, and then you'll be free to be someone else. But it doesn't work like that.

At the gates she asked for Holy Mother. After a long wait, the old lady in grey who had ordered Papa Dicty around appeared and waved the gatekeeper nun away with her stick. 'Why couldn't you come and find me, young lady? What are you, a princess, that you think I have to come traipsing out to greet you?'

'I've broken a vow, Mother. I wish to rededicate myself. May I enter?'

The holy woman sniffed, turned her back and stumped away. Andromeda realised she was supposed to follow. 'Well, well, a dedication. D'you wish to bathe?'

'N-no. I wish to make sacrifice.'

Holy Mother could be heard muttering crossly, *Hmph, one of those.*

'What's the name of the divinity?'

Andromeda told her the name, which was Melqart.

'Doesn't mean a thing to me. But these new-fangled Supernaturals are all the same, from one end of the Middle Sea to another. What's 'Melqart' supposed to rule?'

Death, she thought, but she didn't say it.

'He is the god of making. Of taming horses, of the ocean, and—'

'Speak up!'

'Earthquakes.'

'That sounds like the Achaean called Poseidon. You speak Greek, don't you? You should call him Poseidon, if you meet him here. We don't worship those upstarts, but as you're a foreigner, I *suppose* I can make an exception.' Holy Mother looked suspiciously at the small bundle in Andromeda's hands. 'Nothing alive, I hope? I won't have animals killed in here, it's revolting.'

She tried to shake her head, and couldn't.

Holy Mother shrugged, and asked no more questions. They reached a door in the rocks at the back of the Enclosure. There was a cave, and a small pale figure on a plinth. The old lady shut out the sunlight, and dragged a brazier from a cupboard in the rock wall. She put together a heap of charcoal and spices, and lit it with a firebox.

'Now you lie down and go to sleep. See if you dream.'

Andromeda knelt. The cave was dry and quiet. This was a very holy place. Light-headed from so many nights with little or no sleep, she slipped at once into a meditation, and didn't see the Holy Mother leave.

She saw the Gods of the city where she was born, and the Gods of her mother's people, and the Achaean Supernaturals, falling away like veils.

She didn't know if she was falling back in time, or deeper and deeper into herself.

When she came swimming up from the depths again there was a tall man, with clustering curls and a strong, rich, dark face, sitting behind the brazier. He wore a purple robe, white bordered, he held a three-pronged spear; he looked at her as if he knew her. 'Are you Melqart?' asked Andromeda. She unwrapped her loom weights, the rope of precious purple yarn and her shuttle, and set them on the pyre. She'd meant to burn the tallyboards where she'd written *Dark Water*, as well. But when she'd looked for them, the morning after Mando's singing, they'd gone from behind the bar.

It didn't matter. The new kind of writing wasn't held in those marked boards, it was in her head and hands.

She lifted up her hands to pray, and remembered the name Holy Mother had told her to use. 'Accept the sacrifice, Lord Poseidon, which I make of my free will.'

The rocks cried out, there was a rushing of feet, a sigh like waves beating on a long, long shore. Somebody was crying—

She sat up, with a start: stiff and sore. The man was gone. In his place a pale, small statue gleamed, dim in the darkness. She had fallen asleep. How long had she been in here? It felt like hours. The brazier was cold, the bundle she'd brought with her lay on the sandy floor, still knotted up. She opened it: the loom weights, the yarn and the shuttle were unharmed, not burned at all. She had only dreamed the offering.

No, not just a dream, a vision. Because she knew something she hadn't known before. She could accept what she had to accept, now that it was action, not surrender. Not something done to me, something I choose to do.

I will do it. I can do it. This act is mine.

I more or less carried Pali as far as the goat-hollow, hoping I wasn't making the damage worse. Kefi had bravely stayed in his hiding place, through the earth-tremor. We sent him racing down the hill with the news; both good and bad. The spirits were not visible, but the spring was a welcome friend. We bathed Palikari's face, and got him to drink a little water. We thought that was safe, as he didn't have any chest or belly wounds.

'I wonder if they felt it at home,' said Anthe. 'Lucky for us it wasn't worse.'

Anthe had not seen what I had seen, or felt what I had felt. To her it had been nothing but a minor tremor, frightening but harmless.

I shrugged. 'It seems to be over, anyway.'

The walk home took a long time. When we reached the streets we got him on his feet. It was still midsummer: maybe we could have passed, in the dark, for three lopsided, drunken revellers. But it was very late by then, and we met no one. The waterfront was quiet, the taverna shuttered. Moumi, Koukla and Dicty were waiting for us in the yard.

'Kore?' I said, at once. I couldn't help it: I had to know if she was safe.

'She came home an hour or two ago,' Moumi told me. 'I sent her to bed.'

We took Pali into the kitchen, and laid him on clean towels on the marble-topped table. Lamplight showed my friend's tanned face grey from loss of blood, dark blood all over him; and he'd passed out again. It was just as well, because the next part was going to be painful. Koukla brought more lights, a pot of hot water, clean cloths, and the chest of household medicines. Moumi and the boss stripped off Anthe's sodden, makeshift bandages, and the remains of Pali's clothes, while Anthe and I stood by, feeling useless.

Pali's whole torso was a mass of cuts and darkening bruises, but the shoulder and the great cut across his head seemed the worst of it. Dicty felt his skull, gently, while he cleaned and snipped away clotted blood and hair. 'It's not too bad,' he reassured us, as quickly as he could. 'No broken bones, no damage to internal organs so far as I can tell, no dangerous fracture to the skull. He's lost a good deal of blood, but he'll recover.'

'He was set on,' murmured my mother. 'Cut down from above and behind, see, Dicty? With a heavy sword. And the slash through his shoulder, looks like the same weapon. They could easily have killed him, but they didn't—'

'The rest was done when he was on the ground,' said the boss. 'With boots, fists, and here's the marks of an armoured boxing glove. I'd say at least three men.'

'The cowards!' wailed Anthe. 'How dare they! I hate them! I'll *kill* them!'

Moumi prepared a length of catgut by passing it through flame, and threaded a needle that she'd treated the same way. Koukla poured wine into the smaller wounds to clean them. I'd seen this team deal with broken bodies before: I trusted them. I'd been afraid he was dying, relief flooded me with fury. 'I'll do it for you, Anthe. I have kept the peace, because I know the price we'll all pay. But this means war!'

Moumi stared at me, across Palikari's body. '*Perseus—!*'

She was right, it wasn't for me to say.

The boss looked up from his careful work of searching the head wound, to make sure no dirt or debris remained. 'Means war?' he said, head on one side. 'I don't think so. Strangely enough, I don't believe the king means war. No, the truce still holds—'

I couldn't believe it. I was dumbstruck.

'—if we want it to, at least.'

That's how things were when Kore found us. We had not heard her coming down the yard stairs, barefoot, and she was not carrying a light. She stood there, a dark blue mantle wrapped over her white sleeping shift, taking in the blood-daubed scene.

'What *happened*?' she gasped. 'Great All! It's Pali! Who did this?'

Koukla brought another basin of hot water for the boss, and carried away the one that was fouled with blood and dirt, shaking her head. 'What a mess,' she muttered.

'He got into a fight,' I said. 'It's not as bad as it looks.'

'He was attacked, you mean,' cried Anthe. 'A cowardly, brutal attack. And we know who's responsible. But we can't touch him!'

'You m-mean, the *king* did this?'

My mother gave Anthe a warning look, and went on sewing

62

Pali's shoulder. The boss was swabbing fresh blood from the scalp wound, ready for Moumi to sew it next. 'The king Polydectes is my full brother,' he said, quietly. 'As I'm sure you are aware, my dear. I don't know if people have heard of him, in your great city so far away: but he has made our island both feared and respected. Our agreement, which works most of the time, is that Seatown is my house, so to speak, where my ways are followed. The High Place belongs to the king and his men, and members of my household respect the boundary. If Palikari broke the agreement tonight, which we won't know until we can ask him, I'm afraid I'm to blame, because I encouraged him to go in search of information.'

'But you *didn't* send him!' Anthe broke in. 'That's why we didn't tell you!'

'Thank you child, but I will decide how to answer my brother's men.'

Then for once Dicty's calm gave way. He wiped his hands on a towel and went with stumbling steps to sit on a bench by the dining room, his head bowed, twisting the towel between his hands. 'He would always take the best,' he muttered. 'When we were young, when it was Dicty and little Dectes. The proper thing to do, when gifts are offered to the royal house, is to take a modest share and say, "The rest is to be distributed, among the vassals; for the poor." Dectes always took the most and the best of everything, the best colts, the best weaving, the best fine-worked metal. His hands were always grasping, never open. Our mother died when he was born, you know. After that, every real lady packed up and left. Our father and his women treated the boy with such scorn. So now he is *Poly*dectes, the ruler of many, and he rules by force ... He is the one who understands these times. I was born too late. The old days are gone, and I've tried too long to keep them alive.'

He raised his head, there were tears on his face. 'A city

63

on a hill is not a good thing! All these "High Places" that kings are so proud of these days, are *built on fear*. In civilised times cities are built on the shore, or in fine valleys, without walls, welcoming to strangers. Oh, I know Polydectes isn't alone. The people of Serifos accept him because he is *no worse* than many rulers in the Middle Sea, that's the sorry truth. But I did not raise him, teach him well. I am to blame for that.'

'What could you have done?' asked my mother. 'When he challenged the throne? Gone to war with him? Killed your own brother? That would have been a hateful act.'

'Ha,' said the boss, shaking his head. 'Spoken like an Achaean, Danae of Argos. I did not make the truce for family reasons. *I did it for my island.* For Serifos!'

Kore was not listening to them: she wasn't hearing the old story of two brothers. She was staring at Palikari's battered body with a look of sick horror.

'Why did Palikari go to the High Place? Was it because of me?'

We couldn't answer her. We were trying to think of a lie, and this was written on our faces, when Palikari himself stirred. He half sat up, and gave a moan. 'I was ambushed,' he croaked. 'Anthe—?' She darted over to him and he clutched her, talking feverishly, his eyes wild. 'We have to get away from here. It was a trap, I was ambushed, but the news is good. The king will not touch her. He's heard some story that she's god-touched, marked for sacrifice. The crazy innards-readers in the High Place confirmed it.'

Anthe tried to get him to lie down. 'Hush. Sssh, sweetheart, lie quiet—'

Pali stared around at the bright kitchen, and touched the bandage on his shoulder. 'Oh, I'm home,' he mumbled, in a puzzled voice, and slumped back unconscious again.

No one spoke. The terrible look of fate was in Kore's eyes,

she stood very straight. I had the feeling that she could not see me, she was sleepwalking or in darkness.

'The king is right,' she said. 'The king is right. I am a sacrifice.'

'What do you mean?' cried Anthe. 'What's this about? You're safe with us!'

She is not safe with herself, I thought.

'Kore,' said Papa Dicty, 'I think I should tell you what I have heard myself: news that I haven't yet shared with my family. It's a story from the far east of the Middle Sea, which is making its way around the ports: I heard it from an agent of Taki the shipowner. The big earthquake was not in Libya, it was at Haifa, on the Phoenician coast. They say that the great queen, Cassiopeia the Ethiopean, boasted that her daughter Andromeda was wiser and more beautiful than some Supernatural or other. The earthquake was the result, and the queen is required to sacrifice her daughter to appease the God. Cassiopeia now maintains that she's holding the princess in prison, preparing her for the day of sacrifice. Rumour has it that in fact the girl has escaped, and no one knows where she is.'

'Ooh,' breathed Anthe, '*that's* why you weren't worried about the king wanting her—!'

'Be quiet Anthe.' The boss looked at 'Kore', and added gently, 'I know the name Cassiopeia, of course. She's a very famous ruler. I don't know how much of the rest of the story to believe. Haifa is a long way from here. I was waiting for *you* to tell us.'

'It's all true. I am Andromeda.'

And my heart leapt, even then: because now I knew her name.

She went to Dicty, and knelt in front of him.

'My father, the usurper may rule in the High Place but you are the true king, the guide and protector of your people. Let

65

me tell you how it happened. The priests said that the first quake was a warning. The next would be devastation, another Great Disaster, unless I was given to them. But no one locked me up, so I ran away. The queen did not believe I would run away, princesses of my race do not *run away* ... You have shown me nothing but kindness, and I have brought trouble to add to your troubles. I'm very, very sorry. But it's over, I'm going back.' She stood up gracefully, her head held high. 'I knew when I wrote the "Dark Water" song, when I felt the dead crying to me, that I had to go back. But it was you who taught me to do right, Papa Dicty. I found my courage here.'

Anthe and my mother stared at each other, open-mouthed.

'Hm,' said the boss, at last. 'Princess Andromeda, I hope I haven't taught you to put your neck on the block for no good reason. Priests claim a human sacrifice will stop an earthquake, or end a drought. Have we ever seen that *proved*? I've heard that the priests of Haifa are jealous of your mother's power. Are you sure you trust them?'

Andromeda shook her head, slowly: but she hardly seemed to hear him.

'There are veils and veils, and behind them is the truth. I went to the Enclosure today to re-dedicate myself. I am sacrificed in my heart, I am ready to die.'

She looked us in the eye, one by one, standing so straight and proud. It was heart-breaking. Maybe it was easier for the others: they could tell themselves she was deluded—

Papa Dicty sighed. 'Well, well. We should all be prepared to die. Let me give this thought.' He patted the princess on the shoulder, and stood up. 'Anthe! Get out of those rags and go and bathe, you'll feel much better. Let's finish the sewing and get this young man to bed. Perseus, we'll need your muscle.'

Anthe looked down at the tatters of her skirt, and her

66

blood-spattered bare legs. 'All right, boss,' she said meekly, and took herself off.

Palikari had come round again, by the time we got him into bed. He was able to sip a cup of warm, watered wine, and tell us about the ambush. 'My so-called friend was waiting for me,' he said. 'We were supposed to talk in the cemetery, but he didn't feel safe there, he insisted I had to come further up the steps. I didn't suspect a thing. He told me about Kore, that she was god-touched, and then they jumped me. I thought I was done for. But they didn't mean to kill, they just sliced me up and kicked me around.' He grinned at me. 'I've got a message for you, big kid.'

'About Kore?'

He began to shake his head, and winced at the pain. 'Our business ... I'm to tell you, Polydectes the king says, *Next time, don't send a servant, Perseus, and don't hide behind an old man. Come yourself.*' For a moment the boss was out of it, and I was no longer a 'big kid'. We were two young men, my friend had been beaten up, we were both furious. Pali set the cup down and lay back. 'When you *do* go up there,' he remarked, reflectively. 'Do me a favour. Take me with you, great prince. And let's be armed, eh?'

'You bet we will.'

Palikari closed his eyes.

'I'll sit with him for a while,' said the boss. 'You go back to that shining girl of yours. See if you can convince her she's not dead yet.'

Koukla had gone to bed, the lamps were out. My mother, Anthe and Andromeda were in the dining room, in firelight by the great hearth. It was the dark before dawn, a chill hour even at midsummer. Anthe had changed into clean clothes and was combing out her wet hair. Moumi had made some sage tea. Andromeda was looking tired and shaken, but

67

strangely calm. They were telling her about the harsh underbelly of the truce. The mines worked by kidnapped children, the brutal soldiers preying on villagers. Moumi poured me some tea. I sat holding the bowl, breathing fragrant steam.

'What kind of metal is it, in the mines?' asked Andromeda. 'Is it gold?'

'No, mostly the new, black metal,' said my mother. 'Serifos is rotten with it.'

'Oh yes, I've heard of that. It's very important. So Serifos is rich?'

'The *king* is rich,' Anthe dragged her comb viciously, and glowered into the red smoulder of the fire. 'Not the rest of us. He plays his Mainland friends off against each other, keeps the wealth, and we're supposed to be grateful. The people see him as a necessary evil. They call our boss "Papa Dicty", they look up to him, they *revere* him, but they accept the usurper. The boss himself, you heard him, half-believes that Polydectes has the right to rule. Because gentleness is out of fashion. Because kindness and reason are signs of weakness!'

'There's something else you should know, Andromeda,' added Moumi. 'Polydectes wants me for his wife. He hasn't been able to touch me: I'm his brother's adopted daughter. But now that Perseus is a man, he feels he has to challenge my son, and claim me. I think that's why Palikari was set upon. The king wants *us* to break the truce, because that would be a triumph over his brother. But he's getting impatient.'

I'm not a man, I thought. Not really. I'm not anything like ready.

Andromeda nodded. 'I see. Impatient.'

Then no one spoke. The princess, who had not yet looked at me, seemed to gaze inward: as if looking at her own death, the fate she freely accepted—

'Why didn't your mother try to save you?' whispered Anthe.

'Anthe!' murmured my mother.

'No,' said Andromeda. 'It's all right, I don't mind. She couldn't say no, Anthe. She came to Haifa, she married my father Kephus, knowing what she'd have to accept.'

'The child sacrifices,' said Moumi.

'Yes.'

In the terrible times, right after the Great Disaster, hideous things had been committed in our Turning Islands, and in the palaces of Kriti. The legacy of those nightmare years was still with us, making cruelty and rule by force acceptable. What the Phoenicians did was something else, something worse. They practiced child sacrifice, not just on rare occasions but regularly, without shame.

They'd always done it. It was a scandal we'd heard about even on Serifos. But the Phoenician cities were extremely rich and extremely powerful. And Cassiopeia was a great queen.

'She knew it was horrible, and she let it continue,' said Andromeda. 'To keep her power. How could she refuse, when they told her it was her turn?'

The wall paintings were rising out of the night, their faded colours woken by the grey dawn. The caique had been for Andromeda, I realised, not for us. The boss had known who she was, and he'd been afraid the king would take her and send her back to Haifa, for some kind of reward—

'Do you think there are people searching for you?'

Andromeda shrugged. 'I suppose so. I made it look as if I'd gone south, into Africa. My nurse, who helped me get away, comes from the desert. She's back with her family: she should be safe from retribution. I took a ship to the west. When I was doing it I thought I had everything planned, but I didn't. I didn't think about what my mother would do when she found I was gone. I just ran. Then I met the refugees in Naxos. They couldn't have known me, they were from a country on the edge of the quake zone, far from the city. I paid their fares with gold: not because I was generous, but because I was scared and ashamed ... I suppose the shipowner may have given me away. I paid him with so much gold. He didn't know who I was then, but he must have realised by now. It was his agent who told Papa Dicty the rumour that Andromeda had escaped.'

'Taki will have melted the bracelets down,' said Anthe. 'If he thinks he harboured a runaway princess he won't have told anyone. It would be bad for business.'

'It doesn't matter, Anthe. I'm not running any more.'

We were silent, brought back to earth: but she continued, almost cheerfully. 'There's a festival when our rains begin. It's in the tenth month. That's when I'm to be given to the monster ... They call it a sea-monster, because the quakes come from the sea, I don't know what it is really, but I know it will kill me. I'll have to find a ship going east, as soon as the wind changes.'

There would be no eastbound ships as long as the summer wind was blowing.

I have a month, I thought, with desperate hope. A month to convince her not to go back. But I knew why she was refusing to look at me. She had tried to run, we had fallen in love, but it was no use. Her fate had tracked her down, and it would not let her go. I thought of war on Serifos, and I felt as if I was being torn apart. A ray of sunlight struck across the floor. Mémé the cat walked in, yawning, and stopped in surprise to see us up.

'We should go to bed,' said Moumi. 'We're going to be dog-tired, later, and we have a restaurant to run.'

She was right. Dicty's must open as usual. Good food, good conversation, a welcome for strangers: life the way it ought to be. We must not be beaten.

Before I went to bed I went to Dicty's office. I opened the safe, and took out the tallyboards where she had written down the 'Dark Water' song. The dancing marks seemed to be alive: the living, immortal souls of human words … Andromeda had told Dicty, so casually, that she had invented a new kind of writing. Could that be true? Yes, I thought. It's true. I felt the presence of a mysterious power, greater, *more real* than all Taki's treasure, or all the black metal in the islands. A power that might change the world. How could the girl who had created this new thing be marked for death?

I thought of the crying and weeping I had heard, when I was on the hill with Anthe. Andromeda must have been in the Sacred Enclosure then. I imagined (no, I knew!) that the spirits of rock and tree and water had wept at the moment when my beloved dedicated herself to death, of her own free will. Why would the spirits weep, if she was right to sacrifice herself?

I had been running away from the Gods all my life. My mother had insisted on teaching me all she knew about the Achaean Supernaturals. She said I needed to understand what I was. Me, I'd never cared. I wanted to be like the boss, who was far too rational to believe you could appease an earthquake by human sacrifice. He honoured the Great Mother, without fuss, and ignored all the rest of them. He loved life, he tried to do right. That was the religion for me.

Now I wanted to understand, and I couldn't.

I remembered her on the dockside at Naxos. Her black eyes snapping when she offered to hold my tunic, while I dusted off the louts who had insulted Moumi. I didn't feel any of the flustered panic of being in love. I could see no way out of our troubles. I just knew that I would stand by her, and she would stand by me. It was enough.

5

Moumi woke me to take my turn sitting with Palikari. It was the night after the attack, he had a fever. I crawled up from a black, dreamless pit and stumbled to the wellhouse. As I stood in the yard, dripping, scouring my head with a rough towel to get my brain going, I saw a shooting star, a lance of brilliant gold. It dived across the starry sky and seemed to plunge into the sea, just beyond the headland that shelters our harbour.

Something's coming, I thought. Good news, or bad?

Later I went for a walk out of town, as far as Moni and Aten's farm. The wheat terraces gleamed, most of them already shorn to dry, glittering stubble. Grapes were swelling, jewel-coloured under the vineleaves. The sky was clear from horizon to horizon but the air quivered with tension, as if a storm was coming. It was earthquake weather. On the way back I sat and talked for a while at the bar we called the Yacht Club, a hang-out for the young people, off-islanders, who were wandering around the Middle Sea for sheer adventure. They asked after Pali, they knew he was off work. I said he had a fever, he'd be laid up for a few days: nothing serious … Had the attack on Palikari changed everything, or was it just another skirmish in the truce? I knew which option the boss preferred; or I thought I did. Peace at almost any price.

Was he right?

I was worried about Anthe. Today she'd been muttering to Koukla that it would be easy for a girl to dress up, get herself 'invited' into the High Place, and get close to the tyrant king: with a fish-gutting knife in her clothes, or hidden in her hair. And maybe a girl should do it, before Papa Dicty started arming the Seatown lads with boathooks, or before any stupid so-called heroes she knew got hacked to dogmeat just trying to get through the gates of the citadel. Koukla hadn't told the boss, she didn't want to worry him. But she was afraid our wildcat was serious.

I could not make up my mind to go home. I left the Yacht Club and walked over the headland, with the strange idea that I wanted to see where that shooting star had landed. The first inlet was one of the places where people went to bathe, but there was nobody down there, only a rowing boat drawn up on the sand. The oars lay inside. Out on the water a big pleasure boat was moored, a real monster, all shining paint, and polished metal that looked like gold. It had three raked masts and a sleek tall prow, bearing the name *The Magnificent Escape*. I'd never seen it before, but I knew what I was supposed to do. Time had stopped, the bathing inlet was a reflection of itself, like colours in a film of oil, deeper, richer than any colours in life, and yet ungraspable.

The Magnificent Escape looked like a pleasure yacht, but it felt (how can I explain this?), it *felt* like one of those spirits in the goat-hollow. I had passed a boundary, into that other world; and maybe the strangest thing was that I wasn't surprised. I'd seen this coming.

I pushed the little rowing boat off, climbed in, and rowed out to meet my father. When I reached the yacht's dark blue, glossy flank two sailors dressed in white slung a ladder of silvery metal over the side. I looked for some way to make my boat fast, but there was none. I shipped the oars, stood up, and grabbed hold of the ladder.

The sailors had very short hair and clean-shaven faces. One was a dark African, the other was so pale his eyes looked transparent. Their spotless whites were strangely styled, but they behaved exactly like snooty servants. The way they led me into the opulent wheelhouse was designed to tell me that they knew what my tunic had cost, they couldn't believe my tasteless haircut; and that I wasn't someone with whom their master would normally deign to associate. 'Please allow us to attend to you, sir,' said the pale one, giving my dusty sandals a once-over of supreme disdain.

There's a way to brush someone's clothes and wash their feet and hands, before a meal or a social visit: so that you make it dignified on both sides, friendly and kind. There's a way *not* to do it. The sailor-servants were experts at the second version. I was grateful to them for steadying my mind. By the time they'd finished treating me like scum, my fear and trembling had vanished. They showed me along a companionway done out in a fabulous, fine-grained red-brown wood; opened the door of a stateroom, and ushered me through.

The sailors didn't come in. The door was shut behind me. A very big man, magnificently built, sat at his ease, his legs crossed, his arm along the back of a couch. He had a fine head of red-gold hair, and a curling beard. He was dressed in spotless white, in the same strange style as his servants: loose trousers and a stiff, long-sleeved jacket with gold braid on it. I knew

I was looking at my father, great Zeus, ruler of the Supernaturals. The God who had once deigned to visit the princess Danae in her prison-tower, and set my life in motion. I am tall and strong. He was on a different scale: not only bigger than any human being ought to be, but you could feel that most of him was *elsewhere*, uncontained in this picture; this image. I had an urge to fall on my knees: I fought it down.

'Very nice,' he said, after a thoughtful appraisal. 'Very nice indeed.'

I knew about his habits. My old man *collects* half-mortal children, the way a mortal filthy rich potentate might collect beautiful vases, or rare insects impaled on pins. He breeds us as a hobby. That wasn't what my mother had told me, but it was what I'd worked out for myself. How nice that I had won his approval. I didn't thank him for the compliment, though I'd have loved to say something sarcastic: I couldn't trust my voice yet. I would not kneel, but he scared me to death, and he knew it.

'Sit down, please. I have to talk to you, about matters that concern us both.' He gestured to another of the couches. The stateroom seemed to go on forever. From about half way up, the walls were made of something transparent that shone with a high polish.

'A lovely part of the world, Serifos. One of the best kept secrets of the Middle Sea, in my humble opinion.' The chieftan of the Olympians cocked his head, considering the view through his clear walls. 'It's slipped my mind: do they worship me particularly here? Is there some little ritual I could attend, since I'm passing?'

'I wouldn't know. That would be up in the High Place. In Seatown we have the Great Mother's Enclosure, that's our only place of worship.' I knew I shouldn't mention the old religion, but I was trying to have the guts to stand up to him.

'Ah yes, the Mother.' He scowled, playfully. Playful like a

thunderbolt ... I was two people. One of them was in real danger of bursting into tears, wetting himself, hiding behind the couch. But the other Perseus, the one who felt no fear, didn't want to let go of being mortal. I didn't *want* to be on easy terms with this golden bully.

'She used to call us her pets, you know. Tell me, son, do I look like a domestic animal to you? *Do I look like a pussy-cat?*'

Now that he mentioned it, there *was* something animal about him, more vast animal power than divine wisdom in his splendour. But there's standing up for yourself, and there's plain stupid.

'No, you don't.'

He raised a mighty eyebrow.

'Sir.'

'Quite right. Well, the "pets" are in charge now. The Mother's day is over, we're going to *develop* this place. We're going to make the human world *buzz*. You'll see.'

I nodded, because he seemed to want some response and I had none; and he laughed so that my mortal heart shook like a leaf. 'Don't look so doubtful. You will see it all, Perseus. From your place in heaven ... But back to the here and now. The tyrant king Polydectes is about to invite you to a party.'

Oh I see, I thought. *That's* why he's here. He's going to tell me what to do. I'm facing the crisis of my life, my father has come to give me advice—

'The king of Serifos hates me. Why would he do that?'

'Pay attention. Polydectes will invite you to a party, and at this party he'll announce that he's given up his pursuit of the Argolide princess, your dear mother. He has turned his mind to a more useful match, and he expects his vassals to chip in with a horse or two towards the bride price. That includes you.'

'I'm not his vassal!'

'Of course not. Be quiet and listen. He will then tell the

company, in the most offensive way, that he knows you can't possibly contribute. The foster-son of a taverna keeper owns no horses, and hasn't a hope of ever seeing that kind of money.'

I fired up at this, because it was an insult to the boss. The God raised a big, well-cared for hand. A white jewel in the ring on his middle finger sent out sparks of rainbow-refracted light. His thumb-ring held a ruby the size of a sparrow's egg.

'Don't fly into a passion! I know that you have been fostered by a prince, a rare and virtuous man, for whom I have the greatest respect.'

My mother had told me that he was a polite old devil. Not that *she* remembered any politeness, but it was part of his reputation. I hadn't believed her.

'The insults are meant to make you lose your temper. Polydectes will then suggest that instead you should bring him the head of the Medusa, a monster with snakes for hair whose glance turns anything she looks on to stone. A whole army petrified in an instant, imagine it. He will say that if you are not too cowardly to achieve the quest, and if you deliver the Medusa to him, all accounts between the two of you will be settled. That will be his offer. You are to accept.'

'I see.'

The terrible lord of thunder looked at me sternly: luckily I had my mortal self under control. '*I see* is not an adequate response, Perseus. You must know the story of the Medusa, any six year old in the whole Middle Sea knows it.'

I had heard of the Medusa, but I wasn't going to give him the satisfaction. 'In one ear and out the other,' I said. 'I can't never remember all those fancy monsters.'

'Ah well,' he muttered to himself, 'brains aren't everything ... The Medusa, Perseus, was once the most beautiful woman in the world. She offended the gods, and was turned into a monster. She lives with two sister-monsters, also endowed with the snake-hair and the petrifying glance. The three of them are called the Gorgons, only Medusa is mortal. Her head has long been considered a highly desirable item by warlike princes. Champions and heroes have tried again and again to win the prize: they're all stone. So will you be, if you look her in the eye, my half-mortal child. Make no mistake, Godhead itself is no protection from the Medusa's power.'

'I understand,' I said; not risking another *I see.*

'No,' said Zeus, with a strangely human smile. 'You don't understand at all. These are mysteries ... But you'll know what to do when the time comes. You are to accept the challenge, that's all you have to grasp for now. We'll go on from there.'

Go on *where?* I wondered.

My father shrugged his great shoulders. 'In reality, by the way, Polydectes has not given up his outrageous, insolent pursuit of your dear mother. He's obsessed, but he's afraid to challenge you. You are my son, and he has some dim idea of what that means. He thinks you'll go off after the Medusa and never come back. That way, in his limited reasoning, he'll be able to take the lady by force, and incur no blame. He believes his brother will aquiesce once you are out of the way, and the very cosy set-up he has on Serifos will continue undisturbed. Now repeat your lesson.'

I wondered how much I would remember, when I was back in the mortal world. I'm genuinely *not* good at remembering things I don't understand. But that was his problem. I repeated my lesson. Party invitation, insults, horse-gift. The monster who turns people to stone. The challenge, which I was to accept.

There came a soft tap on the door.

'Come in!' he called, and the two servant-sailors appeared, one of them bearing a small table, the other a covered tray. The scent of fried fish and fried opotatos arrived with them. They ignored me, discreetly making sure I knew it, set the table in front of him and laid the cloth: deftly arranging oil and vinegar, a small green salad and a carafe of chilled white wine; beads of snow-melt on its rounded sides. The African lifted the cover from a huge platter, offering for display a fish as long as my arm, wrapped in airy golden batter, and surrounded by fabulously expensive mountains of opotato, cut in batons and fried to perfection.

I think the opotatos make it too much of a show-off dish, myself.

'Ah,' cried Zeus, beaming and rubbing his hands. 'Fish and chips! One of the sublime dishes of the world; and believe me, I know. First invented in my Aegean, of course. Invented here like *every* idea of value! Don't ever let anyone tell you about Ur of the Chaldees, Perseus. *My Aegean* is top of the cradle-of-civilisation class! And here, now, in the mortal realm of time, *you* are going to help me put it there.'

For a moment I knew what all this meant. I *knew* why the chief of the Achaean Supernaturals was talking to me about Polydectes' social plans, I knew that somehow the flying marks were part of it ... Then it was gone again.

He held out his hands to be washed. 'Oh, ah, Perseus. Won't you join me?' The table was laid for one. Sublime truth fell away, he was just another big cheese, dying to get at his dinner. I work in a restaurant, I said what I was supposed to say.

'I'd be greatly honoured, but I've got to be going, if you'll excuse me.'

'Must you? Ah, very well. I'll see you out.'

My father rose up like a thundercloud, and casually pointed a finger at the servants, table, food. The array shook itself and froze. Time had stopped for them all: the sailors, the dishes, the drops of melted ice. It dawned on me that Zeus's sailor-servants were not human beings. They were like the yacht itself, like his huge human body: appearances, part of his game, and this made me shiver.

What am I? I thought. Am I more real than these toys?

He came out on deck with me, affable and relaxed, smiling in his beard. 'Let me give you some advice. Your relatives, now. Some of them are reasonable, most of them are no-account. A bunch of drunks and squabblers, I'm afraid. Hermes, my courier, is a very safe young man. Make a friend of him, he'll be useful to you. You can trust your half-sister Athini; but watch her temper. Steer clear of my wife, obviously. Do not, under any circumstances, ever, tangle with your aunt Afroditi. I mean it.'

I was tempted to think this warning meant Afroditi might be an ally; but his tone of voice convinced me. 'I'll remember that.'

I was on the metal ladder, he was looking down. 'Beware of hunger. Beware of tiredness. The body you are wearing is a fine one, but it is mortal, and those things will cloud your judgement. Oh, and beware of alcohol. Same reason.'

Everything was coloured mist, reflected light, a veil over things that wouldn't fit into the mortal world. But there was mighty Zeus, leaning over the side of his pleasure yacht: giving me banal advice. Just like a human absentee dad, not knowing how to say goodbye. I felt a crazy, stupid pang of longing—

'Sir?' I could never call him father. 'Sir, what does it mean? The Medusa, a beautiful woman, a monster with the snake-head? Why do I have to do this?'

He smiled and leaned down, and touched me with his fingertip, on the forehead, between my eyebrows. The world exploded: writhing, coiling, squirming into fantastic patterns, a nest of vipers the size of the universe. I fell into the snake pit, I kept on falling, out of the reflection, back into the things I knew.

I rowed to the shore, I left the boat on the sand. Halfway up the headland path I felt something leave me, I looked back and the inlet was empty. *The Magnificent Escape* had vanished.

Everything looked strange, as if I'd been gone a very long time: but the shadows were hardly longer than they'd been when I left the Yacht Club. When I reached home the staff were setting up for an evening at Dicty's, as usual. Conversation was subdued, people greeted me uneasily. They didn't know what was really wrong with Palikari, but they'd sensed trouble. Anthe was running the kitchen, in a bad mood. She told me that Andromeda was with Pali. She said, *D'you have to keep asking where she is every single minute, Perseus?*; and I said *yes*.

The boss was in the furnace yard, cleaning his tools (which didn't need cleaning) and talking to Moumi. 'All well?' he asked, when I walked in.

'All's well enough,' I said, automatically. Our watchword. They were staring at me, and I wondered what they saw. Which was real? This world, or the other?

'What happened to you?' said my mother.

'I don't know. Maybe I fell asleep on the shore.'

I sat on an old packsaddle, and told them about *The Magnificent Escape.*

Moumi put her palm to my forehead. It was burning, as if I'd been too long in the sun. I found out afterwards, when I looked in her best bronze mirror, that I had a dark, rosy mark there, which took days to fade.

'Bathe, and then go and sleep it off, Perseus. You'll feel better in the morning.'

6

The invitation arrived a few days later. It was delivered
very properly, very old-Style – like a memory of
how things were done before the Great Disaster. The
king's embassy arrived with two horsemen bearing green
branches and six musicians on foot, playing the lyre and
the double flute as they walked (but not well). The herald
had no Achaean staff of office, just a wreath and garlands.
His hands were empty except for the traditional gift of scented
oil. They stood on the waterfront, and requested permission
to speak with the master of Seatown. Papa Dicty hadn't been
treated with such honour since the leadership challenge of
long ago.

The people of Seatown watched from indoors. They'd
cleared the streets when they saw the herald's party coming:
not sure what was going on. But the staff at Dicty's were very
excited. The king was sueing for peace! Our troubles were

over! Papa Dicty was going to share Polydectes' throne, the way things ought to be!

'First the stick, then the carrot,' said the boss, dryly. 'I suppose if we decline the invitation we may expect more violence. I think I'll call a Town Meeting.'

So we called a meeting, and everyone from within a day's journey turned up. The Sacred Enclosure was packed. I sat with my mother and Dicty, going over what I planned to say: remembering the time when I was a kid, and climbed up with my friends to peek over the fence. And we were spotted, and yelled at, and chased ... Town Meetings had been rare in my lifetime, rare enough to be fascinating to little boys. Now I was one of the grown-ups, about to speak in public, but I didn't feel privileged. I felt like a stranger, uneasy and awkward among these people I'd known all my life.

I thought of Andromeda, who wasn't here. I felt I was looking at the world through her eyes: seeing human life like a game you've forgotten how to play.

We had the opening ceremony, Holy Mother and the sisters retired to their incense-smoky alcove at the back. Dicty made the first speech, and kept it short. 'The king my brother has invited my daughter's son, Perseus, to a celebration of his wedding plans. Apparently he is courting a Mainland princess, of a very respectable family: it sounds like a good match, and a useful alliance for our island. As you know, Polydectes has been a suitor to the lady Danae, and this has caused some strain. He wishes his new plans to mark a return to more cordial relations. I believe that Perseus should accept the invitation, but I felt you should have a say in the matter, dear people.'

Murmur, murmur, murmur, then a share-fisherman stood up, a modest fellow with a small stake in a fishing boat co-op. 'I'm glad to hear this news, Papa Dicty, and I'm sure you're right. We should always let bygones be bygones when someone wants to make up. Do you agree, dear people? And if so, who should we send with lady Danae's son? He can't go up there alone, that would look very poor and shabby.'

That set the ball rolling. Balba the great weaver rose majestically (she was not fat, but *massive*), and folded her brawny arms. 'After all these years,' she said. 'Suddenly young Dectes is behaving the way a king ought, involving us in his business. It's about time. I agree, a company should go with Perseus. But can we trust the king?'

A farmer from one of the villages cried out, forgetting the proper forms. 'He takes our children! We've lost two sons, and our only daughter. I know they're still alive, but they are as if dead to us. How can I forgive that? How can you be taken in by this so-called invitation, are you insane? He's a monster. I say *turn him down*!'

There was a swell of voices agreeing with him, a tide washing in the opposite direction, *Don't talk like that! He does what has to be done! He's the king!* The Seatown butcher, a huge dark-bearded man with a twisted leg, who used to scare me to death when I was a child, thumped on the floor with his stick. 'Quiet down! Quiet down!'

Dicty stood up again. 'Clearly, our feelings are divided. I think that's to be expected, but there is a deciding factor. Please listen to what Perseus has to say.'

So I stood up to make my maiden speech. 'I'm going to tell you why I think we can trust the king. I had a strange dream, I think it was a vision, which foretold every detail about the invitation, before it arrived—'

The boss wanted them to know what had happened to me, and I could see the justice of that. I'd been wide awake on board a yacht that didn't exist in this world: but *strange dream* seemed the right description, something they would understand.

Murmur, murmur murmur. 'Have you told your dream to the sisters, Perseus?' demanded the pastry cook who supplied our breakfast fancies.

'The sisters know the difference between a common dream and vision,' called someone else. 'There are signs. Did *they* think it meant we should trust the king?'

'If it's important, he should take this to Holy Mother!'

'Perseus can't have had a vision, he's not the type. He's a *bruiser*—'

'A big hulking lad like that, look at him!'

The pastry cook had made herself known, the hecklers just yelled without standing up. Of course, normal people who had *strange dreams* brought them to the Enclosure to be interpreted. It hadn't even crossed my mind—

'It wasn't like that. Er, it wasn't hard to understand, it was very straightforward. I just know that the marriage party is safe, kidnapping is not on the king's mind—'

I floundered, wondering what it would have meant to one of them, my friends and neighbours, if they'd met Great Zeus. Would they have *survived*?

Balba came to my rescue. She surged to her feet again, and glared them all into silence. 'May I speak? Some of us here are devout, some of us aren't. Some of us believe in the Supernaturals, some of us stick by the old ways. But whatever we think about it, Perseus and his mother are god-touched. And not in an unlucky way, or they'd have drowned like kittens when the lady's father (she bowed towards my mother) threw them in the sea in a box. I believe that settles the question. The boy's dream can be trusted.'

The townsfolk muttered *god-touched* to each other, and quieted: mysteriously satisfied. Sometimes when people said god-touched, they simply meant 'he's crazy'. I thought of the mark on my forehead, and a nest of whirling vipers.

'Well, that's about all I have to say.' I sat down quickly.

'Never mind,' murmured the boss. 'You'll do better next time.'

There was a pause. Then they plunged, with relief, into the practical issues. I should go, but I shouldn't go alone. The boss had not been invited, nor had my mother. The meeting couldn't decide if this showed a lack of respect, or tact. But our matriarchs and other substantial citizens were certain it meant *they* couldn't go. They couldn't sit down at the table with Polydectes, and without Papa Dicty!

Humbler members of the older generation said they didn't feel they were up to it. So it was agreed it would be appropriate to send unmarried young people, but then nobody wanted their own sons or daughters to be in the party. Suppose my 'strange dream' was one of those *tricky* oracles, meaning the opposite of what it seemed to mean? The young men (the few of them qualified to be at the meeting) were keen, but felt the girls should stay at home, for safety. The young women had exactly the opposite opinion. Someone suggested drawing lots. Someone else (I think it was the butcher), said drawing lots was *invariably* a recipe for disaster, quarrels, and blood feuds lasting hundreds of years. And so on, and so on.

The Holy Sisters sat at the back, drinking tea and quietly chatting. Their only contribution was when Holy Mother strongly suggested we ought to walk up to the High Place. We didn't have horses, and mules would create a poor impression. Donkeys would be worse. We might make an offering at the ruined hilltop shrine, that would be proper. Some flowers and choice fruit, nicely arranged; maybe a dance, and a hymn or two . . .

It's not that the sisters are greedy for food offerings. They're rich, they give all the offerings they get to the poor. They just love the thought of a procession: it makes their day. But she was right about the mules.

At last they hit on the idea of asking the Yacht Club

kids to escort me. The off-islanders who hung around that waterfront bar were in no danger from our king. Many of them were very well connected: Polydectes wouldn't dare to touch them. A messenger was immediately sent to sound them out. Of course they agreed. They were party animals, and the spice of danger didn't put them off at all.

It was all settled in about four hours, not bad going for a Town Meeting.

Seatown got into a ferment of excitement. People came to the taverna to congratulate Dicty on happier times ahead. They praised the wise way my mother had dealt with Polydectes' unwanted advances: as if the new marriage was Moumi's idea. Matriarchs brought out heirloom finery for the wedding-shower guests to wear. The Yacht Club kids were auditioned (which they thought was hilarious) by Seatown's dance teacher; crowds came to watch the rehearsals in the Enclosure. The best flowers and fruits that could be found were earmarked by a committee, for our garlands and for the offering. Competition between the gardeners was cut-throat.

The restaurant was very quiet, even more so than usual; though trade was always slow after midsummer. 'I see how it'll be,' said the boss. 'Perseus will bring back his grisly trophy, I'll become Secondary King, and nobody will eat here. They'll be embarrassed to have the king's brother cooking for them, and I'll go bankrupt!'

There was so much I wanted to ask him. What did Great Zeus really want with me? What if we went up to the citadel, and Polydectes *did* ask me to fetch him the Medusa? What then? But we'd never talked about those issues. I didn't know how to start, and the boss gave me no help. He was in a strange mood: sometimes more irritable than I'd ever known him; or else muttering hopefully about his brother. 'Polydectes

87

may still repent,' he'd say to Moumi. 'He may come to his senses.'

My mother would nod, but say nothing. She'd withdrawn into herself, not talking much to anyone, since I'd told them about meeting my father.

Palikari would miss the party. But everyone took it for granted that the two young women of Dicty's household would be in the chosen band. I had no say in the matter, apparently. I made an idiot of myself trying to convince Anthe that she ought to have her parents' permission – which she couldn't have got hold of in time, because they lived on Milos. She rolled her eyes. 'Oooh, Perseus! You told the Town Meeting there was no danger at all. You didn't *tell a lie* in Meeting, did you? And how d'you think it's going to look if you turn up with the Princess Andromeda on your arm, and no chaperone?'

'I don't think that's funny,' I said.

'You're right. This is not funny at all. I love you both and if anything goes wrong I'm going to be by your side.'

I decided I'd better frisk her party frock for that fish-gutting knife.

I told Andromeda she had no reason to get involved in this. She just asked me what I thought she should wear. 'My own clothes are for travelling, and Anthe's things don't fit me, but I've been offered some lovely dresses.'

'Wear what you wore when I met you, on the dock at Naxos.'

She laughed at that idea, and we went to review her wardrobe, taking a jug of cool watered wine, and a fistful of almonds and dried apricots. On the white roof, in the rich sun of late afternoon, we spread out a glowing array of heirloom robes. We talked; I don't know what we said. I know it was nothing about how I felt, or how she felt. But I was wrapped in a dream, where we were lovers who hadn't yet said the word:

and I thought she was dreaming with me. I told her how glad I was that I knew her name. She said, you always knew my name, I told you my name on the *Afroditi*, the night we met. It's *S'bw'r*. I couldn't say it, she made me keep trying—

S'bw'r

S'bw'r

She'd been like someone returned to life, since she'd told us she was bound to die. But summer would end, the wind would change, and my fate might descend on me this very night. We would never speak what was in our eyes, we would never touch each other, because there was no time. All we could do was smile, and tease each other, and say things that were secret messages; until our family called us to come downstairs.

Twenty of us walked up the hill, ten boys and ten girls, wreathed and garlanded, dressed in our best: slightly salt-foxed Mainland finery from the Yacht Kids' sea chests, the treasured robes loaned by our weavers. Frothing white skirts banded in red and gold, fringed scarves woven with cherries and apples, tunics blazoned with sunbursts and dolphins; brooches and pins, heavy old bracelets and necklets from ancient dowries. The matriarchs had been determined we were going to make a good show.

I wore white, with a purple stripe. Anthe had a new dress in her favourite saffron yellow, with a pattern of green leaves. Andromeda's antique tunic was the colour of damsons: a laced bodice went with it, with little flames woven around the neckline. The girls had chosen her to carry their offering, and given her a wreath of white sea-lilies; her black hair fell in shining, natural ringlets. She walked beside the lad who'd been given the job by the boys' side; carrying her fruit basket, smiling and laughing.

She looked like a sacrifice.

There was nothing left of the shrine but its foundations. We made our offering among the tumbled stones: we danced and sang, and prayed aloud for the health and fortune of the prospective happy couple. What kind of wishes for the king anyone had under their breath, I leave to Great Mother.

The gates of the citadel were open, but the guards were out in force, drawn up in double ranks; in full armour. I was proud of us as we strolled between them, discussing cheerfully whether we should sing another hymn to edify the king, or should we save it for later. Not a sign of nerves, not even when the heavy gates had snarled shut, and we were trustingly helpless in the tyrant's camp.

The High Place didn't look all that impressive, oddly enough. I'd never been inside a fortress before, but I could tell that's what this place was, plain and simple. There were no shops, no restaurants, no markets, no *streets*: just the spaces between the barracks, ranks of storehouses; and a great wall of timber, stone and thorns all around. The only significant buildings, apart from Polydectes' stone-built house, were the new temples, and they looked raw and poorly finished to my eyes. No trees or gardens around them. No coloured paint or whitewash on the walls. It seemed the High Place folk didn't bother with decoration of any kind: either that or they didn't know how to do it. You're not so fine, I thought. What we have is better than this. But I tried not to look around too curiously, I didn't want to be spotted behaving like a spy.

The banqueting hall was more impressive. It was a big, imposing room, rather dark but lit by many hanging lamps. We filed in and got announced by the steward. I watched the man adjust his condescending attitude, as the Yacht Club kids gave their names to be shouted out. He'd been expecting the lower orders. We had our hands and feet washed, we tried to look relaxed. There were no women present, apart from the girls in our party, but that wasn't a danger sign. The king had no wife, no mother, no sisters. There was no ladies' court at the High Place.

Some of my company were Achaeans, or from well-off families on other islands; some from further afield. They all knew what to do at a private feast. Anthe and I relied on our restaurant training. We sat together: Andromeda had a place at a higher table. She'd given her name as 'Kore of Africa, a traveller', but she'd been treated like someone of rank.

At least I could watch her. She was safe, between her partner from the offering ceremony, and another Yacht Club lad: two handsome young men from the Twelve Islands, who called themselves Gliko and Niki. They seemed to be looking after her all right. They were making my girl laugh—

Which upset me, stupidly.

The courses came thick and fast, I counted fifteen (too many for good taste). I couldn't fault the baked and grilled meats, the rest was dismal. The wines were poorly kept, the honey was stale and the mixing water was not spring water, or iced either; but there you go. I hadn't expected the cuisine to compete with Dicty's. Polydectes, having made sure I was given a lowly seat, had not so much as looked my way. He sat in his big armed chair at the table on the dais, looking down on us all, and talked to his friends.

I had never seen the king before, except at a distance. I tried to judge him, as if he was an opponent in a boxing-match. The tyrant who'd been a shadow over my life was not much taller than his brother. But he had presence, and plenty of hard muscle. He was about ten years younger than Dicty, as I knew: his hair and his well-clipped beard were dark, untouched by grey. His eyes were hazel-brown, they caught the light.

Finally a dessert was brought in: butter, cheeses, cakes and nuts, fresh fruit and dried; sweet wines. I saw a stir of expectation on the high table.

The show was about to begin.

Polydectes rose, and held out his cup to be filled. I saw him shake his head, fussily, as the steward tried to give him a liqueur. He was an abstemious man. I'd noticed that he'd eaten sparingly, and taken his wines with plenty of water.

'My lords!' he began, in a strong voice: he didn't need a herald repeat his words. 'My friends, my guests. Especially the charming ladies; whom we welcome. Although up here we follow modern fashion, and think ladies should stay at home—'

He was looking at Andromeda. She paid no attention, she went on eating a piece of cheese, looking bored. I'd seen him glance her way often, with curiosity and calculation. Was he thinking of the reward he could get for delivering her back to Haifa? I was grateful to the innards-readers, if they'd told him he mustn't touch.

'I thank you all for joining me, to celebrate my marriage plans.' (Cheers and whoops: some of the 'nobles' were completely tipsy, and the Yacht Club kids too). 'But as you know—' He bared·his teeth in a grin. 'A wedding isn't all pleasure, it's a business negotiation. A man has to haggle with a fine young lady's parents, same as if he were buying a round of succulent cheese in the marketplace.'

His courtiers roared with laughter, and banged their cups.

'How would *he* know?' muttered Anthe. 'He's never paid a bill in his life. These cheeses are stolen, I bet. Like everything else in here.'

'Sssh.'

'Now since the lady I desire is Hippodameia, daughter of the great king of Olympias, I'd better make my bridegift a hefty present of horses!' More roars. *Hippodameia* was a Greek name meaning something like 'Horse-Tamer'. I bet she looks like a horse, I thought. And she's being sold like one. 'I know you're going to help me out. I expect a horse from each of you! Imported bloodstock, if you please, no nags. What do you say? Is that too much to ask, my noble vassals?'

This has been rehearsed, I thought. Everyone knows the lines. And so do I ...

One by one the tyrant's followers got up. Each of them said he would give a horse, and not just any horse. We got the name of the stud farm, the sire and dam, the colour of the animal's hide, its conformation, top speed, the honours it had won; the trainer's name and reputation. A seriously expensive wedding list of mighty chests, firm hocks, short backs, round eyes, proud crests: which got harder to believe as we passed down the pecking order. I'd drunk as little as I could get away with, and I have an iron head, but I felt very strange. I was watching from the outside, I *knew* all this—

'Ah, now we come to Perseus. Did you hope we were leaving you out? Don't be embarrassed! As the least of my vassals, I know you can't afford a horse. Your foster father's a taverna keeper, which I'm glad our parents didn't live to see, but I suppose old Dicty's found his own level. Where would he find that kind of money, eh?'

The high table yelled with laughter.

'You're absolutely right,' I said, loud and clear. But I didn't stand up. 'I'm stony broke. What do you suggest?'

'Give him your *mother*!' shouted one of the so-called nobles. 'Let him have that secondhand princess as Hippodaemia's bathroom maid.'

'I'd like a pretty yeller-haired bathroom maid myself!' bellowed another of them. 'I'll have her after you, Sire. Before we pass her around the barracks, eh?'

'Bit long in the tooth, but she'd do with the lamp blown out—!'

Anthe had grabbed my knee under the table. She seemed to be trying to gouge out the bone with her fingernails: but I didn't need extreme pain to help to keep my head. I knew the insults were meant to shake me. But I took note. Tall older bruiser, with a boxer's nose and ponytail. Fat slob with pasty double chins; scrawny young blood with the armlets and the goatee beard. I won't forget you three, I thought, as I sat grinning uncertainly – a pitiful oversized clown, too dumb to tell the difference between raucous fun and damned insults.

Polydectes was wrapped in a showy mantle in the Serifos *sunburst* style, a gold and yellow sun the size of a bonfire splattered over his chest. If I looked like an idiot, he looked like a strutting cockscomb. But I knew he wasn't, and his friends weren't fools either. I knew them by what they'd done to Serifos. The king was a tough, cunning, ruthless man in the prime of life, and the men around him were the same. He was no pushover. Yet he was speaking words my father had told me I would hear, and he didn't know it. He thought he was in control of this, but he was not—

'Your mother's safe,' he said gravely, after waiting for the laughter to die. Making out the insults weren't his design: as if his men would have dared to speak like that about Danae without orders. 'The gift I want is very different. I'm going to set you a challenge, my fine young fellow. Bring me the head of the Medusa, with the eyes that turn men to stone. Do you think you can manage that?'

(Afterwards, some tale-tellers said *I* made the offer. I boasted I could get him the Medusa Head, trying to make an impression: and Polydectes called my bluff. This is not true, and no one who knows me at all believes it ...)

There was a hubbub of excitement. Polydectes' men were going *oooh!* because they'd been primed for this moment. The Yacht Club kids hadn't known what was coming, but they'd heard of the Medusa. She'd been a famous challenge – until so many champions had failed to come back that the quest went out of style. Anthe and Andromeda were in shock for a different reason. I'd told them practically word for word what the king would say.

'*The Medusa,*' whispered the girl on the other side of me, a traveller from Kéros. 'Great Mother, Perseus, your tyrant mustn't get hold of that monstrous thing! A weapon that can turn armies to stone! He could rule the Middle Sea!'

'Don't be dumb, Kia,' muttered Anthe. 'He doesn't want the Snakehead, he wants rid of Perseus. No one comes back alive from that so-called quest.'

I ignored them. I was fascinated, detached, watching it all unfold. I said what I was supposed to say, shrugging and grinning like a yokel.

'All right. I'll give it a try, if you like.'

Polydectes smiled. I saw that he was *hungry* to be revenged on Dicty; and on my mother for refusing him. But just getting me out of the way wasn't enough, there had to be a twist . . . He's being used, I thought coldly. He's doomed.

'Accepted!' cried the king, with a flourish. The sunburst mantle flashed.

The hall burst into wild applause. The Yacht Club kids were banging and yelling too, not to be out done. They didn't care that we were unarmed, outnumbered, and things could still turn nasty. They're pretty crazy, boys and girls alike, the young braves who wander the Middle Sea looking for fun. 'PERSEUS!' they shouted. 'PERSEUS! PERSEUS! PERSEUS! THE SNAKEHEAD! PERSEUS!'

As if I were the star of a ballgame team, and the Medusa Head our winning goal.

There was another dessert course, salty this time, with more wines. As it was laid, I saw Polydectes speak to the chief steward. The man came over to me, smirking. 'Young sir,' he murmured, with fake deference and a pitying grin, 'the king has asked me to tell you, feel free to take your leave now. An entertainment is about to start, and we don't want to shock the young ladies. It's dancing girls, you see.'

There's nothing wrong with dancing girls. But I knew that the 'entertainers' here would be kidnapped villagers, untrained, unwilling, humiliated ... And there was nothing I could do.

'The king hopes you'll call on the High Place for weapons and supplies. We know your foster father won't be able to equip you, we wouldn't want to put him out.'

'That's all right,' I said. 'We've got plenty of meat cleavers.'

Herding drunken Yacht Club kids was like filling a sieve with water. Somehow, I don't know how, we got them out of there. Outside the hateful walls it was still black night, though dawn couldn't be far off. Anthe had left a bundle of torches by the road, with the offering-baskets. She and Andromeda lit them and handed them round. Gliko gave one to me, and punched me in the shoulder. He was very happy.

'Go, Perseus!' he crowed. 'The Medusa's Head! That'll make your name!' He peered into my face. 'Hey, you look a bit glum. You can do it, can't you?'

I shrugged. 'I suppose.'

'Tha's the spirit. Your tyrant's *an idiot*. Glad I was there to see you take him on.'

He winked at Andromeda and launched himself after the pack. The away team went dancing, stumbling and singing down the hill. Anthe had gone with them.

I looked at her, she looked at me.

'They'll be sober in the morning,' she said.

'I'm sober now.'

'I know you are,' said Andromeda.

We let the bobbing lights vanish and then followed, slowly; heads down and silent as a pair of tired mules. Neither of us said a word until we reached the cemetery. We sat on the low wall, and she took my hand. The eastern sky was grey, the fading night was cold.

'What's it like where you live?' I asked.

I could hardly see her face, but I felt her smile.

'Our city's on the coast. To the east and north and south, you look out and the land goes on and on, forever. It's an ocean of land, the caravans sail across it. But I had never left Haifa, before I ran away. Except once, by sea, to visit Eygpt—'

'I meant where you *live*. The palace?'

'Oh … It's not at all like here. Nothing's square, except the gates. Nothing's stone, except the doorways to the public rooms, the throne room, and my father's house, and the halls of judgement. There are gardens on terraces high above the ground, and there's the bathing place, which is underground and spring fed. There are far too many towers, some of them very tall and spindly, with windows like little black eyes. From the outside it looks exactly like a gathering of giant termite's nests, painted white—'

She could talk now, because she didn't have to lie. She'd been our silent mystery girl when she was still fighting for her life.

'I don't know what a termite is.'

'It's a kind of ant. They make huge nests like blobby towers of earth in our fields: as tall as you. They look half-melted. But they don't have windows.' She looked at the toes of her sandals. 'Termites eat anything.'

I noticed that being by the graves didn't bother her. She was no more afraid of the dead than I was. 'I didn't like the way that brute kept staring at you.'

'You mean the king? He won't kidnap me. Men like that don't meddle in priests' business. All those horses … Why are horses so important, Perseus?'

'Status symbols. Signs of power. They're important to the Greeks: not to us. But Polydectes wants to *be* a Greek, an Achaean. That's why he's obsessed with my mother.'

'I dream of horses. I don't know why, I've never ridden one.'

The east was growing brighter by the minute. I let go of her hand and rolled my torch on the ground to put it out. Andromeda's had already guttered. She used the charred end to draw lines and curls on the rocks at our feet.

S'bw'r . . . I whispered it. 'I wish *I* had a secret name. I would tell it only to you.'

'But you do. I think you've spent your life hiding your secret name from everyone, except maybe your mother. Pretending it doesn't exist, and you're not him.'

'I don't know what you mean.'

'Son of Zeus.'

'Oh, that . . .' I shrugged it off. There was something I must say, and the half light gave me courage. 'Andromeda, you *can't* go back. What about the new kind of writing? What'll happen to that incredible, wonderful idea? Don't you care that it will be lost? What if no one can ever write down Dark Water again, and bring it back to life, from little flying marks, what if people never learn how to do that again—?'

She shook her head, listlessly, without looking up. 'I thought like that. Now I know it doesn't matter how talented I am, how clever, how "special" . . . Anybody's child is special. I didn't tell you did I? Before I ran away, my mother tried to get the priests to take *her*, in my place. Of course they said no. A sacrifice has to be young, and virgin. But she'd have died for me. She truly loves me, in her way.'

'Then she'll protect you.'

'No she won't. She thinks she brought this punishment down on us, but she's still a queen, who has to plan for the future. If she refuses to give me up, then even if there's no earthquake, I'm *useless*. I'm god-touched now. I can't rule our country, I can't make a match that will give us a great alliance. There's nothing she can do with me.' Andromeda shivered. 'It was very unpleasant, at home. It was p-partly to get away from her guilt and remorse ... No. That's a lie. I ran because I didn't want to die. I still don't want to die. But I've accepted it.'

'What about your father?'

'Kephus?' She almost laughed. 'Daddy's very sorry this had to happen. But needs must, if the priests want a princess. He has plenty of other children.'

I'll kill him, I thought. I'll smash his teeth through the back of his skull.

But it's easy enough to say these things, think these things, when you're big and strong, and you've never done anything worse than knock down a lout or two.

'Do you believe in the Gods?' I asked, abruptly.

I could see her clear dark profile, a frown gathering between her level brows. The curve of her lashes, shadowing her cheek. 'I believe they are not what we think they are. That there are veils on veils, between us and them—'

'I don't mean do you believe they exist.' Suddenly I was shaking, I couldn't stop. 'I meant do you believe in the way they tell us to behave, Zeus and the rest; the way my mother taught me. Never mind what they do themselves?'

'What is it? What's the matter?'

'I *do* believe,' I said. 'I never thought about it before, but now I *know*. If I kill an innocent person, the Furies will rise from hell and pursue me, and tear my soul to shreds.'

I had heard Polydectes speak his lines. Visions, strange dreams: shadows I could see and other people couldn't ... I couldn't run away from all that now. I knew the other world was real. More real than earth or stone.

'Everything my father told me has come true, *it's real,* Andromeda. I'm supposed to go and kill the Medusa, a beautiful woman who offended the Supernaturals and got turned into a monster. D'you know how she offended? I didn't know, but I've found out. The Yacht Club kids know all about it. Her *crime* was that a God raped her. The way my father raped my mother.'

'Oh, Perseus—'

'She never did me any harm, but I'm to track her down and kill her, this wretched woman in her misery, because the Supernaturals are playing some game. My father thinks he can make me, but I can't do it. I won't do it—'

Andromeda tried to calm me. She stood up and held my head against her breast, imprisoning my clenched fists: she stroked my hair and kissed me. 'Perseus, Perseus, my hero, my dearest, my love—' I freed myself, so I could see the light in her eyes. But the way she was looking at me twisted like a knife. How could she look at me like that?

'It's *all right*,' she said, like someone soothing a hysterical child. 'You're not going to kill the Medusa. It's not murder, it's just an impossible task. You're going off on a quest to get killed, for some reason of your father's that we don't understand. And I am going back to Haifa, because I must. We are both dead, you and I. We are ghosts.'

She smiled at me sadly, gently, full of wise, hopeless love—

'You don't understand me at all!' I shouted, furious.

I pulled my hands away, left her there and went storming off down the hillside.

7

I ended up at the gates of the Enclosure scratched to bits, dust and thorns all over my party clothes. A spray of morning glory flowers, fluted horns of lilac, blue and violet, nodded from the fence beside me; newly opened to the sun. The gates weren't barred, they rarely are. I went inside, just because it looked quiet in there. I couldn't see any sisters around. They must be working in the herb and vegetable gardens, or in the hospital. The Town Meeting benches had been stored away again. I walked about on the beaten earth, trying not to think about Andromeda. I couldn't bear her attitude, all that shining love and noble resignation. I wanted her to run for her life, and take me with her.

I looked at the old wooden door to the bathing place, which always seemed like a door into the centre of the earth. You had to stoop to get inside; I'd have to bend double now I was grown. Once there'd been a hot spring in the caves, with healing powers. The water wasn't hot any more, the flow of all our underground water had changed since the Great Disaster. It was still sacred. People were brought to bathe if they were very ill, or mad. They came when they had something important to do, like buying property, getting married, confessing a crime; or before a child was born.

We could bathe, we could bring our dreams to be interpreted. Every other Great Mother ritual was totally secret. Maybe there *weren't* any rituals, I thought. Maybe that was what you found out, when you became a nun. The big secret, new sister dear, is that there isn't one. All we do is tend our gardens, and look after the sick and poor. I thought of what Andromeda had said, *there are veils on veils* ... Great Mother herself was at the back of the nuns' smoky alcove, on a plinth of dark red stone with veins of black in it; which was supposed to have been brought here from Fira long ago. She knelt on her heels, her arms folded under her small breasts. She was carved from a kind of stone the colour of oatmeal, polished very smooth; she was only about two hands high. She was older than the plinth, maybe by a thousand years, but Great Mother's statues always showed her as a young girl, hardly more than a child.

Once her features would have been painted, and the painting renewed at ritual times. There was nobody qualified to do that now: Holy Mother was never going to let Popo get his hands on Her. But I could feel her watching me, although all I could see was a jaunty, cheerful nose in a smooth shield of a face, with a pointed chin.

What should I do? I thought. It wasn't a prayer, and the cheerful little girl didn't answer it. But I thought I'd kneel for a moment with her—

'Perseus! Good heavens boy, *what* have you been doing to yourself?'

I nearly jumped out of my skin. It was Holy Mother. She'd

crept up behind me, the silent way she can, and was standing there leaning on her cane, looking disgusted.

'Uh, nothing. I ran down the hillside, I don't know why.'

'Huh. You got drunk at that party, obviously. Have you come to bathe? You'd better, before your mother sees the state of you.'

I had not thought of it, but she was right. I had come to bathe. I nodded.

'Well, come on then.'

I followed her, bending double, into the bathing place, stripped off and oiled myself with the holy oil while she lit some tiny lamps: pointing out where I'd missed a bit, and grumbling on Koukla's behalf about the state of my best clothes. I knelt, humbly naked, in the worn old bathtub; the remains of red paint with a black design barely visible in the gloom. The old lady opened the holy water tap, took her personal bronze scraper, thin and fine as a leaf, and went to work. She had no respect. She might as well have been washing a dog, a dirty overgrown puppy, the way she pushed me around. But it was soothing, somehow, although she made me yelp. I felt like a little boy being bathed by my mother. I felt I'd be *seriously* clean after this, and my mind would be miraculously clear.

The cold douche was so cold it made my eyes water.

'There you are. Out you get, rub yourself down. I'll fetch you a clean tunic, and don't worry about the customary donation.'

'Thank you.'

'I'll put it on Dicty's temple tithe. Item, scrubbing one enormous child who can't see a plain path when it's set down in front of him.'

'Sorry.'

Holy Mother wasn't very old, no older than the boss, and that's hardly middle-aged in the islands. We say we're like our olive trees, at our best between seventy and ninety. But she'd been born with a case of curved spine, which our people consider a sign of a vocation to holy orders. With her slow walk and her cane, and the long grey veil swathing her, she seemed ancient.

I had a feeling she worked on it. All proper Holy Mothers ought to be bent and crabby, and senior to everyone.

'Holy Mother, what happened when the Princess Andromeda came here?'

'None of your business. As long as it's not immoral, foreigners may use their own forms of worship here. What *happened* is between the young woman and her God.'

She shuffled off, muttering about my disgraceful curiosity, and returned with an armful of old clothes. I wanted to ask her, please, what should I do? Should I obey my Supernatural father, take off on a quest and commit murder? Commit the murder for my own reasons? *For Andromeda?* Should I stay on Serifos, kill a tyrant, unleash the destruction of war and break my *real* father's heart? Or should I run away from the whole mess? Take a berth on the next ship out and never look back?

These seemed to be my miserable options, and she was the holiest person I knew. But I didn't manage to get started in the secret dark of the bathing chamber. When we were out in the sun again, me wearing a too-short poorbox tunic the poor had declined through good taste, I knew it would be useless. I wasn't going to get any help in here. Great Mother had gone off somewhere, and left her pets in charge.

But I tried.

'Holy Mother, is it ever right to commit murder?'

'Of course not. What are you? Four years old?' She looked at me sharply. '*Have* you killed someone unfairly? Did things turn nasty up there? Oh, *Perseus*. You're going to cost your poor family a fortune in hooliganism-fines. You'll have to say it was the heat of the moment, you'll probably get away with that. Claim that you're truly sorry and agree a price with the family, that's all.'

I gave up.

'What do you think of the black metal, Holy Mother? Is it a bad thing?'

The old lady sniffed, and led the way to the gates. 'It's fine for farm machinery,' she said. 'And common weapons, I *suppose*. Absolutely useless for ritual purposes. Put it in a bone dry cave, that stuff rots faster than human flesh.'

So much for old time holiness.

I walked into the hills, because anywhere in town I'd run into friends and neighbours buzzing with the news of the Medusa's Head Challenge. At first I walked because I couldn't stand to go home. I couldn't face Dicty or my mother, and I didn't ever want to see Andromeda again. If we were *dead*, what was the point? We should part now.

After a while I just walked, lost in hopeless plotting.

Andromeda would never break the vow she had made in the Enclosure. I *could not* stop her from sacrificing herself . . . I knew how it would be done. She hadn't told me, but I'd got it out of Dicty. He thought the description could be relied on: Taki's agent was extremely trustworthy. Princess Andromeda would be chained to a sacred rock just off shore, and left there for the monster, or the tidal wave: which would devour her and subside with no further damage. If the priests were to be believed.

I'd asked him how long it was supposed to take.

The boss had shaken his head. 'A matter of hours, I believe. There are big seas on that coast at the end of summer, without anything supernatural involved.'

I saw myself rescuing her from that rock. I'd get to Haifa, be out there with a boat. I'd row up when the priests had left, cut the chains and snatch her away before she drowned.

No use, she'd hate me and she'd be right. *She was god-touched.* Whatever that meant, it meant something real. More real than those conniving priests could imagine. Die in her place? No use, that would be an insult too, the duty was *hers*. If I wanted to save her, I had to deal with the God.

Somehow, in that short span of time when she was on the rock, I had to make it so that her people didn't need the sacrifice.

When Great Zeus had ordered me to accept the Medusa Head challenge, and told me that Godhead itself was no protection against the Medusa's power, an idea had leapt at me, almost the moment I heard those words. I'd been brooding on it ever since.

How would it sound, if I told her?

I'm going to kill an innocent woman to save your life, Andromeda—

No! No!

Find the Gorgons' lair, spot the mortal one, chop off her head—

No. Stop that.

I can't do it.

I *won't* do it. I won't kill an innocent victim of their games—

How do you tell which is the mortal one? What kind of blade do you use?

I woke out of my walking daze in uncleared forest. I didn't know what time it was, I couldn't see the sun. The sky was a blank strip of blue, so intense it shaded to violet, the black shadow of the trees on either side confused my eyes. I didn't know where I was ... Of course I knew where I was. I must know! Serifos is a small island, I could walk across the 'trackless forest' of our highest peaks in an hour or so. But the path under my feet looked strange.

My shoulders prickled, I looked behind and saw nothing move, but I knew I was in danger—

There was light ahead. I made for it with relief, and came out of the trees into a high, stony place. Black slopes of ilex and pine fell into hazy brown distance; the shining sea was all around. The Turning Islands, my Kyklades, were spread in every direction, an island everywhere you looked, haloed in silver mist, floating between sky and ocean. The path wound between big red and rusty boulders. There were two people standing in my way, in a narrow place where there was no room for me to get by. The light was dazzling, I couldn't make out the figures clearly, though I was within a few paces of them. I was afraid, and that made me angry.

'Hey. Are you going to get out of the way, or what?' I demanded.

My vision cleared. I saw that the taller of the two was dressed as a warrior, in polished black: a tunic as if carved from obsidian, leg and armguards strapped around white, sculpted muscle; a black breastplate. She had a shield on her back and a sword at her hip, and her face was so icily beautiful I couldn't look at it. The young man with her wore a traveller's cloak and hat, and carried a herald's staff. His sandals had wings at the heels. He looked more human than the woman, but it was hard to keep his smooth, bright face in focus; it seemed to be in constant motion.

I knew who they were. I refused to fall on my knees. I wanted to run, but no one can run from fate. The other world had reached out to claim me, and there was nothing I could do. I hated to be in their power, but I *needed* them.

'I never get out of anyone's way,' said my half-sister Athini, in a dangerously gentle tone. 'What are you going to do about it, Perseus?'

'Oh, well,' I made as if to turn around and head back into the woods. (I was showing off: there was no risk that they'd let me go.) 'There are other paths.'

'Stay where you are, brat!' snapped the Goddess of Wisdom,

with a hand on her swordhilt. I remembered I was supposed to look out for her temper.

'We need to talk to you,' explained the young man whose staff and winged heels told me he was Hermes, the Divine Messenger. 'Or rather, you need to talk to us. We're here to equip you for your quest, didn't Father Zeus tell you?'

'He didn't tell me anything beyond Polydectes' feast.'

'But you know you have to slay the Medusa?'

I could not let go of my anger. 'For the sake of argument,' I said. 'Let's say I know that. Let's say I have to chop this woman's head off, because you Supernaturals say so: and I don't have a choice. But it sounds like murder to me. You can't just tell me *she's a monster*, as if that explains everything. Why does Medusa deserve to die? Hasn't she suffered enough? *Why* do I have to do this? I don't understand.'

Athini came up close, in one stride. Her blinding face looked into mine, I felt her touch on my brow, same as when my father had pushed me off his yacht, into the whirling snake pit. 'You have to do it because *you don't know*,' she said.

I backed off, stumbling and shaking my head.

'Thanks. That's very helpful.'

'Don't bother with the sarcasm, Perseus. These are mysteries. Just pay attention.'

'The Medusa is innocent,' said Hermes. 'She was once the most beautiful creature in the world, but she offended one of the Supernaturals. She was transformed, as you have heard, into a hideous monster, whose glance turns anyone looking on her to stone. She banished herself to the Garden of the Hesperides, at the far end of the world, where she lives with the two Gorgon sisters, Sthenno and Euryale. They have boar tusks, snakes for hair, and they are winged ... Medusa has never willingly harmed anyone, but what you do will not be murder, far from it. For the Medusa it will be a joyful release.'

'Which doesn't mean the monster won't put up a fight.'

Athini unslung the shield from her back, and drew her sword. 'And you are not immune to the petrifying glance, Perseus. You have to do it like this.' She demonstrated. 'Look into the shield. *Do not* look at the Medusa. Look at the Snakehead directly, and divine or mortal you are dead stone. Look into the shield. In reflection she is not a monster, I assure you. One sweep, and leap back. Her blood is poisonous, by the way. *Don't* get the blood on your skin.'

I thought I knew how to handle a sword and shield. I thought I was pretty good, tell you the truth: although I'd never drawn a weapon in anger. But when my half-sister went into action, that was utterly different. I was awed.

She held out the sword and shield. 'Now you try.'

God help me, I thought: but there was no escape.

She schooled me till I was dripping, and let me stand for a breather. My poor-box tunic was drenched, my legs were trembling. Athini was cool and dry as marble.

'Not bad. You can borrow the shield. I'll have my sword back, thank you.'

'Apart from the blood,' said Hermes, who'd been watching the training bout carefully, and making helpful comments (I mean, really helpful). 'There are the Gorgon sisters. Sthenno and Euryale are not mortal or human, and never were. You can't kill them, don't try. The only thing you can do is get away from there, very, very fast. You'll need to borrow these.' He stooped, swift as thought, and unfastened his sandals.

I slung the shield of Athini on my back, and took the sandals. The wings on the heels were fixed with little golden bosses, they were folded like a sleeping bird's. I'd seen Yacht Club kids wearing winged sandals, with the feathers done in cut leather, dyed white or gilded . . . This was where the idea came from; this was the real thing.

'Don't put them on,' Hermes advised. 'Put them in, er—' he took a dubious look at the sweat-sodden poor-box tunic

'—in the breast of your, er, training kit. Practise where you have plenty of space. No buildings or tall trees around, and no steep hillsides you might smash yourself into. But don't worry, it's intuitive, you'll soon pick it up.'

I held the sandals, not sure if I should really stuff them away.

'And there's this.' Hermes produced a slim bundle from under his cloak, unwrapped it, and drew a weapon from a plain leather sheath. It was a strange thing, between a sickle and a hooked dagger; the length of a foot-soldier's short-sword. 'This is the *harpe*,' he said. 'It's Chaldean. It wants to help you. *Please* treat it with respect.' The blade was well-forged bronze, without any inscription, the edge had a silvery, wavering gleam. 'The metal's specially treated. It'll sever Medusa's head at one blow, which is vital. You won't get a second swing at her.'

'All right,' I said. 'I'll remember that.' I tucked the sandals under my arm. He slid the *harpe* into its sheath, wrapped it up again and put it into my hands.

'Keep these things hidden until you're off the island. Your enemy, Polydectes, doesn't know that he is in our hands. He believes you were either fathered by a cunning mortal who sneaked into the tower; or else by some minor deity with no great power, whom the king of Argos had offended. He thinks he's sending you on a hopeless venture. *Don't* let him know you've had our help.'

'I won't.'

Athini stood with her arms folded.

'How about "thank you", Perseus?'

I did not feel grateful. Stunned, yes. Dazzled, definitely. Winged sandals, Athini's own shield! Great Mother. But I didn't feel like *thanking* them for the loan of these staggering treasures. They were supplying the gear they needed me to have, so I could do their bidding. Why should I thank them for that? I used my commonsense. I bowed very low and made the right noises. Athini looked slightly mollified. Now's my chance to find out something I personally need to know, I thought.

'You've been very kind and generous and thoughtful. I'm overwhelmed, Great Athini, Divine Hermes. But, er, there's one thing. Excuse my ignorance, but which Divine Person did she offend? Which of the Supernaturals did something so terrible to the most beautiful creature in the world?'

Until my father had told me I had to kill her, the Medusa had just been a name to me, just one of those hair-raising monsters that litter the Middle Sea, some of them real; some of them as fake as a stuffed mermaid. But I knew how the Supernaturals ganged up on each other. If it was true that the Medusa would be released by my blow, the Person who had turned her into a monster was not going to be pleased. I had to know whose Divine toes I would be stepping on. I knew *I'd* be the one in trouble with Whoever it was. Not Zeus, Hermes and Athini, oh no. That's not the way it works.

Hermes grinned, which worried me. 'Ah, hm . . . We're glad you asked that.' He glanced at Great Athini. 'That's a very good question, isn't it, sister?'

Athini was not amused. She came up too close again, gripped me by my upper arms, and fixed me with that terrifying, glorious gaze. '*I* did it. Something most improper happened to her, in one of my temples. I detest that kind of thing and *I lost my temper.*'

'All right,' I said, hurriedly. 'That's fine. Thanks. Just wanted to know.'

She stepped back, and resumed her businesslike tone. 'We come to the journey. The Gorgons live in the Garden of the Hesperides. Do you know where that is?'

I told her what the Yacht Club kids had told me, when I asked. 'The Gorgon's lair is in North Africa. Almost as far as the

Pillars of the West, and back from the coast a bit, somewhere. There's a huge mountain range. It's in the foothills, I think—'

She sighed. 'You *think*. And how are you going to get there?'

I'd been working it out. 'I'd take a boat over to Paros. Get a berth from there to Libya, and then coast-hop westwards asking the way as I go. I'll get better directions when I'm in the area, I'll be following the trail of the other champions.'

No points. Athini and Hermes were shaking their heads.

'No, no, no,' said Hermes. '*Do not* head south. That's the way to join the statuary. You're forgetting that Polydectes is your enemy, and you're forgetting this is not a mortal quest. You must go down to the River, to find your way back to the Garden.'

There was no river in the Medusa lore I'd picked up. 'Er, which river?'

Hermes looked amazed at my slow-thinking. 'The dark one, of course.'

'Ask the nymphs,' Athini advised. 'They'll help you.'

'*Nymphs?*' I felt a shift in the air, in the light, and panicked, because I knew they were about to vanish, leaving me bewildered. 'There's a nymph for every tree and stone on Serifos, and what do those fragile creatures know? *Which* of them do you suggest I ask—?'

Athini looked at Hermes. 'He really is one of us,' said the Goddess.

She smiled on me, for the first time: a smile so fierce and glorious it nearly knocked me off my feet. 'My father's half-mortal children are frequently supercharged dolts, Perseus. They see what mortals can't see, they feel what immortals can't feel: and they go crazy, torn between the worlds, and have to be put out of their misery. You will not share that fate, you are too wise. We salute you ... The Stygian nymphs are different from the simple spirits you know. The Graeae, the elder goddesses, will show you how to reach them. But they won't do it willingly, you'll have to trick them.'

A bright cloud, like a sun-filled mist, fell between me and the Supernaturals.

'The Graeae have one tooth and one eye between them. If one of them wants to eat, she says pass tooth, if one of them wants to see what she's eating she says pass the eye. Your best plan is to steal the eye and the tooth, trade them for a passage—'

The Divine Messenger's voice came from far away, it was fading, it was gone. *Trade the eye and the tooth for a passage—*

I was alone on the stony height.

'I don't understand!' I yelled. 'WHY ME? You know everything, you have all the power. If you want the Medusa's head, WHY DON'T YOU JUST TAKE IT?'

'That's what we're doing, Perseus,' said Athini's voice. 'You are our action.'

The confusion I'd felt before Athini and Hermes appeared had vanished, I knew where I was. It was hot noon. I had a pair of winged sandals in the front of my tunic, Athini's shield on my back, and a wicked-looking curved dagger, wrapped up in a bundle of cloth, that the God Hermes had treated with great respect. I decided the *harpe* was safely disguised by its sheath, which was attached to a plain leather belt. I strapped it round my waist (the poor-box tunic's belt was a piece of cord). I used the cloth to wrap Athini's shield. I couldn't do anything about the shining white feathers that poked out of the neck of my skimpy tunic. I plodded home, looking as if I'd stolen somebody's prize fancy chicken.

There was no one in the yard when I let myself in. Kefi was singing in the stable, accompanied by some mighty honks from Music. I could hear voices from the kitchen and the dining room: our staff, my family, Andromeda; getting ready for the evening. I had a strange feeling that if I went into the restaurant they wouldn't recognise me. They'd say you can't be Perseus. He vanished, long ago ... I sneaked through the house like a ghost, and reached my own room without being spotted. Brébré was alseep on my bed. I laid out my treasures, and sat there cuddling his warm, supple furry body. He licked my chin. A ferret can be a surprisingly comforting pet.

'I'm going away, Brébré. I'm going hunting. You won't see me for a while.'

Athini's shield.

Winged sandals.

The *harpe*.

And a bucketful of instructions which were fast escaping from my brain. Find the Stygian nymphs, steal the eye and the tooth. Practise where there are no trees. Could we go over that again, Hermes? I can't memorise things I can't understand.

The feathers felt like feathers, the wings were no bigger than a pigeon's wings. Hermes was limber and tall, but very slim. Do Gods weigh anything? Would his sandals carry me? Perhaps they'd only have to carry half my weight, as I was only half mortal. Someone coughed. The boss was at my door, his cooking apron round his waist.

He looked older, worn and bowed by trouble. Maybe it was because I'd just seen his brother. I stood up, holding Brébré, and felt that I towered over him: I'd been taller than the boss since I was ten, but I'd never felt bigger than him before.

'Anthe and Andromeda told you?'

'That everything happened as Great Zeus foretold? The king challenged you, and you accepted? Yes, they did.' He saw the loot on my bed, and looked at me quizzically.

'Equipment,' I croaked. 'I had another encounter with the Supernaturals.'

'I see.' He moved the shield aside, and sat on my bed. '*Can you do this, Perseus? Can you kill the monster?*'

'I think so. If I'm careful. I'll have help.'

I longed for his advice. But there was something between us – something the boss had seen at once, when I came back from that meeting with my father, and I hadn't spotted until last night. Polydectes was finished. He was doomed.

I was such a kid, I'd wondered why Papa Dicty was in a strange mood. Now I understood. The Gods were going to destroy the king, for reasons of their own, and I was to be their instrument. And in spite of everything, I think he still loved his brother.

He nodded, sighed, and smiled at me sadly.

'I've been thinking, Perseus ... I could forge a press that would turn out hollow tubes of wheat paste, like sausage skins. It wouldn't be too hard. Tubes would absorb the sauce better, it would make for richer dishes. What do you say?'

'Sounds great. When can we start?'

We both knew I wouldn't be helping him in the furnace yard again.

'I should have left Serifos,' I said. 'As soon as I was old enough to be a threat to him. Is that what you were waiting for, before Andromeda came? For me to realise I had to leave? Well, I'm leaving now, Papa, so maybe it'll be all right—'

'You're a good boy.' He patted my hand, and sighed. 'Sometimes I wish I'd made different choices, long ago. I wish that I were king of Serifos now, and you were my heir. But it won't do, thinking like that.' He looked at me straight, man to man, and that gave me a shock. 'You are *not* my grandson, son of Zeus.'

'I wish I was,' I blurted, like a kid. 'I've been raised by the most noble, wisest prince in the Kyklades. I wouldn't have had things any other way. I'm *proud* of your choices, I'm proud of everything you've taught me—'

Then I felt as if I was making a funeral oration, so I shut up.

The boss got to his feet. 'We are in the hands of the Gods. It's not the most comfortable place to be, but let's make the best of it. We're in for a big night. The Yacht Club kids are gathering, eager to throw their money around and bask in your reflected glory. Hurry up and bathe, and—' He looked at the poor-box tunic. 'Change into something decent, before you come down.'

Palikari was back at the bar, with the remains of a black eye, his left arm in a sling, and a half-healed scalp-cut hidden by his vine-wreath: knocking out the best Kitron Slammers in the Middle Sea, one-handed. I was at the front of the house. My mother was being gracious with the guests and keeping everything in order; Andromeda was serving tables at speed, and cheerfully fending off personal questions. I had never known how much I loved my life, the bustle and the chatter, the sheer *fun* of running a good restaurant on a busy night. The Yacht Club kids got wilder and more inventive about what had happened at the High Place. Pali and I had a good time being mysterious.

'C'mon, Pali, who beat you up? *Was* it Perseus?'

'Couldn't possibly comment, ma'am.'

'The Medusa's Head! The man's insane! So what did you say to him, really?'

'I said, er, I'd give it a try—'

I avoided my mother. I was scared to face her. I was afraid she blamed me for the pain I'd caused Papa Dicty, I was afraid she'd heard the tale that I'd been stupidly boasting, over the Medusa challenge ... The evening wound down. We cleared up. Bundles of used linen for Koukla, plate scrapings for the pigs and goats; better class of leftovers packed up for the poor. Put the chairs on the tables, sweep up, sluice down the floor, swish the water out into the yard . . . I looked around about midnight and found that Moumi had gone off to bed, and I hadn't spoken to her.

I went out into the yard. Andromeda was sitting in the dark, on the stone bench by the wellhouse. I sat beside her, feeling nervous. She'd been refusing to look at me again, all evening. The mules stirred and whickered to each other in the stable, Mémé trotted along the wall, on her nightly rounds. I remembered how embarrassed I'd been when I first brought the girl who wore solid gold to this humble setting.

'I'm sorry about this morning.'

'No,' she said, wearily. 'You were right, I didn't understand. *You're* not going to certain death, son of Zeus.'

'Not like you, Princess Andromeda.'

She looked up at the stars, that glinted like white fire though the branches of the tamarisk. 'How does it feel to know that you're immortal? Is it a good feeling?'

I shrugged. 'I don't think about it. How does it feel to know you're going to die, Andromeda? I don't know what *immortality* means, I don't know what will happen, nobody has explained it. I don't even know if I'll still be Perseus, on the other side . . . How is that different from dying?'

Somehow, this exchange cleared the air. She smiled at me, and I told her about meeting Athini and Hermes on the road: the weapons training, the loot. I told her the last, strange thing Athini had said. You are our actions.

'Feet and hands,' said Andromeda. 'We use them to walk around and pick things up, and never tell them why. If they had voices, perhaps they'd ask us, *Why do we have to make these moves, that don't mean anything to us . . . ?* Do you feel better about being sent to murder someone now?'

'I don't feel *better*. But when Wisdom and Thought in human form stop you on the road, and tell you there's no need to have moral scruples, what can you do?'

'When the Lord of Ocean and Earthquake says he wants your life—'

I winced. 'Did you *see* him? I mean, when you re-dedicated yourself?'

'Yes.'

'I thought so.'

Everything was so hopeless, and so filled with piercing sweetness. I took her hand, I kissed her fingertips, she leaned her head on my shoulder. Her hair smelt of rose-oil. 'Andromeda, come with me?'

'Come *with* you? What do you mean?'

'I know you have to go to Haifa, I know you have no choice. But I'm leaving the island too. We could travel together, part of the way?' She sat up, and looked at me. The last lamp had been put out indoors, I could only see the liquid gleam of her eyes. 'You could write down my instructions, in your new writing. I'm never going to remember everything.'

'Perseus, what would be the use of that? You couldn't read them.'

'No, but you could read them to me. Will you come?'

At the back of my mind was the thought that if she was with me I still had a chance to save her, but I wasn't going to tell her that. I didn't even believe it, I just couldn't bear to leave her. Another day, another hour, was worth everything—

'All right,' she said. 'I will.'

8

Andromeda dreamed of horses. It was a cloudy dream of impressions, then for a moment everything would become clear; more than real. There were horses all around her, brown and chestnut and bay. She walked between them, thrilled by their size and strength, not at all afraid. When they bent their heads to look into her face, their eyes were gentle and eager. She was to bridle one of them. She used the hank of purple yarn that she had tried to sacrifice, it seemed to be knotted together with her loom-weights. She slipped the bridle over a horse's muzzle – it was like catching a thought – and leapt onto its back. The long spring from the ground, up into the air, felt like magic. But she knew it wasn't magic. It was simply that she had never used this power to leap, before. She had been timid without knowing it ... Then she was in the Outer Court of the Women's Palace at home. She was sitting crosslegged in a sunny alcove, by herself, writing on a white cloth stretched in a frame. She could hear the sounds of the city, faintly. Black horses ran down her arms, and through her hands. They raced over the cloth and were fixed there, flying marks. But they were still alive.

Perseus.

She woke from the dream, full of an idea: something about horses and the flying marks being one and the same? It slipped from her grasp. Was Perseus a horse? Or was he the flying marks? She smiled: according to her idea he must be both.

No, that was wrong. She knew what the horses in her dreams meant. They were the presence of the God: the lord of making and breaking, horse-tamer, who was going to kill her. She wrapped her face in a scarf of soft hair, and pressed it against her eyes. 'It is just,' she whispered, and lay still. If any mother's child must be killed to appease the God of Earthquake, it had to be Andromeda.

The day had been breathlessly hot. The little room had grown cooler while she slept, but it was still bright. She sat up and looked around. In the window niche stood a small red jug, holding three ears of corn, one blue cornflower and two white daisies. Her bundle lay against the wall, by the open door. The weights – which she'd never used here, she had no standing loom – were in there, and the purple yarn.

'I'll miss you,' she said, to the room. 'You've been a true friend to me.'

She got up, twisted her hair into a knot, and sat on the floor to look at her pieces. She'd washed the stiffening size out of them, and left them spread out to dry. None of them was bigger than a hand towel. She held up each of the three and looked at them carefully, feeling the joy of creation – the joy that almost makes you forgive the mistakes, the uneven places, that you can always see. She did not give her pieces away lightly. A gift had to mean something, and it had to be *right* for the person. For Palikari a green and yellow stepped design, which meant a field of ripening wheat in the language of patterns; and the white convulvulous motif, twining around it. For Anthe no pattern, just uneven patches of pure colour: this had been more difficult than she'd thought it would be.

That's the contrast I wanted—

And here, the balance is good—

She lingered over Papa Dicty's, thinking of her dream. The flying marks were not like horses. They were like weaving. The new kind of writing was made from the marks for actual things, *ox, jar, cart, horse, house*. They only appeared in fragments, but together they added up to a message in sounds . . . The way that choosing where a weft colour will show, and where it will be hidden, makes a picture in the finished cloth. It was easier in the Minoan language than in her own. She folded the completed pieces, and went to look at the new work on her little frame loom. It was barely started, it would never be finished. It would have been an intricate pattern, not a picture. You can put so much more meaning into a pattern. Dark blue, for his eyes. A sheeny chestnut, and a lighter, golden brown. She needed a hundred more shades, far more than Seatown could provide. She knelt there, fighting tears: remembering 'Kore', and the night Perseus had leaned in her doorway, asking her if she ever slept? Moments that ought to have been the beginning of a life story, but were the end—

It is just, it is just.

When she was sure she could smile, she combed her hair and went downstairs.

The north wind of summer had started to fail, taking all the freshness from the island's air. Andromeda had been on Serifos for two months. The shipping season was not over; in Haifa the rains, and the festival of sacrifice, were still far off. But it was time, maybe past time, for her to be on her way.

The kitchen was closed, the staff had a holiday. The

restaurant would not be opening this evening, because of the excessive heat. The hearth fire burned low, crusted with grey ash. She quietly joined Papa Dicty and his household at the family table. They would eat later, they had a guest with them now. It was an old man called Yiannis, a smelly old seadog: a very faithful customer, not so good at paying his tally. He raised his cup to Andromeda, calling her 'Kore', and she gave him a friendly answer.

The table was spread with stiff, dirty scrolls of sheepskin, partly unrolled. They must be the old man's star-charts. He was showing them to Papa Dicty, Pali and Anthe. Perseus and his mother were pursuing a different conversation. Andromeda watched the faces of mother and son, and listened. Lady Danae was concerned about dangers closer to home than the Medusa's lair.

'Perseus, the king doesn't want the public blame for your death. But if you are set upon in an alley in Paros port, and dropped in the harbour with a boulder tied to your feet, all people will know is that you didn't come back—'

Perseus glanced at Papa Dicty, and spoke low, 'I'm safe from the king, Moumi. The Gods have decided to set me up against him, because they need me for this chore.'

'You're part of their plans,' said Danae, equally low. 'Don't think that means you know what those plans are. Don't think it means you can trust them. You can't.'

They were like brother and sister in this light: two blue-eyed Achaeans, conferring before a battle, Queen Danae giving advice to her young general—

The Gorgons' lair was in Africa, but Perseus must not go south. He'd been told that he must find the Stygian Nymphs, before he could reach the Garden of the Hesperides. There was a river called the Styx, on the Greek Mainland, which Papa Dicty knew of. It was both a real place, and – to the Greeks – the river of death: the Dark Water everyone must cross. But the days when islanders had known all the routes around the Mainland were in the past. Yiannis was being consulted about coasts that were now rarely visited. Beyond the busy, divided Achaean nations, in unknown northern lands—

'I *think* the river's up in the north west, Yiannis. There's a place of pilgrimage, I *believe* the port is called Parga—'

Andromeda reached for a scroll. She made out a wavering line that had once been incised and filled with black. Beside it, at intervals, a scatter of pricked holes, half obliterated by grease and dirt. Anthe leaned over and traced the line with her finger: a very clean, cook's finger, the nail cut short and square. 'That's the horizon. Or it could be the coastline. I don't think he remembers.'

'Is he going to be any use at all?' murmured Andromeda.

'Don't know.'

'Oooh, no need to apologise, cap'n,' the old seadog was saying. 'I ferget things, it's our age, sir.' He had his nose to another of the scrolls. 'I ferget what the patterns meaned. A rat et one bit, and the salt-rot gnawed off another bit. I'm not what I was. How many days sailing, to the north west coast ports? Could be, ooh, twenty. Lemme think.' His free hand, with a life of its own, pushed the wine cup coaxingly towards the jug. 'I'm tryin' ter jog my mem'ry, as you're sech a noble, *gen'rous* company.'

Nobody else was drinking. To any sane human being unwatered wine would have been unbearable in this heat. Anthe filled the old soak's cup, but she'd lost interest in his mumbling. 'Did you remember anything more about nymphs, boss?'

The heat lay heavily on them, though the dining room had been shuttered all day. Papa Dicty passed a hand over his bald head. 'Hm. Styx, Stygian ... The Styx runs underground through a famous cavern: hence the association with the dead, perhaps. There's an oracle, where the Greeks question the departed.'

'They question dead people? Eeww. That's disgusting!'

'Not *corpses,* my child; ghosts. One has to feed them with blood, I seem to remember. But perhaps that's another—'

'The Supernaturals didn't mention an oracle,' Palikari broke in. 'Maybe I'm missing something, but if these nymphs are the nymphs of the Dark Water, won't Perseus have to be dead to talk to them? He's dozy, sometimes, but he's not that bad—'

Perseus grinned, ruefully. 'Thanks, Pali. You too.'

'The Supernaturals describe things in their own terms,' said lady Danae. 'We mortals know that stones and springs, rivers and trees, *may* have spirits inhabiting them. To the Gods, that's everyday reality . . . Perseus lives in both worlds, Pali. If he can reach the Styx, he'll be able to speak to the river spirits.'

Perseus stared at his mother. 'I didn't know you knew about that!'

She laughed, and sighed. 'You used to talk about it, my dear. When you were a little boy, before you decided you didn't want to know—'

Andromeda thought of Perseus's secret life, the birthright he was both ashamed and proud of; like the power of his fists. Their eyes met.

They'd been ready to leave for days. Everything had been so simple. But then they'd learned that the regular ferry to Paros was laid up, in dock for repairs. There was a dead calm, a shortage of long-haul rowers, cargo ships were not taking passengers. So the household went on talking, talking, asking the same questions over and over. They meant well, but it made the waiting even harder to bear—

'What about the "Graeae"?' asked Anthe. 'What are they, and *where* are they, in our world (another question asked too often, and never yet answered). 'The sisters with a tooth and an eye between them. He has to talk to them, too. What did you say about the "Graeae", boss? You knew something—'

'I recall the name, my dear, that's all. Grey Sisters, Elder Goddesses: the sailors used to talk about them, when I was a child. Ancient, cunning and dangerous, that sticks in my mind. But *where* they are, or *what* they are, I've forgotten if I ever knew—'

Yiannis perked up. 'Wozzat? Grey Sisters? Ooooh, now I know something about *them*! And I would tell ye a terrible tale, only I find my throat is dry.'

'Yiannis!' exclaimed the boss. 'You'll give yourself an apoplexy, in this heat.'

'The women say that, Mother bless 'em, but what do women know about drink? It don't *harm* me. It cures my shakes. An' *helps my memory.*'

Anthe gave the boss a questioning look. He mouthed *one more.* She filled the cup again with thick, dark, unwatered wine.

'Aah, thank yer, young Anthe. *Now* lemme see.' Yiannis reached for his precious scrolls, inspected and returned them, one by one, to the breast of his well-seasoned tunic, which stank of ancient fish. He smoothed out the last, with watery-eyed pride and joy.

'I uster know the stars. I was a steersman once, you didn't know that, did you?'

When he was drunk enough, Yiannis always remembered that he had once been a steersman, a great navigator, famed throughout the Middle Sea. Maybe it was true, or partly true. He had those charts, which weren't the usual gear for a common sailor—

'Good heavens,' said lady Danae, politely. 'Yiannis, we never guessed!'

'Aye, well, it was long, long ago. I fell in the world, from the helm to the bilges. It's a terrible thing to have a weakness.' He looked at his cup, which was mysteriously empty again. Pali and Andromeda grinned at each other. Yiannis was a magician: you never, ever saw him lift his cup. Anthe moved the jug away.

'The Graeae are the terror of the sea, tha's what. Ancient and merciless, we face those Grey Sisters every time we leave port. Nobody has sympathy with what we sailors suffer, and where would yer be without us? But let me tell you about this one time, an' I'm sure it was off Parga. Between the eye and the tooth, now that's what we call bein' tween a whirlpool and a fang of rock—'

His straggle-bearded chin sank down, his gnarled finger traced a lost path, pricked onto a salt-stained, rat-gnawed blackened scrap of memories. 'It were off *Parga*, it were. You know what that is, a whirlpool? Horrors, horrors. When the waves is fifty man-heights over your mast, and the wind is ripping the skin from your back. When you see your ship bein' drawn into a great spinning eye-hole in the sea, and the only way past is between it an' the great fang of the Tooth, oooh, then you won't forget the Grey Sisters.'

The chin sank to rest with a soft thump. Yiannis gave a snore, and rolled quietly from the bench. He was an expert at dropping out of sight, they would often find him in the morning, peacefully asleep in a corner.

'Maybe he really knows something,' said Anthe. 'We gave him a cup too many.'

Brébré, who had been sniffing around the table, sneaked up and took a quiet chew at the last star chart. The boss lifted him, dropped him onto the floor, and rolled the cracked scroll. He would give it back to Yiannis in the morning.

'I don't think so, my dear. We were talking about Parga, then he tells us that's where the Graeae are. I'm afraid he just wanted to please us.'

'Good news,' said Perseus to Andromeda. 'I went up and down the waterfront again while you were sleeping. I think I've found us a berth.'

A thrill went through her: like falling, like flying.

She was bound to die, but they were running away together—

On the last morning she woke from forgotten dreams (if there were horses, they'd galloped away before she opened her eyes), and took her gifts down to breakfast. It was a feast. Spiced sausage pie, fried eggs and cheese; mountain greens in oil and sharp wine. Papa Dicty's own fresh bread, yoghurt and honey, a platter of fruit cut and arranged; the pastry cook's finest. Andromeda would have stuffed herself if it had choked her, out of pure love. But she had an appetite, and so did Perseus. They ate until their stomachs begged for mercy; grinning at each other. Once, Palikari and Anthe started talking about the defence of Seatown. How they would meet the threat if the king turned nasty while Perseus was gone, the plans they had for the outlying villages ... Papa Dicty was quite angry with them. He wouldn't have unlucky subjects at a farewell meal.

Then Andromeda brought out her presents.

For Anthe the piece with splashes of orange and yellow, blue and red, on a ground of unbleached wool. 'Is this really mine?' said the wildcat, uncertainly. The flying marks worked below the colours astounded her. 'Your new kind of writing! Oh, Andromeda, I love you! I'll treasure this for ever! What does it say?'

'It says *honest colours*,' said Andromeda, gravely, and everybody laughed. The colours Anthe had added to the ancient painting were still on the wall.

For Palikari the ripening field, the convulvulous motif, and flying marks that said, *faithful flowers*. At the last minute she'd been afraid that her message was too personal and he'd be offended. She was wrong. Palikari came around and hugged her, wet-eyed. 'You may be a princess at home,' he said. 'But to me you'll always be Kore the mystery girl. You're my best mate, bar the wildcat and that great hunk of yours. Look after yourself, and er, be safe—' He broke off, in confusion. What could he say?

'I'm all right,' said Andromeda. 'I know I have to do this, so I'm *all right*. Thank you for making a waitress out of me. Thank you for being my friend.'

For the boss there was a platter of wheat ribbons and a smiley fried fish, above a red furnace surrounded by smithy tools: the two groups divided by a short line of flying marks, all on a deep yellow ground. The wheat ribbons weren't a great success. But she had wanted to make him laugh; and tried to give him the signs of kingship.

'Now this deserves pride of place!' cried the boss, laughing. 'I shall frame it and hang it above the bar. What does my writing mean, dear girl?'

'It says,' explained Andromeda, '*Dearest guests, PLEASE do not take your room towels to the beach. Ask for a beach towel at reception.*'

'Hm. Really? That's rather a lot, for such a small number of marks.'

'It doesn't,' she confessed, blushing hard. 'It says *The Good Master.*'

The boss smiled at her, with the same kind, yet piercing look she remembered from the day she'd come to his house as a fugitive. 'Great Mother bless you,' he said quietly. 'Don't give up all hope, Andromeda. Fate takes strange turns.'

For lady Danae she had a circular piece of very fine, bleached linen with a knotted fringe; a wreath of cornflowers, wheat and daisies embroidered in the centre. 'The linen is the first good thing I ever made,' she said. 'I brought it with me. The flowers and the writing I added here, for you. It says *The Queen Of Summer.*'

Danae took the cloth, and kissed it. 'You have given me a promise, *Kore,*' she said, in Achaean Greek. 'Keep it, and I will be very glad, my dear daughter.'

There was a clutch of smaller presents for Koukla and Kefi, and the restaurant staff. She'd worked the beads, and some of the silver coin she'd brought from Haifa into braided wrist-bands and necklaces: she left them for lady Danae to distribute. It was a wrench to see them go, all these little things that had given her hours of refuge, steady work to ward off the fear and grief. And had served a double purpose now: making this morning easier, saving her from trying to *say* what these people meant to her.

Goodbye to Brainy, and Music and Dolly. Goodbye Mémé and Brébré. She ran upstairs to fetch her bundle, and there was the *Perseus* weaving, still in her loom. She was leaving the frame behind. She'd thought of hiding that strip of cloth, so there'd be something of herself in this room, in his house. One day Perseus, hero of the Medusa Challenge, would discover it, and remember *Kore* ... She couldn't bear the idea. It would be like leaving a bit of dead flesh for him to find. She cut the warp, and stuffed the lost scrap into her bundle.

Our bags were already on board the little cargo ship, called the *Octopus*, that was going to carry us to Paros. We walked along the waterfront in silence: she with her bundle, I with mine. I was thinking that those pieces she'd woven, and the tallyboards in our safe, were very precious. They would be all there was left of Andromeda's discovery, if I failed ... I was wondering if the boss had guessed my secret plan. I thought he had.

The news that 'Kore' was probably Princess Andromeda of Haifa, a runaway human sacrifice, had got around, and of course everyone knew about the Medusa Challenge. We'd been expecting some kind of a crowd to see us off. It was one good reason why we'd said our goodbyes at home, in private. I *hadn't* expected to see our baggage on the quay, and the crew of the Octopus hurrying to get cast off.

'Hey!' I shouted. 'Wait up!'

The sailors saw us, and redoubled their efforts. I raced along the quay, Athini's shield, which I had wrapped in a sheepskin, jolting on my back. The winged sandals were in the same bundle: I was never going to let the Supernatural treasures out of my hand's reach. The crowd of tale-tellers and idlers yelled encouragement. The Octopus was moving, clear water between her and the dock. I leapt across the gap like a lunatic.

'What are you doing!' I yelled. 'Did you forget you have passengers?'

The ship was a Parian, and so was her captain, a man called Sika. I didn't know him personally, but he was a respectable small trader. He stood on his fish-scale glistening deck, scratching his beard and looking very uncomfortable.

'I changed my mind, er, young sir. We've no room. Can't take you.'

'But I *paid* you! Well over the odds, and in goods. You have the stuff on board!'

He looked at his crew, hoping they'd help him out. The men just looked away. 'I'll reimburse you, sir, only we can't do it now, got to catch the breeze.' He lowered his voice. 'Look, we could take the noble young lady, no problem with that. But you'll have to get off the boat, I'm sorry sir.'

'Suppose I won't?'

'Then I s'pose we'll stay in port.'

I heard one of the sailors mutter *god-touched*.

The crowd on the quay was loving this. Maybe I should give them a real show: draw the *harpe*, wave it around, order the captain to carry us at knifepoint. 'Set me back on the quay,' I said, resignedly. 'I don't feel like another long jump. But you'll regret this. We *are* god-touched, we're on a sacred mission, and now the Gods are going to be offended with you. Are you sure you still want to put to sea?'

All sailors are superstitious, and I am Perseus. But the crew of the Octopus were not shaken. 'Go home, lad,' said the captain. 'It's nothing personal.'

The busybodies dispersed, leaving us alone.

'There's something wrong,' said Andromeda.

'You bet there is. He took our fares! What a crook!'

We had far too much luggage: two chests full of warm clothes, food supplies, tradegoods to save the coin we carried; everything our family's tender care could overload us with. I'd have to borrow a handcart, or go and fetch a mule.

'No,' she said. 'There's something wrong with *this*. Why was it so hard to find a passage to Paros? Why is the ferry mysteriously in dry dock? Perseus, it isn't an accident. Someone powerful doesn't want us to get off the island.'

I'd been thinking the same. Maybe we'd all been thinking the same, and praying we were wrong. But who could be trying to stop us? I had *Athini's shield* on my back. I could not be trapped here. How could I be trapped here?

I felt as if I'd run up against an invisible wall.

'It's not *us*,' I said, reluctantly. 'It's me.'

I told her what the Parian captain had said.

We had been fretting at the delay, and clinging to the idea of our voyage, alone together. The thought that she could leave and I couldn't was a cruel blow.

'We'd better go back to the taverna,' said Andromeda, through stiff lips.

The boss decided to send for Bozic. 'We should have sent for him in the first place,' he said. 'Time enough to rely on strangers when you have no choice.' I didn't like the idea, because it would leave my family with no means of escape, but I saw that he was right.

Our caique was back in her usual hiding place up the east coast. Kefi went running off to that two-hovel fishing village; while Pali went out to do the rounds of the bars and shipping offices, to see if he could find out what was going on. In Seatown most of the shipping offices were *in* the bars. They were single-handed operations: if you had the price of a jug of wine there was usually no problem getting inside information. He returned with nothing. Nobody would talk.

'They won't admit there's a problem,' said Pali. 'They're just not taking passengers, or they're fully booked (which isn't true). Or they're waiting for a consignment that hasn't arrived.' Unfortunately Taki's agent, the most reliable source, was not in port. Apparently he was on Naxos.

We spent an anxious night, because Kefi didn't get back until the next day. When he turned up he reported that the caique was gone, and the village was 'deserted'. If 'deserted' was the right word for the fact that Kefi hadn't found anyone at home in those two shacks . . . He was thoroughly frightened, convinced the king had taken the boat, and was about to descend on Dicty's and kill us all.

We opened the restaurant again, just to be occupied. There weren't many customers. Andromeda went to her room as soon as we'd cleared up, the rest of us sat in the yard. Kefi kept whimpering, '*Trapped! Like rats in a trap! Trapped! Like rats in a trap!*'; until Anthe told him very sharply to shut up.

'Perhaps we should apply to Polydectes,' Moumi sounded almost serious. 'He has ships. He offered to equip Perseus.'

There was one other harbour on Serifos, at Megalivadi in the west: deep water in a narrow bay. It belonged to the High Place, it was forbidden territory.

'What if the king *is* behind this?' I asked. 'He's the only real enemy I have. But if he wants rid of me, why would he stop me from leaving the island?'

'Either the king,' said Pali, 'or you have competition on the Medusa Challenge, Perseus, and somebody's rich relatives are putting you out of the running.'

'That's ridiculous!' snapped Anthe. 'Anyone who stops Andromeda or Perseus from leaving is in trouble with the Achaean Supernaturals. The captains are *sailors*. They're terrified of getting on the wrong side of a black cat. Exactly who do you think could have got to them?'

'Who indeed,' murmured the boss. He stroked Mémé, frowning. 'This isn't Polydectes, Perseus. Your mother may be right about his murderous plans, but he'll wait until you're off the island. Let's give it a few days. Bozic has no doubt vanished on one of his smuggling escapades, he'll be back. And the *Afroditi* will be here soon.'

The Blue Star *Afroditi*, of course: the ship that had brought 'Kore' here, and carried the earthquake victims. She would be calling at Serifos very soon on her way down the line for the last trip of the season. She could take us to Naxos. It was cutting the timing fine for Andromeda, but at least we could rely on Taki. No power in the Middle Sea told *him* what to do—

I felt no relief. The invisible wall was still there.

The *Afroditi* duly arrived, and we went out to her on one of the lighters. The lightermen wouldn't take our heavy luggage. They said the chests could be fetched on board if we got a berth: only they'd heard Taki was poorly, and he wasn't taking on passengers, he didn't want the trouble of them. We'll see about that, I thought.

But it felt ill-omened, a backward step, to board the *Afroditi* again.

Taki seemed to be in perfect health, a big broad-chested

sailor, oiled and adorned like a prince. He received us in his office, a fine saloon on the upper deck: though not as fine or as strange as the stateroom on *The Magnificent Escape*. We explained that we needed a passage. The shipping magnate played with the weights of his antique, Minoan assay-scales and asked after everyone at Dicty's, down to the household gods. He was very pleased to meet Princess Andromeda again; under her own name.

He knew everything. He'd even heard about the 'new kind of writing'.

'I have a *very* promising little girl, mother's a slave, but that's no odds, she's my darling. Six years old, very pretty, brainy as a barrelful of monkeys. What d'you think? Could she learn how to do your new trick, noble Andromeda?'

'I don't know,' said Andromeda. 'The problem would be finding a teacher.'

Andromeda was the only one who knew the craft, and she would be dead in a month, if the God of Earthquake had his way. 'And you might want to think about the consequences,' she added, bleakly. 'If you're fond of your little daughter. The flying marks have not brought me a long life, or happiness.'

Taki cleared his throat, and arranged the executive toys on his desk again. Normally our shipping magnate had a heart of stone. It gave him no trouble to lie to anyone. But he was stumbling over this interview. There was something on his mind that made him twitchy as a guilty muleboy.

'About our passage to Naxos?' I prompted him.

'It would be a great favour,' added Andromeda.

'Ah. I'm afraid it can't be done. Not, er, not this season.'

So even Taki was against us. But there was one chance—

'I have gold,' announced Andromeda, as we had agreed beforehand. 'I have no more treasure *on* me, but you will be paid very, very well for setting me on my way to Haifa. I can promise that.'

'Noble lady,' sighed Taki. 'Your money is no good. I can't help Perseus with this senseless Medusa Challenge.' He glanced meaningfully at the portable shrine, bolted to the paintwork opposite his desk, where his Supernatural sponsor was honoured: and raised his voice. 'I don't approve of young men throwing their lives away, haring off after monster this and treasure that. I'm thinking of your poor mother, Perseus, and Papa Dicty, going down in sorrow to their graves. Don't argue with me, it's a serious moral issue.' The shipping magnate glowered righteously. 'Someone should put a stop to the whole ugly, macho, violent business. It's barbaric, if you ask me.'

This, from the man who thought human sacrifice was a fine, modern idea. But I wasn't tempted to argue. I'd got the message, finally.

'*I* won't take you, and neither will any captain, merchant, trader, or pirate who wants to keep on the right side of me. Sorry, but there it is. Do you take my meaning?'

We did. We understood everything. Our difficulties made perfect sense, now.

'What about me?' wondered Andromeda. 'Would you give me a berth? Though you know where I'm going?'

'I'd rather not,' said the great man.

I had the strange feeling that he'd done his level best for us. We told him *thank you* and *goodbye*: the lighter took us to the quay.

Hera,' said Andromeda. 'Hera,' I agreed, bitterly.

The shrine in Taki's office, that he'd made sure we noticed, was dedicated to the Goddess Hera. He was a Hera-worshipper: a devotee of my Supernatural father's estranged wife, whom Zeus had told me I must avoid at all costs. Not that I'd needed the warning. I knew from my mother that Lady Hera would do anything to spite Great Zeus's plans: especially if one of his mortal 'girlfriends', or half-mortal children was involved. Somehow, through a dream or an omen, she'd ordered the lord of the Middle Sea's shipping to stop me from leaving Serifos: and he had obeyed.

'I was *sure* he worshipped Afroditi,' I muttered.

But my father had warned me against Afroditi too.

We left chests to be picked up later. Neither of us ever wanted to see them again.

The boss said, 'Taki. I knew it,' and retired to his furnace yard. He could be heard banging things savagely in there, through the long, hot afternoon. Palikari and Anthe had a perverse scrap, with Pali defending Hera, and Anthe snarling about the Supernatural First Lady's witless attitude. *Why doesn't she just leave him, like a normal person would? Why doesn't she have her own collection of human toyboys?* Moumi tried to make peace, and made things worse. Andromeda and I sat by the banked-down summer hearth. There was nothing left to say, so we said nothing. I listened to the sounds of Koukla wheeling a cart of laundry, slapping out wet tablelinen; shouting for Kefi to stoke up the outside stove so she could heat her smoothing irons. Ordinary life, going on—

The tenth month had seemed a long way off when Andromeda had agreed to come with me; at least part of the way. It wasn't so far off now. She didn't have to say it, I knew she couldn't wait any longer. She must leave: I was trapped. Our parting was no longer somewhere ahead, out of sight. It was here.

In the end I went to my room and lay there, my choices going round and round in my mind. The winged sandals. Could I use them to leave Serifos? Would Hera prevent me? Could I fly along beside Andromeda's ship to Haifa, and fight the priests? I did not doubt my own destiny, but I couldn't get past the idea that we must part, *here and now.* I would get off the island somehow, but it would be too late. I would reach Haifa with the Medusa Head, *too late . . .*

I woke in the dark. I'd fallen asleep, and someone was climbing noisily through my window. Luckily I didn't leap onto the intruder: I struck a light first. It was Kia from the Yacht Club. She sat on my floor in a heap, her pretty brown hair all over her face. She was wearing a yellow singlet smeared with treebark, and a little purple sailor's kilt that didn't leave much to my imagination.

'*Kia*? What are you doing in my bedroom? Are you drunk?'

'Heeeheehee. In your dreams, lover boy.' She parted her hair and grinned at me. She didn't *look* all that drunk. 'Yours is the only room with a window on the street.'

'I know. I planned it that way. What are you doing here?'

'I'm the best tree-climber, and we didn't want to wake the house.' She stared at the *harpe*, which was unsheathed in my hand. 'What is *that*? We've got a surprise for you. A ship! Come and let the boys in, they're hiding in the alley.'

'It's a Chaldean dagger. I'll get the boss—'

'No! Don't wake the grown-ups! You have to let us explain.'

She insisted on waking Anthe and Palikari: Anthe ran to fetch Andromeda. Pali and I went with Kia, down to the kitchen yard. Niki and Gliko, the lads from the Twelve Islands who had been flirting with my girl at Polydectes' feast, sneaked in from the alley with a covered lantern. We gathered behind the wellhouse.

They'd found us a ship. The captain had agreed to take us, but on the quiet—

'*He* doesn't care about the great Taki,' hissed Gliko. 'Only we do, so we'd like our help to be a secret, if you don't mind.'

Andromeda nodded, eagerly, without a word.

'Done!' I whispered. 'But why can't we wake the boss, or my mother?'

'Er, we're not sure. Your friend said just to tell you two.'

'What friend?'

'He says this ship won't be stopped by contrary winds,'

broke in Niki. 'Which Someone might be trying to arrange. She's *manpowered*. The captain's an Achaean.'

Manpowered: I knew what that meant. 'You mean she's a warship.' My hope plunged again: I might have known this was too good to be true. 'I know why warships take on stray young men, Nik. Are you sure this captain isn't going to press-gang me into service with the Achaean fleet?'

'It's not like that! It's more mysterious than that!'

'You have to come *now*,' Gliko insisted. 'The *Argo*, that's her name, will be long gone at dawn. Your friend says some of the crewmen have been doing a little night-hunting, er, for deer, so they'd rather be away before daylight—'

'There are no deer on Serifos. We ate them all, hundreds of years ago. You mean the "Achaean captain" is raiding our herds. Who is this "friend"?—'

The kids seemed puzzled. 'Dunno,' said Gliko. 'Didn't get a straight look at him.'

'*Perseus*', breathed Andromeda. 'We're wasting time!'

We hugged Pali and Anthe. I had the Supernatural loot on my back, and a wallet with a few necessities; she had her bundle. We took nothing else. The Yacht Club kids led us to the end of the waterfront and onto the headland path. We passed the inlet where I had met my father, and climbed down into the next bay. I saw the ship, long and black against the starry horizon; riding without lights (a pirate trick). She definitely looked like a warship. But there was something *strange* about her ...

A small boat was waiting. The kids came no further, we crossed the sand alone.

'Great Mother keep you both,' called Kia softly. 'Hey, if you don't like the company, jump ship at the first port! That's what I always do.'

The figure in the boat tossed back his cloak. I saw Hermes's bright, glimmering face. 'Who is it?' whispered Andromeda, gripping my hand. 'Do you know him?'

'This is Hermes,' I said. 'He's my half-brother, and he really is a friend.'

The courier of the Gods rowed us out into the calm, his oars shattering reflected starlight. 'Now, this ship. We borrowed her from, er, somewhere else. The *Argo* is *fast*. At this season, with the ships of your times, you'd never make it now by natural means: so we had to cheat a little. The young people won't remember me clearly. It was better your mother and the noble Dicty didn't know, it would have added to the confusion—'

'I don't understand.'

'It's a little tricky. The captain's name is Jason. He's a freebooter, a bit of a pirate. He'll get on your nerves, try to keep your temper. One other slight difficulty: he's agreed to take you, but he's supposed to be a friend of Hera's. So watch out for that.'

We were expected, a rope ladder came tumbling down the black hide of the ship. She was riding strangely low, the oars were ranked on two decks, I'd never seen that before—

'Just *one* more thing,' said Hermes. 'Keep clear of a fellow called Heracles, if you can. Big bloke, lot of hair, wears a lionskin sometimes.'

'Why him in particular?'

'He's your great grandson. It would be complicated.'

9

We stood together on board the black ship. 'Is this how it feels to meet the Gods?' asked Andromeda, wide-eyed in the dark. 'Perseus? Are we in the other world now?'

'No,' I said. But I wasn't sure. 'Yes ... I don't know. It's different.'

We were taken below. The pirate, outlaw, or possible press-gang captain, was a brawny Achaean, almost as tall as me, his yellow hair bleached whiteish by the sun, cut short and sticking up in spikes. His eyebrows were the same colour as his hair, so was his beard. He wore flashy topaz earrings, a pair of trousers made of canvas with ragged holes in the knees, and a white singlet fastened on both shoulders with gold pins. He obviously thought he was the king of style in this get-up: I took an instant dislike to him.

He met us in the well between the rowing benches, explaining grandly that the Argonauts were a band of brothers, and the captain didn't have a private cabin. When he'd taken one look at Andromeda he lit an extra lantern, all the better to ogle her.

'So you're Perseus, the massive hero, beloved of the Gods.'

We couldn't see the rowers, there were screens on either side of the well. But we could hear the pumping, pounding, regular thunder of the beat, over a slamming sound I couldn't identify. (It was the sliding-benches, a new invention; I found out later.) It didn't seem as if anything human could be making that noise—

'I wouldn't know about that,' I shouted (there was no chance of normal conversation). 'They asked me to do an errand. Not much to it.'

'I like your attitude! Thanks muchly for the meat supply your foster-dad's island is kindly providing, by the way. And gorgeous here is your girlfriend?'

Andromeda gave him stare for stare; which he did not like.

'We're travelling together. She's a friend.'

Jason grinned, 'All right, I'll mind my own beeswax. Many of us on board the *Argo* have left some kind of hell behind us. Let's get to the man-talk.' He spread his arms. 'Welcome aboard, Perseus, son of great Zeus! Glad to have you on the team!'

He would have hugged me, but I dodged. 'On the team?'

'Well, yeah?' said Jason. 'What did you think? You're a son of Zeus, you don't have to audition, lad. We have fifty oars on the Argo. *Fifty*, how about that? In a custom shell, only one in the world. She's *unbelievably* powerful. You can take a back-up seat on the top shelf next shift, try our style. You'll earn your own cushion in no time, I'm sure.'

Thunder, thunder, slam, slam ... So this was the secret of the *Argo*'s speed. Fifty oars, in a designer hull. A rowing bench meant *slavery* to me. The worst kind of slavery, where the only way you get free is by dying. It was the horror of modern war:

feeling the shock of battle, not knowing what was happening, going to your death trapped below deck without ever striking a blow. I forgot I was supposed to humour this guy. I didn't care if the crazy Argonauts were doing it for fun, the idea of joining them was repellent.

'You've got the wrong idea. I'm not here to join your crew. We're asking for a passage to the port of Parga. It's on the north-west coast of the Greek Mainland. I was told you're willing to take us?'

Jason was staggered. 'You don't want to join us? You can't be serious! We're *the Argonauts*. We're the future of the human race!' He swung back his elbow and fisted the air a couple of times, in what was probably the crew salute. '*Manpower! Manpower!*' He grinned. 'Scared of showing yourself up? Well, one of you has to work for your keep, I don't take passengers.' He leered at Andromeda 'Beauteous babe, if *you* can't handle a bireme oar, you'd better persuade hunky here. Or it's over the side!'

I would have to do it, and just hope to Great Mother this clown would remember I hadn't signed up for life . . . But wise Andromeda saved me.

'He can do better than row,' she said. 'He can *cook*.'

Jason's stubby white eyelashes quivered. I hadn't noticed how much he looked like a smug, sleek, bronze-hided pig. He folded his arms, deep in thought. 'Hm. The cook quit, and the cooking rota isn't working out—'

His brow clouded, he looked puzzled. 'Hold on. Did you say *Parga*? We weren't heading north . . .' Then he threw back his head and laughed. 'Hey, it's an adventure! Strange, spooky things are always happening to us, we're the Gods' favourite playthings. We have our secret objective.' He tapped the side of his piggy nose, and winked. 'But we're in no hurry. We don't care where we go, as long as there's a fight to be fought, or a feat to be accomplished. We'll take you to Parga, why not?'

I knew the *Argo* was god-touched. I could feel it. More than touched, she was rotten with it. But Jason was mortal, I could feel *that* too. He was being used, and I needed to know how much he understood—

'Do you know *why* you were brought here to pick us up?'

Jason grinned. 'Oh, yeah. I know all about it, now I think. You fell foul of Hera, and I'm her blue-eyed boy. Is that worrying you? So what! Me, I *love* living on the edge. She has a huge crush on me, bless her. She'll forgive.' He leaned over to nudge me in the ribs. 'It's a toss up, eh? Offend one of them, please another. Between you and me, I'd back great Zeus against his old lady, any day of the month.'

I didn't like being nudged. 'How long will the trip take?'

The captain became a different person. He frowned, he consulted a metal instrument on the centrepost. He opened a locker, pulled out a scroll and spread it wide. It was an exquisite sea-chart, like no chart I'd ever seen. I saw my Kyklades, and the Mainland coast, I had a glimpse of the shocking distances; before Jason glowered at me, and adjusted his fleshy arm and shoulder so I couldn't see the inked lines.

'Hm.' He muttered, and measured with the first joint of his finger.

''Bout five, six days. Can you live with that, great Perseus?'

Yiannis had said twenty days or more. Wow.

'We can live with that,' said Andromeda.

The Argonauts were gentlemen-adventurers. They had no servants as such, they did their own chores. The hired cook had been their one concession, and he'd been badly missed. A constant supply of hot food for the rowers was part of their speed formula. We worked in a tiny shack above decks, forward of the steering-oar housing, grandly called 'the galley'. It was nonstop; and boring too. Grilled meat and flatbread, grilled meat and flatbread, in immense quantity, morning, noon and night.

Seasonings? Fruit? Vegetables? Forget it. The Argonauts never went to market, on principle. They carried no tradegoods (though they were well supplied with coin), and picked landing spots where there wasn't a town or a farm for miles, so that they could pretend the country was uninhabited, ruled by monsters, plagued by witches; any excuse for thievery.

It was no wonder the ship felt god-touched. Jason had a high proportion of half-mortals on his team: sons of Gods, sons of nymphs; even of the North Wind. Some of them ignored our arrival, they just took the food and ate like starving machines. Some were friendly: Castor and Polydeuces, the twins who had two fathers; one mortal and one a son of Zeus; Orpheus the musician; Atalanta, the only sister in this band of brothers. Some, like the great brute called Heracles, whom I'd been warned to avoid, seemed to be completely in a world of their own.

None of them questioned who we were or why we were onboard. Jason had called me *son of Zeus*; but Hermes must have told him that. The others knew nothing. What was stranger was that *we* didn't know *them*. We'd never even heard of Orpheus, and he was *amazed* at that (although for an artist of genius, he's not vain). I began to think it was a good thing, for this particular voyage, that they avoided the ports. The heroes of the *Argo* might have been very strangely surprised by what they found there—

There was another 'deerhunting' raid two days out of Serifos, but we didn't dare to go ashore. We were afraid we might never get back on board, if we once stepped on mortal earth again. Either the god-touched black ship would vanish; or else we would.

We spent our free time on the roof of the galley, haunted by the everlasting slam-swoosh-thump, slam-swoosh-thump of the oars; watching the sea and sky. Andromeda had copied down my instructions onto tallyboards before we left Seatown. She read them to me, and we tried to make sense of them; without our family's distracting comments. Find the Graeae. Get them to tell me how to reach the Stygian Nymphs. Get the Stygian Nymphs to tell me the special route to the Garden of the Hesperides; located somewhere in north Africa. Kill the Medusa, without looking her in the face. Get away very quickly with the grisly trophy—

Either I'd forgotten more than I remembered, or a lot of information was missing.

'How am I supposed to sneak up on the Gorgons? They can't be blind, if they can look at people and turn them to stone.'

'Maybe they look at people by accident. But they'll hear you.'

'Unless they're deaf. But how do I escape, after I've killed the Medusa, even with winged sandals? The other two have wings, and I can't kill them—'

'Perhaps they have wings but they can't fly,' suggested Andromeda. 'Like ostriches.'

I didn't know what ostriches were.

'They're very big birds, with legs longer than Atalanta's. They can run faster than horses, but they can't fly. Perseus, try to concentrate. What about the Head itself? How do you carry it if it's dripping poisonous blood? How do you manage never to look at it?'

'How do I keep it from looking at innocent bystanders?'

Sometimes the Medusa Challenge seemed like a ghastly joke.

I loved to hear her voice and to watch her. I felt that shiver down my spine again as her eyes, her mind, turned the flying marks back into meaning. I'd pore over the boards, fascinated by those dancing signs. 'Do you think you could teach *me* to read?'

'Maybe,' she said, sadly. 'If we had time.'

When darkness fell we stayed on the roof: we had nowhere better to sleep. The Argo's huge oars beat onward, remorseless, mechanical as a waterwheel. The Argonauts had a mast and kept it stepped, but they never raised the great square sail unless there was a steady breeze in exactly the right quarter, and rarely even then. Not one of them, not even the captain was much of a *sailor*, in the normal sense. Which made it all the stranger to be travelling so fast, at summer's end, when any normal sea journey was faltering, losing days to calm and fretful squalls—

'You're very sure you can do it, Perseus. How are you so sure?'

'I'm not. I'm fatalistic.'

I watched the glow of moonrise in the east. The eighth-month moon was waning, and Andromeda was still with me. At Parga she *must* find a ship heading east. She must set out on her last journey, among strangers, all alone. I was awed by her courage. I wanted to tell her that I loved her, and that I wished we could stay here, poised between worlds. I wished time might stand still. We were sitting with our backs against the rope-locker that shared the roof of the galley with us, holding hands. But you can hold someone's hand, and feel that they are completely out of reach—

'Andromeda? Do you *believe* that your sacrifice will stop the earthquake?'

Silence, then she sighed. 'You don't know about human sacrifice, do you?'

'N-no.'

She let go of my hand, and drew her knees to her chin. 'The priests *always* say the child-sacrifice was effective, Perseus. They always say it was necessary and right, whatever happens. I don't know what the Gods themselves think. I don't know what the Gods really *are*; except they're not what the priests tell us.'

'Papa Dicty says people get the Gods they deserve.'

'I don't think the Gods are only in our minds. That wouldn't make sense, would it, son of Zeus? It's more as if, as if our minds are in the Gods. The Gods and our minds are made the same, and live in the same world—?'

'That's what I've thought. I've never worked it out in words, but that's how the otherworld feels, you're right. But then *why*—?'

Why go back to Haifa, when you know the damned priests are lying? I didn't finish my question, but she started up, in a desperate, trapped movement. I saw her kneeling, fists clenched, her eyes gleaming in the moonglow and the starlight.

'Why go back? You really want to know? Because I don't know if there'll be an earthquake or not, but I know for certain that if I'm not chained to that rock, *another girl will be.*'

She caught her breath. I knew she hadn't meant to say 'chained to the rock'. She hadn't told me that, she had spared me the details—

I was born to save you, I thought. There's no other reason why I'm alive. And I felt, right then, with *passion,* that the Supernaturals knew it too—

'But that's not all.' She wiped her eyes, with the side of her hand. 'It's not just that. It's a mystery, Perseus. I can't explain it, but I did see the God. And it's strange, but I'm not worried about getting to Haifa in time. I feel I'm bound to be there, the same as you are bound to reach the Medusa's lair. Maybe I'll have a strange dream, like the day you met your father, and I'll find myself at home again.' She stopped, and I thought she was surprised at hearing her own words, 'I still dream of horses,' she murmured. 'I've been seeing them in daylight, in the foam of the waves, since we were on the Argo. Maybe they're Ocean God's seahorses, waiting to carry me away—'

The oars thumped. The stars looked down, with changeless bright eyes.

'Let's try to sleep,' I said. 'Put your head on my shoulder, and I'll be your watchdog. I'll keep those horses at bay.'

I lay awake and thought about being immortal. I must lose her, no matter what: the same as Castor and Polydeuces must lose each other. All I could do about that was pray to the Gods to have pity, and let me cross the Dark Water, the same as mortals do. Let me be with her on the unknown shore; even if I didn't recognise her (I'd heard that the souls of the mortal dead forget everything). But I had something new to dread.

White horses in the waves?

Andromeda was seeing things mortals shouldn't see, because it drives them crazy.

It was this ship. It was getting to her. I was glad we'd be leaving it soon.

I avoided conversations with Jason, *not* because of the strangeness, but because he was so irritating. He was still convinced I longed to be an Argonaut, only I was too shy to admit it. He kept cornering me, and 'confiding' in me about the great plan. Fantastic adventures distracted them, but they were basically heading for the Black Sea, the eastern end of the known world. I couldn't resist asking what they planned to do when they got there? Pick up this overgrown rowboat and carry on, see if they came to another ocean? Or just turn around and head for the Pillars again, for a little more exercise?

'You don't get it, god-bothered dude. The *Argo* is *cutting edge*. When we do come back from this wild, rake-helly adventure we'll be famous. More famous than we are now, even. I'm going to found my own shipping line, take over the Middle Sea. I'll have the capital for that. We'll be bringing home a *huge*, *undiscovered*, secret prize. The details of which we're keeping to ourselves, so don't bother asking.'

'I don't know, Jason,' I said, shaking my head. 'The secret

undiscovered prizes I've seen you go after so far, have not been secret to their actual owners. I think you're just planning to night-hunt some unlucky Black Sea farmer's big fat sheep.'

The captain of the *Argo* gave me a very suspicious look, and changed the subject. 'Where d'you want to be let off, by the way? At the pilgrims' port, or somewhere quiet? As you know, we don't like ports. We're too hot for them to handle.'

It was the fifth day. Two nights ago we'd passed the cape of Kithera, southernmost landmark of the Achaean nations, and there we'd left the world I knew behind. We'd made one shore raid since, but that had told me nothing. It could have been the Mainland, or one of the northwest islands. We'd never had another chance to look at Jason's charts, and probably wouldn't have learned much from them: we weren't master mariners. We were at his mercy, which I didn't like at all. I suddenly wished I'd been more grovelling—

'Somewhere quiet would be very good.'

'Right,' he said. 'It won't be long now.'

I told Andromeda what the captain had said, and we started cooking the noon meal. We had flatbread and meat down to a fine art, and there wasn't much room in that hutch, so she went out to get some air while I finished up. Meat broiled and resting, a stack of flatbread ready to be fresh-grilled; a gravy with wild onion, garlic and cucumber (the twins and Atalanta had brought back the wild vegetables for me, from our last landfall). The Argonauts would hate the sauce, but I knew it would do them good.

I went to look for my girl, and found her on the foredeck with the captain. They were alone except for Heracles, who was staring doomily at the horizon, picking at the lionclaws under his chin. Castor had told me he was depressed for a reason: his boyfriend had been left behind with some nymphs, or something. But he made me uncomfortable, no matter what his problem was. Beyond the churning of our oars, the waves were dark as unwatered wine.

'C'mon,' Jason was saying, 'why not? If not me, who's the lucky guy?'

Andromeda could look after herself. But I didn't walk away.

'Well,' she said, coolly. 'If you *really* don't know, let's see if you can guess. Some people think he's just a bruiser, and sometimes he plays up to that. But secretly he's wise. Secretly he *thinks*, and I like that. He's kind, and gentle, and he has a sense of humour. He's tall, broad-shouldered, not at all fleshy. He has chestnut hair, that curls around his brow and at the nape of his neck in clusters, like ripe grapes. I think his skin must be pale in winter, but in summer it's shades of copper and golden brown. His eyes are dark blue, his nose is straight, he has a cleft in his chin—'

'Aw, *Perseus*—' cried Jason, pretending to be amazed. 'That baby? Trust me, Andromeda, forget the loser. Let's drop him at Parga, and then—'

'I need to know about the meal,' I said, loudly. 'Are we serving at the benches? Or are they eating in shifts today?'

Andromeda turned and grinned at me, wickedly. She knew I'd been listening.

'Good news. Captain Jason says we could be on shore this evening.'

She headed off. I stood and looked at Captain Jason.

He held up his hands, in mock terror. 'Hey, don't hit me! What did I say?'

'Not that Andromeda cares, because she's too far above you to even know you exist. But don't ever, ever bother her again, you pig-nosed spikey-haired —'

He leered, delighted to have got me going. 'They're all too far above us, my little son. Even if they're willing as your babe. That's why I'm married to the Argo, me.'

I should have hit him, it was a wasted opportunity.

*

Andromeda stayed at the rail for a moment, when the two heroes had stalked off in different directions. White horses, sombre-eyed, looked up at her. They were very close now, very real. She took a scrap of blue and chestnut weaving from the breast of her tunic, and cast it away: watched it fluttering down. Goodbye Perseus, goodbye. What should have been the beginning is going to be the end. No use hanging on to hope—

Maybe Jason had known what he planned to do with us all along; or maybe I sealed our fate. Either way, the weather took a hand. The day had been clear and fine. Before sunset we were close to a rocky coastline, with mountains beyond: no sign of human habitation. Then an easterly wind got up, there was a sudden overcast, and the sea began to heave in the blind swell that forebodes a storm. It was soon clear we couldn't make landfall, and the Argo was in for a rough night. Rain started pelting. The steersman was under shelter, but we'd been driven off the roof. Everything moveable in the galley was stowed. We crawled under the bolted-down table with our bundles of possessions, to sit it out. Luckily neither of us was prone to seasickness. Waves were smacking us in the face, it was pitch dark. We could only hope the rowers had managed to turn the *Argo's* head, back out to the safety of the open sea.

The door burst open. The Argonauts pulled us out. We thought the ship was foundering, but we were ready for that. I had my supernatural gear strapped to my back, Andromeda had her bundle tied around her waist ... There was light, splashing over us from the lantern Jason was holding. I had never seen such waves. I'd thought old Yiannis was gibbering, when he said *fifty times higher than your mast*. Now I knew, that's what it felt like.

'You two,' yelled Jason. 'You get off here.'

'*What*—?' I screamed.

'This storm. It's a little love-tap from my lady Hera, blessed be her name. I better do what she wants. But I'm giving you a dinghy. Oars, everything, because that's the kind of guy I am. You should have no problem, son of Zeus!'

We were chucked over the side, and a boat the size of a bathtub was chucked after us. I heard the Argonauts cheering as we managed to scramble into it, in a lull between squalls. Then the storm came back with fury, and the *Argo* vanished, as if she had never been. The world was nothing but roaring, boiling darkness and cold masses of saltwater, pounding on us, blow after blow. We could hear waves breaking on rock, a terrifying sound, but we could see *nothing*. We'd been thrown into the sea, in a wooden box. The thing I couldn't possibly remember had happened, and I *did* remember. Choking dark closed over me, I felt my Moumi's heart beating, I heard the nails being hammered down. And deeper than the crash of breakers, another noise, a sucking whirling, groaning roar, the sound of death itself—

He was standing on a spit of grey rock. I was Perseus, he was in two places. In front of him was the hollow among naked boulders where the old creatures crouched together. They were eating. Their meal would have been a cannibal feast; if they had been human. They were the Grey Sisters ... Limbs and bones, skulls and ribs lay about them, some stripped bare, some clotted with white, water-logged meat. On one side of the spit, a black roiling abyss. On the other, a fang of stone.

I did not remember how he'd come here, but I remembered about the eye and the tooth. I crawled, and the cold grey rock slithered from under my feet and hands. I was crawling on the waves, they tipped up and threw me back, he just crawled again. The Graeae could smell me. They peered around, sniffing hard: black eyeless sockets under wild white hair. I kept out of sight of the one eye. I remembered my mother telling me to be polite ... He said what about the goaty ones, they're *rude*. Moumi said, then be a little rude to them. True politeness is making people feel at ease with you, however strange they seem. Be natural, Perseus. The Graeae were as different from the naiad of the goat-hollow spring as death is different from an opening flower. But they were natural creatures, just the same. He crawled through the bones and took my place.

'Pass the tooth ...' I croaked.

The Sister across from him was mumbling on a drowned child's hand. She gulped it, and passed the tooth. I reached for a hunk of pale, dripping flesh.

Andromeda crouched in the bows of the tiny dinghy, gripping an oar with both hands. She'd lost the other. On one side the whirlpool, on the other the fanged rocks. She dared not look anywhere but straight ahead. Think, she told herself. She had tried this only once before. The bathing inlet, a sunny day, Palikari showing her how to use one oar. Push the water *back* in one direction, the boat will go *forward* in the opposite direction, same line. Now the other side. You're getting it, Kore. *Back* on the left, *back* on the right, evenly, evenly now; and that makes straight on. You've got it, Kore. She pictured it in her head, lines and forces, that helped. *Push* back. Boat goes *forward*—

She dared not look behind her. She knew that Perseus was there, curled in a ball, seas crashing over him. He was gone, he was in another place, he was having a strange dream. Wherever he is, she thought, he'll stand by me.

'Perseus? *Perseus?* Can you hear me? Can you guide me? I daren't look on either side, have to keep looking ahead—'

'*The eye.*'

What? Oh! He's right, I'm too close to the whirlpool!

'*The tooth.*'

Too close to the fang of rock—

It was lucky she'd lost the second oar, she could not have handled two. She could do this, with monumental concentration. The cold waves that slapped her, the ache in her hands and arms and shoulders would get to be unbearable: but not yet. The wooden shell bounced through the huge waves, somehow it was never swamped. Keep looking ahead, push back the water, boat goes forward: left side, right side, eye side, tooth side. We are getting there, we really are. If there's a sheltered beach beyond these rocks, we'll live.

Andromeda caught a mouthful of seawater. She choked and coughed, clutching her precious oar. The veil of spume parted. For a moment she saw, in moonlight, what lay beyond the reefs. The cliffs, black and gleaming, rising straight from the white shock of the waves. She looked back, over her shoulder. Perseus was staring at her, his mouth an O of horror, his eyes blind with visions. 'The eye!' he croaked. 'The eye!'

Stand by me, she thought, and deliberately plunged her oar.

The Eye

And again,

The Eye

And again,

The Eye

One more stroke: the clawing fingers of that black maw caught the dinghy, and flung it inwards. Andromeda's oar was ripped out of her hands. She threw herself onto the bottomboards, grabbed hold of Perseus; and the whirlpool swallowed them.

Serifos was untouched by the storm that had swooped on the Ionian Coast, six hundred long miles away by the sea roads.

Danae could not hear the wind that gave Jason cause to toss his passengers overboard. She was kept awake by anxieties closer to home. Hard to believe the children had been gone such a short while ... She stood in the kitchen yard, with the people who'd taken shelter at Dicty's, a pitchfork in her hands: hoping there'd be no more trouble tonight, and thinking of the white linen embroidered with cornflowers and wheat ears, inscribed *The Queen of Summer*. The story of the Summer Queen tells how the child of the Goddess of Harvest, Dimitra, was kidnapped by Winter, the king of the dead. But the blossoming girl was found again, she came back to her mother. Spring always returns ...

Did they tell that story in Haifa? Danae had never had a chance to ask Andromeda. Probably they did, because it was as old and true as the Dark Water song. It belonged to no nation, although Danae had learned it with the Achaean names, in the Greek language, when she was a child.

You gave me yourself, *Kore*. You promised to return.

She did not pray to Zeus. She would never *pray* to Perseus's father. She prayed to his wife, to Hera the Protectoress. Anthe thought the Achaean Goddess was nothing but a vindictive shrew, but Danae knew better. Maybe she bargained, maybe she just pleaded. You know I never harmed you willingly, great lady. Be just. Have pity on my children, my dear boy and my dear girl. Let them live.

10

I lost the otherworld horror of the Grey Sisters, I was back with Andromeda, and the whirlpool had us. Hang on, I screamed, and she clung to me: while I struggled to keep my arms and legs thrust against the sides. There was a weight on my back, dragging me outwards, terrifyingly strong. If I let go, or if one flimsy plank burst we were dead, instantly dead. We were thrown around like a child's toy boat in a yelling black downspout, flung from rock to rock, around and around, falling, falling—

Then the dinghy was right side up again, the tumult faded, and I was breathing air. That's all I knew, until I felt the bottom of the boat bumping against something; gently, gently. There was a grating sound, familiar but uncanny. We separated, and got to our knees. The darkness seemed complete, but I had a feeling of great space above us, around us. I groped over the bows. 'Pebbles,' I reported, hardly able to believe it.

Our boat was being nudged by quiet waves onto a shingle shore.

We climbed out and I pulled the boat further up; instinct for an islander. Then I grabbed her again, or she grabbed me. We wrapped ourselves around each other: icy bodies, saltwater kisses, setting me on fire, the first we'd ever shared—

'D'you think we're dead?' I whispered.

Being dead did not seem too bad, at that moment.

'No,' said Andromeda, her nose against the hollow of my throat. 'We're not dead. I know that for sure, because we're still together, son of Zeus.'

That cooled me off. I let her go; but I kept a tight hold on her hand. We sat on the pebbles. 'I met the Graeae,' I said. 'I got the tooth all right, but I didn't fool them for long. I had to take the eye . . . to take the eye, and run for it—'

'That's what you said. *Take the eye.* I thought you were telling me to steer into the whirlpool, so I did. As far as I could steer at all. I had to believe you, because we were going to be smashed to death. We must be under the cliffs now.'

'What cliffs?'

(In a flash, in my mind's eye, I saw the spume parting, the black wall—)

'There were cliffs beyond the reef, no break in them . . . The whirlpool must have swept us into a cave. Perseus, how are we going to get out?'

The blackness had turned to charcoal. I could see shards of light, far away and far above us: but I couldn't see much of the cavern itself, only that it seemed huge. There was no sound of the sea, no sign of the roaring funnel we'd fallen through. At our feet was a river, running strong but silently. The gleam of moving water vanished into blind dark; I could not see to the other side. I wondered what would have happened to us if we had been carried to that shore.

'I don't think we want to get out,' I said. 'I think this must be the Styx. This is the cavern where the sacred river runs underground, just the way the boss described.'

'We had to get past the Graeae to reach it,' said Andromeda, wonderingly. 'Between the eye and the tooth. Old Yiannis *did* know something.'

We were battered, freezing cold, soaked, our mouths and throats parched by salt. But we were where we were supposed to be. The weight on my back, which had nearly killed us in the whirlpool, was the sopping wet sheepskin. I struggled with the knots in the cord I'd used to fasten it to my shoulders: and there was Athini's shield, the winged sandals, the *harpe*. I wasn't meant to lose them.

Andromeda unwound the cloth bundle from round her waist, and found more practical treasures: a skin of fresh water, two flatbreads wrapped around some grilled meat; a firestriker and tinder in a tarred, stoppered jar. I was very glad to see the water, I wouldn't have liked to drink from that river.

'We lost the tallyboards with my instructions,' I said.

'It doesn't matter.' She had found her loom-weights, and a hank of rare, purple yarn, in the last fold of her waist cloth. 'I wonder why I brought these?'

'You never know. They might come in useful.'

The firestriker wasn't much use without fuel, but she struck a light anyway, and held up a scrap of burning tow. We saw a river beach backed by a jumble of boulders, driftwood and debris caught between them; just like the shore of a river above ground. We rinsed our mouths, drank a little water, and started collecting wood. At least we might get ourselves warm and dry—

I stretched my cramped limbs and counted bruises. The gloom grew transparent, as my eyes became accustomed. There were bones among the rocks, pottery shards, lumpy little votive statues. Old shoes, a broken bracelet. And more mysterious things: crushed cylinders of bright-coloured metal, beaten very thin. Tatters of stuff like insect wings, but very tough. There were a lot of strange small coins, neither copper nor silver; some kind of base metal. I started collecting them out of curiosity. Then I remembered that the Greeks put a coin under a dead person's tongue, so they'll have the fare for Charon's ferry, and I dumped them—

'People must throw things into the cavern,' I said. 'From up above. The river carries them and drops them here.'

Andromeda?

I'd been sure she was right beside me, but she was kneeling by the river.

'Andromeda? Don't drink that!'

'I can hear the horses coming.'

'*Andromeda*? Come on, wake up, we need wood.'

'The horses and the flying marks are one and the same, you see.'

She came back to herself, and stopped frightening me. We took armfuls of wood back to our mooring place, and I used the *harpe* to scrape tinder and split some kindling. I hoped the sacred blade wouldn't find this disrespectful: but necessity is a holy thing. The fire we built wasn't much, but it was wonderfully comforting. We crouched beside it in our salt-soaked rags like shipwrecked sailors; and shared the meat and the flatbreads. I'm afraid I got most of the meal. Andromeda said she was hungry, but she soon lost interest. I was still *starving* when every scrap was gone. I went off into a dream about wheat ribbons boiled and then soaked in butter, with stewed vegetables, chopped sausage, a little hot spiced oil. A yoghurt and garlic sauce on the side—

'If only we had something to *cook.*'

'Everything was battened down. I brought what I could, I didn't think we'd need a whole kitchen. If this was a proper shipwreck there'd be shellfish.'

'Sea urchins. Oysters. Grilled crab. You're going to make me cry.'

'I don't like sea urchins.'

'I bet you'd eat them now, though.'

She laughed, looked over my shoulder, and gasped.

'*Perseus!*'

The cavern should have been darker around the light of our fire, but it wasn't. I looked round and saw a party of young women coming towards us, through the clear gloom: striding free and proud, dressed in black and gold; white arms and shoulders bare. I would've thought they were athletes, bull-dancers, champion swimmers, nothing so wispy as *nymphs*: except that I knew at once they were not human.

'Hello Perseus,' said the foremost of them, a tall girl with dark red hair bound in gold ribbons. She wore a short tunic worked with a pattern of pomegranates across the breast; a bow on her back, and armlets like a woman-warrior.

She sat down easily by the fire. 'We've been expecting you. I'm Minthe.'

'Orphne,' said the second nymph. She was arm in arm with someone harder to make out: not wispy, but confusing, like an image wavering in cloudy water.

'We are Eleione, nymphs of the dead marshes; we are many.'

'I am Lethe,' said a gentle voice: a girl in a long black dress with gold borders, who seemed very young; she had huge dark eyes and a dreamy smile.

'I am Styx,' murmured the last of them. Her hair was loose, a drift of charcoal mist around her white face. She stooped and kissed me on the forehead, gravely and kindly; her breath was cold. 'I run over there.'

'Are you the Stygian Nymphs?' said Andromeda.

Of course they are, I thought.

The five beautiful faces turned as one to stare at my companion — as if they hadn't seen her until she spoke, or as if she had no right to speak to them: which I thought was rude. 'We are some of them,' said Minthe. 'We are many ... What happened, Perseus? How did you *ever* get here? I'm sure Great Athini and Swift Hermes gave you the most unhelpful, confusing directions. Do tell us all about it!'

Orphne laughed, reached out to Andromeda and kissed her. 'Welcome, daughter of Cassiopeia, the famed queen. What a lovely surprise that *you* are with us! But wise and beautiful Andromeda, you look as if you've been dragged behind a chariot! How did a learned and splendid Phoenician princess fetch up by our sister's riverside, so bedraggled?'

'It's a long story,' said Andromeda, ruefully.

'We *love* stories,' they cried, together.

We told them all about it. We fed the fire, and when there was no more wood we all went and collected more. Athini had been right, the Stygian nymphs were special. They were the best company, ideal listeners, I could have talked to them for ever. I never needed to see the sky again. The underworld was world enough—

'How do you do it?' I asked Lethe. 'You make me feel like a poet!'

'We get a lot of practice,' she said, modestly. 'So *many* stories.'

The tall redhead, Minthe, the one who was *very close* with the king of the dead (she'd let this interesting news slip out, once or twice!) gave Lethe a strange look, and leaned over to murmur to me—

'Perseus. Be careful of your girl.'

'What d'you mean, *careful*?' I laughed. 'We have no cares now.'

I had almost asked her *what girl*, and that startled me—

Minthe's breath was clean-scented, she whispered like rustling leaves; it was hard to concentrate on what she was actually saying. 'I'm talking about *Andromeda*. The girl you came in with, son of Zeus. She's mortal. She shouldn't be talking to us.'

I'd known it was strange that Andromeda could see the nymphs and talk to them, but I didn't want to hear Minthe's warning. 'Oh, I think it's all right. We're beside the Styx, aren't we? It's the river between death and life. The veils are thin here, that's probably what makes the difference—'

'A poet *and* a philosopher,' said Orphne, shaking her head. 'It's plainer than that, Perseus my dear. Princess Andromeda is a dedicated sacrifice. In body she's no closer to death in this cavern than she would be anywhere, but in her heart and mind *she is halfway across the river.* So you'd better be careful, that's all, because we'd love to keep her with us—'

Then she took out ripe pomegranates from the pouch she had slung at her waist. 'But never mind. All that story-telling must have given you a thirst. You must be hungry too. Would you like some fruit? You'll find it very sweet.'

I was *perishing* hungry, as if I hadn't eaten for a month. But I wasn't quite so stupid as to accept fruit from the land of the dead. I hesitated, Orphne held out the pomegranate, smiling. Suddenly I looked at the fire, and realised it was nearly out. I'd better get more fuel.

But there was something wrong. How much charred wood, how many circles of ash, on the little stones by the riverside?

How long have we been here!

I jumped up. Andromeda!

'Andromeda!'

She wasn't with me. She was kneeling at the water's edge. The nymph of the Styx, wrapped in her shroud of hair, was beside her—

'Oh, *Jason*,' laughed Elieone, the marshy one, with her crown of reeds and rushes, and gold frogs embroidered on her skirts. 'Our recruiting sergeant! He's so *careless*, but we've no complaints. We love the lads and girls he sends our way—'

'I dread the day he turns up himself!' Lethe, pretended to stop her ears. 'I'll be tired of listening, for the first time in my immortal life!'

I ran down to the water. 'Andromeda! Andromeda!'

She looked up, puzzled: she spoke from the brief past we shared. 'It's Perseus, isn't it? And I am Kore. I remember, the cemetery wall at dawn, my torch guttered; I wrote my name on the stones. We are dead, Perseus. We are *ghosts*, you and I—'

The nymph of the Styx watched me with her river's eyes, beckoning and deep.

'Not yet,' I said. 'Let her go, she's not yours yet.'

I can wait, breathed the river's voice, I am patient, son of Zeus—

Andromeda shuddered, and stood up.

'What was I saying? Perseus, we should get away from here—'

'I know it.'

The Stygian nymphs were gathered by the fire, with its telltale circles of ash: looking guilty and frightened, like little girls caught out. But I blamed myself. There was no evil in them, only nature.

'Exactly *how* long have we been here?' I demanded.

'We don't know,' confessed Minthe. 'We lose track, Perseus. No harm.'

'No harm,' I said. 'No harm at all. But we must get on. We were told you people would direct us to the Garden of the Hesperides? Will you do that?'

'Of course,' said Eleione, sounding hurt. 'We hadn't *forgotten*.'

Orphne giggled. 'Except for Lethe: she forgets everything!'

'The quickest way possible would be good.'

They looked at each other. 'Have you practiced with the winged sandals, Perseus?' asked Orphne.

I'd never had a chance. 'Er, no.'

'Well, you have to use them now. Never mind, it's intuitive. But you'll need this.' She gave me a small round bag with a drawstring. It felt like skin; it seemed to be empty. 'That's the *kibisis*. Don't worry about the size, it grows to fit anything you put inside it, and there's always just enough room. It comes from the east. Put the Medusa Head in there, when you've chopped it off.' She gave me a sly grin. 'You still remember you're supposed to do that?'

No thanks to you beauties, I thought. But they were not to blame.

'Yes I do. I remember everything.'

'You'll also need this.' Tall Minthe stooped to the pebbles beside her, and held out her hands. I could see nothing. I felt cold, curved, metal—

'What is it? A helmet?'

'It's called the cap of invisibility. It belongs to the king of the underworld. Don't worry, he knows you're borrowing it. We're close, Hades and I, as I may have mentioned. He asked me to take care of handing it over.'

She'd mentioned. She'd been dropping his name all over. Hades was a married God, but more faithful than most, he didn't *roam*. I'd heard that his wife (who had her own life), got on well with some of the nymphs around him. I hoped our five were among that favoured band. I knew they'd have been happy to feed on our memories until we were whitened bones, but I still liked them. They brought style and grace to the darkness. If I'd been mortal, I'd have been glad to know they'd be waiting here, when I came back again.

A cap of invisibility, so I could sneak up on the Gorgons; and escape pursuit.

A bag that would contain the Snakehead safely.

I was equiped.

But the rings of ash around the dying fire were frightening.

'Thank you,' I said. It wasn't the same as being kitted out by Athini and Hermes: I had no trouble feeling grateful this time. 'I wish you well, with all my heart, my dears. But how do we get to the Hesperides? And how long will it take?'

I had let go of Andromeda's hand when I took the helmet. I reached for her again, and was relieved to feel her return my grip. But her hand was cold, she didn't speak, and the cavern seemed darker. I felt that I was losing her—

'It will take no time,' said Lethe softly.

'Put on your sandals. Go *through*.'

'My river is at the end of all journeys,' whispered Styx. 'The Garden is where you began. Go there through your beginning, swift as thought.'

I'd seen them walking towards us, I didn't see them go. Andromeda and I were alone. Our fire was dead, the air was still. The silence was so profound that I could hear the sound of the noiseless river, as it slipped through the dark. I sat on the rocks, unfastened my sheepskin and set the invisible helmet on it; so I'd know where it was. I laced Hermes's sandals onto my bare feet. My own footgear had gone when we were thrown off the *Argo*, and I'd never noticed. I slung Athini's shield on my back. Andromeda took the *harpe* from me, and strung the *kibisis* beside it on the leather belt. 'What'll I do with the helmet? If I put it on, you won't be able to see me.'

'It's dark,' she whispered. 'I can't see you now.'

But I could still see her. 'I'll have to carry you.'

I scooped Andromeda up in my arms—

Go to the Garden through your beginning. I thought I understood. The Stygian Nymphs had given me all the clues I needed. I must travel in memory: from the shore of the dark water where life ends, to the beginning of my story. I thought of a wooden box, nailed down and flung into the sea. My mother's shame, my callous, *stupid* grandfather. The Greek word 'Styx' means 'hateful', but this cavern had been a kindly place, compared to my start in life.

'I can't do it, Andromeda. I think I know what they mean: but I'm scared.'

'Remember what you *want* to remember,' she murmured, from far away—

Sunlight.

Little fish, twinkling in the harbour water. Me and my Moumi lying on our bellies, giggling: dabbling our hands and the little fishes coming up to nibble us, the sun on our backs, how it feels to be perfectly happy.

Sparks flying from the boss's hammer, the first time he let me hold the pliers. The mask held in front of my face, the smell of hot metal, my pride.

Sunlight.

Sunlight.

A crisp, golden silence.

The sun burned on my closed eyelids, hot metal. I could *smell* it. I opened my eyes and I was in the dark again. But I was somewhere different. The air was warm, and full of warm scents: dust and cinnamon, musk and dung, spices I couldn't name. If I am where I should be, this is *Africa*! I thought. For a moment I was purely thrilled. I was a little boy, fascinated by travellers' tales: thinking of mighty Egypt; of Ethiopia, Andromeda's ancestral home—

Oh, Great Mother ... Andromeda!

I panicked, terrified: then I realised I was still holding her in my arms. She seemed to be sleeping. I set her on her feet, and shook her gently. 'Andromeda, Andromeda, we're here, we made it!' She opened her eyes, stared straight at me and began to struggle furiously. She was strong and reckless, I had to let her go or break her arms. She stared around, wary and wild.

'Perseus! Where are you!'

I took off the king of death's helmet, and held it under my arm.

'Am I dreaming?' she said. 'Are you Perseus?'

'You're not dreaming. We're here. We must be near the Gorgons' lair.'

If there were mountains they were out of sight. A twilight plain stretched out around us. The sky was the colour of rust, and so was the ground underfoot. I couldn't tell if it was always starless twilight here, or if this was the mortal dusk of an overcast, oppressive day. Not a sign of life, not a blade of grass or a tree, but there were stone figures scattered about. Some had crumbled into shapeless lumps, some were whole enough that you could make out the frozen record of flight ... an outflung cloak, a leaping silhouette; a hand that clutched a mouldering stone weapon. They'd been running and they'd looked back; and that had been the end of them.

One figure, in strange scaled armour, was close to us. I could see the gaping mouth, the bulging eyes of terror. Sometimes the dead preserved by the volcanic ash of the Great Disaster had been found like this. The deep ash looked like stone but it was very soft. When it weathered away the dead – those who'd not been close enough to burn to nothing – were still there, still on their feet. Burned pits for eyes. But the eyes that had faced the Gorgons were intact, globes of stone.

I turned to see what the fleeing dead had seen.

There was a wall. It was massive: easily as high as three men, and built of huge, well-dressed blocks. There were no loopholes, no gates. It curved on either side, seeming to enclose a space no larger than our Sacred Enclosure.

'Well, now for the last trial. Are you ready, my Kore?'

Andromeda was shaking her head. She took a step away from me.

'I'm going back to Haifa now. You have to go on alone.'

'What? No, no Andromeda. It's too late. You'll have to come with me.'

Over the wall with her in my arms, set her down where—?

This was all wrong. I stood there trying to convince myself there was a way I could take her with me. It was no use. I have her in my arms, the Gorgons attack I set her down, how's she going to defend herself—?

'I must go. To the rock of sacrifice. It's time.'

I'll find somewhere to *hide* her, I thought, desperately. I'll put her somewhere she'll be safe, where I can find her again— But though she spoke like a sleepwalker, Andromeda had seen the look in my eye. She took another step backward, and I knew that I dared not touch her. When lads and girls fight – not with each other, not physically, where I come from, but lads fighting lads, girls fighting girls – they scream insults, before and during. It's *your mother's another, your dog looks like a pig, you have stupid hair*. Any old rubbish, childish or vicious. I'd only a couple of times in my life had someone look at me the way she did then: unarmed silent, resolute, ready to kill, ready to die. There's nowhere she *can* go, I thought.

'Wait here! Just be here when I get back!'

I leapt over the wall.

This is a *garden*?

The Garden of the Hesperides was a petrified charnel house. The stone figures, which had been scattered on the plain, were a crowd in here, and none of them was whole. Any champion who'd managed to get this far, had died petrified while being torn apart. The mutilated statues weren't alone, either. There were animals prowling in the shadows. Shapes moved in the withered undergrowth; eyes glinted from tattered creepers. I heard a coughing growl, a chorus of high, yipping barks that went off into weird cackling. It was hard to make out the size of the place. I thought I saw the opposite curve of the wall, not far off at all, but then I wasn't sure. Maybe the garden was much bigger than I had thought. Was that cough a lion?

I'd never met a lion, we didn't have big predators on Serifos: I didn't like the idea of meeting one now. But wild animals were not my concern. Invisible, Athini's shield on my left arm, the harpe naked in my hand, I crept forward.

Something was stirring, like a dry fountain: a murmurous hissing sound—

The three Gorgons were alseep on the bare ground under some dead trees, in a dell in the middle of the enclosure. Is there day in this place? I wondered. Will they wake? How long before sunrise? I walked around them at a cautious distance; very careful where I put my feet. The creatures were man-sized: which made them brawny women, but not giants. They were naked, their leathery hides looked grey in the dusk. Two of them lay curled together like cats; the third was apart. The bat wings folded on their shoulders didn't look big enough for flight: but then, neither did the wings on my borrowed sandals. The snakes all the monsters had for hair were not sleeping. It was their movement I had heard. They slithered over and under each other, three nests of vipers, in a continual rustling stir. I saw a small mouth gape. The snake's throat was red inside, a little stab of colour, and a shock thrilled through me. The snakes must have eyes, if they had mouths—

But they can't see me, I reminded myself.

I guessed that the one lying apart would be the Medusa, who was human, or had been human: not some kind of supernatural animal. But I'd better make sure. Look into the shield, I thought. I moved in, to make that test on the two sisters who were sleeping like cats. It was tough on my nerves. I had to find an angle where I could catch a glimpse of one bestial face and then the other, without getting into a position where I risked being caught by either one's deadly glance. I kept cool, I was patient and I did it. I couldn't see them *clearly* in the shield; there was too much shadow: but I could make out the movement of the snakes, so I knew I was getting the picture.

They were monsters.

So that leaves you, I thought, standing over the third sister.

I was lucky I'd thought about the horror of killing someone. If it had hit me now it would have shaken me badly, and *now* I mustn't falter.

I hope this releases you from torture, lady Medusa. If I'm doing wrong, forgive me ... *Look into the shield*, said Athini, in the brilliant light of a high, stony place. *In reflection she is not a monster, far from it. Then one sweep, and leap back*. I heard her voice: I felt the sweat of that training session running on my body. But the sweat was cold now. I crouched, one knee forward, weight on my back heel. I turned the shield on my arm. I looked into it.

Oh, Great Mother. I saw the Medusa's face. I saw the most grievous, heart-opening beauty in the world, her eyes open, looking out at me, and around her I glimpsed the Garden, the shining waters, the flowers, the boughs of the apple trees bending low, rich with fruit. There was no monster, *I* was the hideous intruder in paradise. Oh, worse. The beautiful woman was my Moumi, young as I first remembered her, looking at me with a girl-mother's tender love.

Oh, Great All, *it was Athini herself—*

It was Athini herself, looking out from inside of me—

I was Athini.

I was the monster.

I had to kill the monster, so I could be Athini—

The snakes rose up, a nest of eyes and whirling patterns, coiling in and out of each other. I saw that they were my thoughts, my mind was a nest of shining serpents: like the spirits of rock and spring, we were many. I saw thought like the flying marks on the tallyboard *racing and mingling*, bright and swift as lightning. I saw that *words are thought reflected*. But these are mysteries: mysteries that don't tell the truth, they are the truth. I did not falter, I knew it was right. I was right to do this. *S'bw'r* . . . I drew back the harpe. I could hear Athini's voice again, coolly saying: 'Her blood is poisonous. *Don't* get the blood on your skin.' I was ready to get out of the way, fast.

One sweep.

—and, and *something leapt*, from the gouting, severed throat. A warrior in armour, who flickered gold and was gone. A huge, beautiful winged beast, who bent his shining head and looked at me, with gentle, eager eyes. His pinions swept in a mighty downbeat, his hooves spurned air. I flung the bloody sickle and pitched myself backward, yelling and frantically clutching the Snakehead by the hair.

Nobody told me about that—!

I was engulfed in the thunder and rush of his passing, and then he was gone. The Gorgon sisters, Euryale and Sthenno, had woken and begun screaming. I was scrabbling around on the ground, one handed, terrified I would put my bare palm, or knee, in the great slick of poisonous blood, whimpering *they can't see me, they can't see me.* They could smell me though, and they could hear me—

I found the harpe. I got the Snakehead into the *kibisis*, without turning myself into stone. I fought a rearguard, retracing my steps: a nasty, naked retreat with no one to give me covering fire. Thank the Great Mother those Gorgons were as bewildered and terrified as I had been, by the living thunderclap that had come boiling out of Medusa. Neither of them had the wit to get upwind and cut me off.

I flew through the dead trees, running in the air, fending off random bat-winged claw and tusk attacks: I reached the wall, and only then grasped that I should have leapt for the sky at once. I shot up, the Gorgons followed on my heels, but in the wide air they quickly lost my scent. They flapped away, screaming at each other, in the wrong direction. I was glad I hadn't had to kill them.

I wheeled, and plunged to earth. I stabbed the harpe into the ground again and again, and scraped it against stone, to get rid of the last trace of poison. I had landed at the foot of the wall, I collapsed with my back against it. The dim plain was unchanged, the rusty overcast was the same. I felt tears on my face, and touched them, puzzled. Why am I crying, I wondered? I thought it was because I would never see the Garden again, the way I'd glimpsed it in Athini's shield—

'Andromeda?'

The scale-armoured warrior, the one who'd been beside us when I left her, was right in front of me. But I couldn't see her. I sheathed the harpe. I'd dropped the shield when I fell to earth: I picked it up and slung it on my back again. I threaded the *kibisis* onto my belt by the drawstring. Where was she? I took off the king of death's helmet, so she could see *me*—

'Andromeda?'

'*Andromeda!*'

I ran around calling her name, but I knew she had gone. There was nowhere to hide on that killing ground. She had gone. She had vanished, back to Haifa and the sacrifice, the way she'd warned me it would happen. But I had the Medusa Head. The peace and glory of knowing *I had done it* welled up in me. I had the means to follow her, swift as thought. I could save Andromeda's life.

11

Andromeda had been dreaming for a long time. She'd dreamed that she and Perseus were taken on board a strange ship that was going to carry them to the river of the dead. They had to cook for a small army of rowers who would eat nothing but meat and bread. She knew the ship wasn't entirely real, nor were the crew. Sometimes you could almost see through them; or they seemed mysteriously small and far away ... It was one of those dreams that's a *good* dream, but you know something's wrong. It went on for days, full of detail. She and Perseus talked and talked, alone together. But in the end the captain threw them overboard, and they reached the river by somehow falling through a whirlpool into a cavern (this part was very confusing).

She didn't remember leaving the cavern. She'd been in the middle of explaining to Perseus that she had to be somewhere else, when she'd found herself alone, walking along a road.

She was crying, but she knew she was not awake. She'd been walking a long time. I don't like this, she thought; like a child. I want to go back to the other dream, the complicated one with Perseus in it. The road had become a courtyard. She was in the Great Outer Court of the Women's Palace, at home in Haifa. It was empty. She knew she was still dreaming, because there were *always* crowds in here, day and night. Men and women both, embassies from far away, palace officials, private petitioners. It seemed to be morning, quite early ... She pushed open the tall blue and white doors to her mother's audience court. It was empty too, but she could hear the sound of weeping. She pressed on, pushing against the empty air that seemed to cling to her and hold her back. The sky overhead was blue and bright. This was a bad omen, because it was the tenth month and the rains should be on their way. The sky should be thick, the air heavy with brooding heat. Her sense that something was wrong grew stronger. The singing birds on the frieze, the flowering trees in their pots seemed to clamour at her, *Run away, Andromeda, run away!*

The doors to her mother's inner apartments were always guarded by the palace regiment, the Royal Ethiopians; who held this honour directly from the Queen. Often two immense and kindly royal cousins, called Aden and Kelmet, would be found on duty here. There was no sign of them: no guards at all. Andromeda was very uneasy, something was terribly wrong. Now she was in her mother's cool, high-ceilinged private rooms, sunlight falling like bright spears through the spaces under the eaves; beautiful things around her. The weeping was closer, everything came back to her but she couldn't believe it was real. She had never smuggled herself out of the palace, she had never escaped in the crowds of people fleeing the threat of earthquake. She had never traded her gold bracelets, she'd never been to Serifos.

She'd always been here, walking along this corridor with

the painted walls of a river scene, her bare feet making no sound on the cool tiled floor.

Her mother was sitting on a carved stool in front of the windows of her bedchamber, very upright, her hands gripping a gold-figured cosmetics case in her lap. There were deep grooves gouged between her fine brows; and on either side of her beautiful dark red lips, as if she'd been holding her mouth like that, calm and quiet, by an act of will, for months.

Cassiopeia was not weeping. It was the young women who were weeping; they were crying because they were mortally terrified. An older woman, another of those royal cousins (all the many personal servants of the palace were minor members of the royal family), was lining them up, chivvying them into place, making them stand straight and uncover their tearstained faces. The girls were all more or less dark-skinned, slim and tall, like the princess. Three of them were Andromeda's half-sisters: children of Kephus by lesser mothers, noblewomen or concubines. The other unlucky teenagers Andromeda didn't know.

None of them was a very good match.

She understood what was happening at once, and knew that her mother must be *desperate*. Cassiopeia was a sincerely religious woman, but she might have tried to get away with 'deceiving' the God. Phoenician nobles offered substitutes instead of their own precious children all the time – and the Gods showed no displeasure. But it was the priests who had demanded the life of Princess Andromeda. The Queen must have her back against the wall, if she was going to try and deceive *them*. It must be today, thought Andromeda, and she trembled. She'd been hoping for a respite.

On the queen's great bed, laid out on the coverlet like a flat dead person, was the covering of gold that the sacrifice wore. A dress entirely made of thin pieces of gold, linked with gold wire and set with jewels; a sacred diadem, with trembling gold leaves and pearl and coral flowers. All to be thrown away—

The queen had seen her daughter, and was staring at this vision in horror.

'Mama?'

Andromeda knelt and bowed her head, raising her joined hands in salute, as she always did when she entered her mother's presence. Cassiopeia was loving but proud. She expected ceremony to be respected, even in private life.

'Let them go. You don't need a substitute. I came back.'

Nothing more merciless than fear.

The chief priests of Haifa had been feuding with Cassiopeia for a long time. They resented the Ethiopian's wisdom, her power over the people, and even her beauty. They'd been plotting for years to increase their own influence and reduce the queen's scope. They were ruthless. They'd seen the portent of the first quake as an opportunity, and claimed Andromeda as a sacrifice to bring Cassiopeia to her knees. But they were also truly afraid. Like Cassiopeia the great queen, they *knew* things. They knew that deep wells were failing, that harvests were smaller, year by year; that the Middle Sea was growing more dangerous and trade was suffering. Fewer ships plied the longer routes, less merchandise was carried. Taki, the shipping magnate of the Blue Star line, had strongrooms full of treasure, but common goods were growing scarcer ... The priests looked into the future, further than anyone. They saw that even a city like Haifa might founder.

They weren't just greedy for material power. They truly believed that the creeping, deadly changes were wrought by Gods who could be bought like corrupt human beings. They believed, like the Achaeans, that Great Fira had been destroyed because Minoan women knew too much; because the Minoans had lived too soft, prizing the peace above war. They believed it could happen again, and this time the Great Disaster would destroy Phoenicia. Andromeda's unnatural learning was displeasing to the Gods. She had to die.

Andromeda knew all this. She was Cassiopeia's daughter, she'd been trained to understand statecraft. But it didn't help.

The wailing and moaning of the palace women left her no dignity. They wanted to bathe her, anoint her with funeral oils, dress her in finest purple. She wouldn't let them touch her salt-stained rags, or even comb her hair. But that was her last victory. She was sealed into the gold dress and delivered to the priests. She was made to walk through the city dressed in gold, and *shackled* – the chief priest of Melqart walking ahead of her in triumph, bearing the sacred diadem. The people crowded to watch her pass by, keening and howling. She was surrounded by the sound of breaking pottery. Vases and furniture were thrown from high windows, fine woven cloth was torn to pieces: all the destruction that was customary at a funeral.

'Don't mourn me!' she shouted, infuriated. 'I am not being murdered! This is my choice! I'm god-touched! This is right!'

The howls, the holy drums and rattles, the smashing of precious objects, the chanting of the priests, drowned her out. She wanted her mother. She wanted her mother to be here, proudly telling the people that Andromeda was willing. That the priests were false, but the sacrifice was *true*. But Cassiopeia and Kephus had retreated to the depths of the palace, leaving Andromeda to look like a dumb animal led to the slaughter; which was so unfair.

She was taken to the rock in a sacred barge. The moaning and weeping of the crowd diminished. She watched the long sweep of the oars, and felt the cool sea breeze. The sky was darker now, and the heat heavy: like a normal tenth-month day. They made her lie down, and fastened the chains to four bronze rings hammered into the rock, so she was pinioned by her wrists and ankles. The rock struck cold through the metal, she could feel the slimy touch of seaweed on her bare arms.

'This isn't your doing!' she shouted. '*I'm* doing this, for the people!'

No one could hear, except the priests and their servants. The chief priest pulled the hood of sacrifice over her face. She felt hands pushing her head about, setting the diadem in place. The drums, the chanting, the solemn moaning of the great brazen horns started to move away, over the water.

'Good riddance,' muttered Andromeda.

She ought to feel that things were right, now. She ought to be at peace.

How long? The sea was supposed to rise up and drown a sacrifice in hours at this season; by the special mercy of the God. But she didn't know how many hours—

The blindfold was a nasty touch.

I flew to Haifa, but not as swift as thought. I soon found out there was no way 'through' this time. I brained myself against one hillside, and one tree . . . after which I looked where I was going. At dawn I touched down at a port on the Libyan coast (didn't find out the name). I tried to get directions from a dockside taverna where they spoke our language. I was ravenous and they let me eat, bless them: although I had no coin they recognised, and I seemed to be insane. I touched down again on the deck of a big ship heading east; where I was taken for Hermes himself on account of the sandals, and that caused some excitement. They gave me water. And once more, at night, in a place I did not understand at all. There were huge sheets of the transparent stuff that my father had on his yacht, crowds of people running around; and roaring, silver winged creatures, that galloped along great brightly-lit racetracks until they were going so fast they galloped into the sky.

I found a bar there, and met someone who was god-touched. He told me, in a strange dialect of Greek, *how* to fly to Haifa, what bearings I should take by the stars, everything; as if it was something people did every day. Hermes fixed up that meeting. He was a true friend in need, the God of Thought; just as my father had promised me.

I reached the Phoenician Coast and identified Haifa, though it didn't look the way my god-touched guide had told me. I saw the earthquake damage as I approached, but the walled city that climbed up the hill seemed untouched. I saw the procession: but I didn't know what it was. I had spotted the palace by its strange white conical towers, pocked with little black windows. I flew straight there and landed in a vast courtyard. There were people, many of them in a red and white uniform, with white conical hats just like the towers. They were milling around like an ants' nest stirred up: they paid no attention to me. I followed the sounds of weeping and crashing to a double door. Two big men in the cone hats crossed their spears in front of me. Their skin was the same shining dark as my girl's.

'D'you speak Greek?' I demanded. 'I need to see the king and queen.'

'What business do you have with Their Majesties?' asked one of them, in Achaean Greek better than mine. I suppose he thought if I'd got this far, I must be more important than I looked.

'It's about the Princess Andromeda. She doesn't have to die.'

Their eyes were red with weeping. 'She didn't have to die,' shouted one of them. 'She had escaped. She came back, poor child. It's too late now.'

'That's what *you* think. I'm Perseus, son of Zeus. I can save her.'

I was a big frantic lout dressed in rags, they could have just run me through. Maybe they felt the presence of the Gods, I don't know. Anyway, they let me pass and told a woman (in a richer kind of red and white uniform) to take me to the Queen. In a pillared room, dark because the windows were shuttered, smoky with incense and noisy with weeping and crashing sounds, the Great Queen Cassiopeia and her husband Kephus were sitting stiffly on two thrones. The woman whispered to Cassiopeia, and the king and the queen came to see the madman.

Andromeda's mother was much older than my Moumi, but she was *very* beautiful, and even then – haggard with grief, her make-up running – she was a figure of great power. Kephus was younger. He wore gilded, fancy-dress armour, and I naturally hated him. I remembered the pain in Andromeda's voice when she said, *Oh, Daddy ... he has plenty of other children.* But he looked formidable in his way. He led the city's army in person, I later found out. I wondered how they saw me. I had the *kibisis* at my belt, with the sheathed *harpe*. The king of Hades' helmet was tucked under my arm, and Hermes's winged sandals were on my feet. Would they recognise the supernatural gear? Would they understand that they could trust me?

'What is your petition, Perseus son of Zeus?' said the king, in Greek.

'I wish to marry your daughter Andromeda. If I subdue the monster, will you agree that she is released from her vow, and free to marry me?'

I was thinking ahead. I could deal with a supernatural monster, but the dedication would be a problem. The priests wouldn't let my girl just walk away—

The queen stared at me: at hope that was hateful because it came too late. 'The sacrifice has been offered. Ask the God if you may marry her.'

Their Majesties swept back to the ceremony they had left, gold and purple cloaks swirling behind them. I realised what

180

all the breaking and tearing meant: it was a funeral. But I couldn't be too late! I had the Medusa Head! Why else did I have the Medusa Head? I grabbed the nearest courtier by his jewelled collar, shook him and yelled at him. '*Where is she?*'

'She is on the rock of s-sacrifice,' he gabbled. 'Y-you can see it from the harbour, g-great prince, m-mighty lord.'

I dropped the man in a heap, and ran. Nobody stood in my way: I think the royal household would've been cheering me on, if they'd known what I was doing. But I remembered the helmet and slammed it on my head, just in case. I reached the big courtyard and leapt for the sky, praying that all the supernatural loot wasn't going to vanish; but that couldn't happen, because I was born to save her—

I saw the priests at the harbour wall, with their horns and drums and gold cone hats. I saw the crowds of mourning, wailing people, and cursed myself because now I knew what the procession had been about. They'd taken her to the slaughter-rock. I saw her lying there, covered in gold. She blazed in the morning sun. Soon as I was over water I pulled off the helmet and chucked it. As long as it was in the sea, some nymph or other would take it back to its owner. Being invisible wasn't going to help me now, and though you couldn't see it, it didn't weigh nothing—

A great yelling burst out behind me. I thought I'd caused the panic: the crowd had just seen a flying man, with a wicked-looking bronze sickle in his hand, appear in midair. Then I saw that the sea out beyond Andromeda had begun to boil.

Sometimes the first warning people have of an undersea quake is a strange long wave, far out on the horizon. They see it but they can't see how big it is, until it's close enough to drag the water back from the shore; until they see the gulfs exposed. Then everybody starts to run ... When the quake is close to land, you see what I saw. There's no storm, the sky is clear and calm: but suddenly the sea roils and churns as if a huge fish, a fish as big as a hill, is thrashing about under the surface. And the killer wave rises right out of this churning, like a monster heaving up from the deep.

I'd heard it described. I'd never seen it happen, until now.

The Haifans were running for higher ground.

They had called the God of Earthquake, and *he was here*.

Great Mother. It was some vicious consolation to see the priests haring it up the hill, as fast as anyone. They'd expected a quiet drowning: not this. I crashed onto the rock, fell to my knees and slashed at the chains. The Chaldean dagger was a good blade, it sliced her shackles as if they were tow. 'It's me! Perseus!' The gold diadem went to feed the fishes. I dragged the hood from her head.

Her great black eyes, a shock of meeting.

'No!' she shouted. 'No! This is mine!'

'Get out of that gold dress!' I screamed. 'You'll sink like a stone!'

I shot away again, slamming the harpe back into its sheath. The *kibisis*, the *kibisis*. I struggled with the drawstring. I had to get my hand inside, and grab hold of the snakes, without touching the severed, bloody stump of the Medusa's neck. The snakes woke and hissed. They wrapped themselves dryly round my wrist and laced themselves through my fingers. It did not feel horrible. It was the feeling you have when you pick up a well-balanced, well-forged sword; and *it knows you*.

Yes! I thought.

Come on, you sea monster—!

You think you are so big. Let's have you—!

Where was it?

How could I show it the Medusa Head, if it didn't show itself? There was supposed to be a monster, a mighty thing with fangs and claws that rose from the deep. The earthquake was supposed to have a supernatural form, like the Grey Sisters; something that I could defeat. I could not turn the

Middle Sea itself to stone ... though I was so desperate, I tried. I raced out over the boiling centre of the eruption, holding the Medusa face, with its petrifying gaze, above the waves. I screamed for the monster to *come out and face me*. But what rose up was the sea itself, a deadly tower of water, racing to shore as it grew. My girl, still dressed in gold, was kneeling on the rock, staring into the sky, oblivious of the great wave, waiting for the God—

Then I saw the winged horse. I didn't see him coming. He was just *there*, all at once, galloping down through the air. His hooves struck the earthquake waves, and they were calm. He trotted over the gleaming sea, his mighty wings curved above his back like a swan's. His neck was stretched out, like a horse eager to greet some rider he knew and loved. I saw him bow his head, into Andromeda's hands.

Andromeda had not stripped off the gold dress. She had no sense of danger, only a crazy sense of defeat. It was just, I was ready! Perseus, don't take this from me—!

She saw the winged horse coming out of the sky.

S'bw'r?

The horse did not speak, but she heard her secret name in the warm breath on her hands. In Greek she was called 'Andromeda', meaning *great thinker*, or else *ruler of men*. A proud name for a great queen's daughter. Too proud: bound to lead to trouble. But in the secret temple language of her mother's people she was just *S'bw'r*, the one who thinks—

Bridle me, said the breath of the great winged horse.

She reached inside the gold dress, and brought out a hank of purple yarn and the loom-weights. Just as in her dream, it was like catching a thought. His soft muzzle nosed into the halter. She drew it over his neat ears, she cinched the weights and leapt onto his back. The great wings beat downwards and they soared into the air.

'Where are you taking me?'

No answer, horses don't speak. The Middle Sea opened beneath them. She saw the Twelve Islands, and the Turning Islands. The ruined cup of Fira, like a hollow, rotten tooth. The mountainous length of Kriti, with two ends jutting up; like a comb. He circled to the north, over the capes and promentories of the Mainland coast. Over the Achaean Nations, he swooped down. Where his shining hooves struck rock, fountains sprang up: springs that had been imprisoned, lost, until Andromeda could ride this horse and free them. *Oh!* she thought ... *This is what I was born to do. I was not meant to die, I was meant to open the springs.*

As if in answer the horse soared again, rising so high that the air was thin and cold. She saw a Greek city, rich in marble buildings, with vivid-columned temples. Rivers of light were springing from it and flying across the lands, weaving a fabric richer than her eyes could follow, vanishing north, east, west, south, to the ends of the earth. She felt the way she'd felt when she was writing down the Dark Water song: but it was not the dead who were calling to her, it was people who were yet to live. And she was part of the dazzling, world-spanning pattern that sprang from that shining city, because she had made the flying marks, because she had made the leap of power—

Then the city was gone, and the flank of a mountain was in front of her, very big and coming up fast. She yelled out, clung to her yarn reins and clutched the horse's flanks with her knees, as he cleared a summit set around with white towers, reminding her of the palace at home – and there the winged horse landed softly, on all four hooves at once, like a huge eagle settling on his nest.

It *was* a palace. There were gilded walls that glittered like crystal, halls and courtyards and gardens. There were people too, tall, splendid people, with unearthly beautiful faces, watching her arrival. She could not see them, or their palace, clearly; but she felt them. Two figures grew solid and came walking towards her. One was a tall, white-skinned woman wearing black armour. The other was an older man, with thickly curling dark hair and seashells in his beard, who wore a long tunic, greenish-purple bordered with white. She'd seen the man once before: through the smoke of a brazier, in the Sacred Enclosure at Seatown. The winged horse bent his head and snorted eagerly. The man in the sea-coloured robe came up and stroked his velvety muzzle, and rubbed him between the eyes.

'His name is *Pegasus*,' he said to Andromeda. 'It means the fountain horse.'

'Is he yours?'

'He is my child,' said the God of making and breaking, known as Poseidon to the Greeks. 'As you are, but differently. But he belongs to himself.'

Andromeda looked around. 'Where is this place?'

'This is shining Olympus,' said the armoured woman. 'Home of the Gods.'

'But I'm not a Greek!'

'Not yet. You will be. You have opened the springs, *S'bw'r*. And mended a family quarrel; you and Perseus together. Well done.'

'Are you Athini?'

'I am.' The Goddess turned to the God, as if Andromeda's part was over. 'Well, is it peace, uncle? Your Medusa has been freed, and I shall place her in honour.' She thrust out her hand, in a brusque, boyish gesture.

Poseidon took the hand, with a warm smile. 'It's peace, my dear.'

Andromeda knew there must be something more. She was coloured mist, and so were the Olympians. They were as real as she, but there was something more, far greater, behind the veils. She and Perseus hadn't struggled, and suffered, just to heal a quarrel between outsize human beings—

'Will there be cities that *aren't* built on hills? In valleys and on the shore, the way Papa Dicty says they should be? Will the people ever be fearless?'

'Sometimes,' said the Goddess of Wisdom, and her dazzling, sorrowful smile filled Andromeda's eyes, blinding her sight. Olympus vanished.

The sea was calm, the waves just washing over the rock of sacrifice. She slipped down from Pegasus's back and stood ankle deep in seawater, to take off the bridle of purple yarn. He blew warmly on her shoulder. She kissed him: he sprang away, and swiftly disappeared into the bright distance.

Perseus was there, waves breaking over his sandals.

'You freed the Medusa?' said Andromeda.

'Yes.' He touched the *kibisis*, which was strung on his belt. 'She's here . . . I thought rescuing you was *my* plan. I was going to turn the sea monster to stone, so you wouldn't have to die. But it was that fantastic horse. He was born from her, when I struck off her head. *That* was how they meant me to save you. Is the horse yours?'

'He's called Pegasus. He belongs to himself. But the springs are opened.'

'What springs? What does that mean?' said Perseus.

'I think I know,' said Andromeda. 'Only I thought I was dying for justice.'

The churning waves had been contained as if in a large bowl, they hadn't reached the quayside. The priests of Melqart, having seen the Lord of Earthquake calmed, were hurrying to reclaim the sacrifice: the sacred barge was already on its way out. They shared a look which said *talk about it later.*

The procession returned to the city: Andromeda in the midst of it, still dressed in gold, the priests trying hard to make out

186

that the triumph was theirs. There was a lot of blowing of long horns, and censing of Andromeda with incense smoke. She ignored the priests, but she didn't ignore the people. She gave them her hands, her smiles, she stopped and talked. Everyone seemed to know where we were going, I just went along with the crowd. Finally we reached a temple precinct, high up in the massive, many-storeyed labyrinth of Haifa. 'This is the temple of Baal-Melqart,' said Andromeda. 'I have something to do here.'

Baal means 'lord', as I found out later. 'Melqart' I can't translate.

Someone must have sent a runner to the palace while we were on our progress through the streets. Andromeda's mother was already there, in a great stone court surrounded by huge, strange buildings. She came through the ranks of priestly servants, in her gold and purple. She'd repaired her make-up but she was still looking shattered. She held out her hands, almost hesitant. 'My daughter?'

The princess and her mother embraced. It was a stately embrace, not a hug. I had the feeling that Cassiopeia, the great queen, did not know *how* to hug. If she'd ever known, she'd taught herself it was a weakness she couldn't afford. Then Andromeda knelt, kissed her mother's hands, stood up again and rounded on the priests, who were hovering around the royal pair in large numbers.

'You didn't have to chain me,' she said, in Greek, to the big fat one in the most elaborate robes and the tallest of the gold cone hats. She spoke as if she knew the brute personally, and I suppose she did. 'I was willing.'

She strode up the court, until she stood in front of a brazier that burned at the feet of a gigantic statue of the God. She stripped off the gold dress, ripping through the soft wires, so it fell from her with a chiming of metal on stone; and raised her arms above her head, holding up the bridle she'd made for

Pegasus. She spoke in a language I didn't know, and dropped it onto the holy fire. Flame leapt up and flowed around her, without touching a hair of her head.

We don't sacrifice to the Great Mother, aside from the occasional basket of fruit. But apparently when this happens, it means the God is satisfied.

'Now I am free,' said Andromeda, standing there in her shipwreck rags.

She glanced from side to side, looking like a real, snotty highborn princess for the first and only time in our acquaintance. 'Someone bring me some clothes!'

Someone brought her a gold-bordered mantle; in a hurry.

Then Cassiopeia said her own prayers of thanksgiving, and burned incense, while Andromeda and I stood by. There was cheering and singing going on outdoors. I thought we should get out there and have flowers thrown at us, be sprayed with wine, *celebrate*. But we were not yet out of trouble. The priests had been organising something. A group of them had scurried off into the inner courts as soon as we reached the temple. Suddenly they reappeared, with a gaggle of old women swathed in white, their head tied up in bindings jaw to chin, as if they were corpses. The big fat priest prostrated himself before the queen, which gave his cohorts a chance to form up and block our exit. He heaved himself upright, looking pleased with himself, and began to make a solemn speech, with holy gestures—

'Speak Greek,' snapped Cassiopeia.

'The noble princess Andromeda may not leave our precincts, Great Queen. She is dedicated to Baal-Melqart, who has spared her to spend her life in his service.'

That was a bad moment. Andromeda looked stunned, completely taken aback. I thought they could do it. The priests could keep her here, it was sacred law. And I was helpless, I couldn't fight our way out, it would be sacrilege—

For a moment the Great Queen felt the same. I literally saw the blood drain from her face, leaving the dark skin grey. Then a light dawned in her beautiful eyes. She smiled, most graciously. 'I'm afraid that's an honour Andromeda is not free to accept.' And she turned to *me*, to my amazement—

'My daughter is betrothed to Perseus son of Zeus.'

'I *am*?' said Andromeda. 'When did that happen?'

'Earlier,' said the queen, firmly. 'You are promised in marriage to the hero who tamed the earthquake. This is the will of the Gods, and you may not refuse.'

'I'm sorry,' I'd forgotten all about it, but now I remembered, and I was scared. 'Andromeda, I can explain, I was in a hurry, I had to, to, you see—'

'Of course, noble Perseus, I accept. A princess has no choice in whom she marries. I shall gladly obey my royal mother.'

The priests saw that they were defeated. I was blushing hard and Andromeda's black eyes were gleaming with pure wickedness—

There was a big to-do out in the precinct. Kephus rushed into the sanctuary, hustling along with him a younger man, who was also wearing fancy-dress armour. A bunch of shiny soldiers clattered after them and clashed their swords in salute.

'Andromeda!' cried Kephus, spreading his arms wide. 'Thank the God you're safe! This is wonderful news! We had not dared to hope!'

'It is sometimes the way of the Mighty Ones,' intoned the chief priest. 'The willingness is all. Sincere submission to the Will of the God, as it is revealed to His Priests, is sometimes all that is required. Submission, and of course a very substantial offering, which is yet to be negotiated—'

Cassiopeia gave him a dirty look.

'Yes, yes,' broke in Kephus. 'Now, Andromeda, you remember Phineus, don't you? Your fiancé? Before this thing with the earthquake God blew up?'

'I remember Phineus,' said the princess, with a brief glance at the warrior. 'I remember you favoured him, Daddy. It didn't get further than that.'

'Kephus—' The queen tried to shut him up. 'This is *not* the moment.'

The king turned on her. 'This *is* the moment! Your Majesty, with the greatest respect, right now your daughter's a rejected sacrifice. She can't remain unmarried after what's happened. If you let them, the priests will have her locked in a convent before sundown. We have to take this very good opportunity—'

Phineus, in his flashy armour, was looking ridiculously hopeful. Cassiopeia was looking daggers. Andromeda was plain exasperated. There was a mad rumour, afterwards, that said I came to blows with Andromeda's so-called 'fiancé'. Or else I turned the Medusa Head on him and his pals, and reduced them to garden ornaments. All nonsense. All I did was stand there. I *may* have set one of my hands on the sheathed *harpe*. They didn't know about the Medusa, but they all knew (or they thought they knew) that I had the power to still an earthquake.

'Father-in-law,' I said, politely. 'You've got to be kidding.'

We had to let them marry us, before we could get away from Haifa. Cassiopeia wanted a huge wedding, we wanted to make it fast. We compromised. The palace secured us a westward passage on one of the last ships of the season: and we did the full royal wedding; shorter version. The best part was when we rode around the city in a chariot, dispensing coin to the populace. We enjoyed that, especially because, as was the custom, this largesse came out of the priestly coffers. The rest was endless, tedious ceremonies: hours of standing around weighed down by gold-crusted robes, and choked by incense.

After the wedding itself we were escorted to our nuptial

chamber by about fifty ladies and gentlemen of the court. They stayed the whole night. Everything's public, for Phoenician Royalty. In a way it was a kindly custom. It was supposed to let two people who'd never met before get aquainted, before the bride was taken away to a country she'd never seen, to live among strangers. We all sat up and talked.

The next morning we stood on the deck of our westbound ship, while the rowers pulled out of the harbour. Andromeda stared and stared, as the city diminished, her dark face set and still. I knew she was thinking of the injustice and cruelty that would continue, and there was nothing she could do—

'Maybe we'll come back.'

'No,' she said, with finality. 'I don't think so.'

The towers of Haifa grew smaller until the anthill palace was a jagged white smear, and we could no longer see the rock of sacrifice. The sea was all around.

12

The ship was the *Panagia* of the Minoan Line. The sailors
called her *Our Holey-one* (*Panagia* means 'All Holy', a
Greek title for the Great Mother). She wasn't unseaworthy, in
spite of this jibe, but she was a battered old lady, unwieldy
under sail; and the rowers were no Argonauts. We had two
cabins and a stateroom, as befitted our rank. In fact we had
the ship to ourselves, aside from the captain, his sailors and a
few marines; it was very late in the season for passengers. We
spent our days sitting under a rather tattered purple awning
outside our cabins, wrapped in rugs, talking, or just watching
crowds of silver drops slither down the tarnished tassels of our
canopy.

There were no storms, but it rained a lot.

I told her that I'd remembered what was really going on,
when I was with the Grey Sisters. How she'd been left stranded
in the wild sea with a quivering, useless hulk, helpless as a

baby. '*How* did you survive that? I just can't imagine—'

'I wasn't alone,' she said. 'You were telling me what to do. I knew you were in that other world, and you were fighting for our lives too.'

She took my hand, and I turned so I could look into her face.

'I was going to die, and it was just,' she said. 'It was my choice. Then I rode Pegasus and I saw everything differently: I saw the power of the flying marks, and what they might mean to the world. But now it's as if *nothing* was really mine. I went through all that fear and shame, I was chained to the rock, because Athini and Poseidon had quarrelled, and what happened to me was the way they made up. I know it's not the whole truth, but it rankles.'

I nodded, I felt the same.

'I thought I had the Supernaturals fooled,' I said. 'I didn't know why they'd given me that horrible task, but I was going to beat them at their own game, and use the Medusa Head to save your life. You *were* saved by what I did, and I should be satisfied. But I keep thinking, *why couldn't they just tell me—?*'

'You saw the Medusa's face in the shield,' said Andromeda. 'I leapt into the sky with Pegasus. It's like pictures in the fire, pictures that tell eternal truths. Maybe they told us what we were doing, the only way that they can speak to mortals. We still know what we did, though we can't put it into words. But we aren't *there* any more, in the world where eternal truths are things you can touch.'

'And now everything seems flat and thin.'

'Not everything,' said Andromeda, and grinned at me.

I pulled her close, burrowed my chin into her scented hair, and held her tight: I could forgive the Supernaturals for pushing me around, as long as it ended like this.

'What did you do all day, when you were a princess? Was it all ceremonies?'

She laughed. 'No! I had my weaving: and my household duties. But mostly I studied: for many hours, every day, with my mother, with my teachers and alone.'

This made me uneasy. 'Did you like that?'

'Yes I did. But I won't miss Haifa, if that's what you're thinking.' She sat up, and gripped my shoulders, fiercely. 'I only came to life when I met you.'

We might have wished the voyage could go on for ever, except that we longed to get home, and be married properly. We had decided the wedding in Haifa didn't count. We didn't want those priests to have anything to do with something so important. We wouldn't be married until we stood together, in the Sacred Enclosure in Seatown, with our friends around us. We talked a lot about that day, and about our friends, less and less about the immense things we'd been part of, as the rainy days went by. The otherworld would never fade from our minds and hearts, but we had to deal with what lay ahead, and we were anxious for our friends and family on Serifos. Had the king been content to leave Dicty's people alone, once I was out of the way? We were afraid that was too much to hope for.

We reached Paros on a calm evening, and the captain said a fond goodbye. He was puzzled by two royal Phoenician passengers, travelling without a single attendant; but we'd brought him good luck. Not a breath of contrary wind, not so much as one white storm-horse cresting the waves. It was unheard of at this season! The Ocean God had smiled on us indeed ... It was dark when the Panagia's boat delivered us to the dock. The Mother Temple of Paros Port was a blaze of lights: people were celebrating the new moon of the eleventh month. We'd left our baggage to be unloaded with the Panagia's cargo tomorrow: we were travelling light. I reached over my shoulder to touch Athini's shield, I checked that the drawstring purse was still at my belt, along with the *harpe*.

The winged sandals had disappeared overnight, when I was staying in the Men's Palace.

'Still there?' murmured Andromeda.

I nodded.

We'd managed to pick up some news from Serifos, on the last stages of our voyage, and it wasn't good. We didn't know what kind of reception committee might be waiting. There was no crowd to hide us, on a rainy evening at the start of winter. We wrapped ourselves in our cloaks, shadowing our faces, we didn't want to be recognised. I knew of a taverna where we should find friends, and information we could trust. I looked from right to left, and something hit me like a rock in the midriff.

'Perseus! Perseus!'

It was Kefi.

Our mule boy saw that it was Andromeda with me, let go and grabbed her instead. 'Kore! Kore! I thought you were dead! Dead like a rat! But Papa Dicty told me to meet every ship from the east and I did, and here you are!'

'Is the boss all right? What's going on at home?'

But he wouldn't say another word until he'd dragged us to a hole-in-the-wall foodshop in a dark alley: just a couple of tables lit by one smoky lamp. A fat old woman sat knitting behind the counter, there was no one else in the place.

'What's the matter with the Sea Urchin?' I asked.

The Sea Urchin was the taverna where we had contacts.

'Not safe!' cried Kefi, shuddering violently. 'Not safe! Nowhere's safe. The king knows you're on your way.' He stared at us, wide-eyed. 'Terrible things, terrible things are going on! We're at war!'

Andromeda and I felt the grip of fate, closing over us again.

Kefi told us that the boss, my mother and the rest of the household had been 'all well enough' when he last saw them, four days before. But he broke down in tears when we pestered him with questions, so we couldn't find out the details. He'd been sent to rescue us, he said, because the boss knew we were bound to travel via Paros, and 'bad Paros people' might deliver us to king Polydectes. The fat woman, whom Kefi called Aunt Noussa, had been letting him sleep under a bench. She insisted on giving us bread and sausage, and a jug of watered wine. Then Kefi took us up the shore by paths through the dunes, for about a mile. Bozic the smuggler was waiting there with his caique. He said he'd take us to Serifos, and try to put us ashore safely.

'Then I'm off. Got things to do. You understand, great lady, noble Perseus?'

I understood. Our secret ally, who'd been our lifeline through the truce, wasn't going to risk his neck in open war. I didn't blame him, but it wasn't a hopeful sign.

The wind was with us. We sailed by Antiparos and Sifnos, keeping clear of any vessel we spotted. In the grey dawn, the lights of the High Place were like a bundle of stars, clearing the western horizon: then we saw tiny pinpoints all over the holy hill, the watchfires of an army. Seatown waterfront was completely dark. It looked strange: there were so few masts in the harbour, and there seemed to be gaps in the skyline I knew so well. Bozic, who was managing both the sail and the steering oar, changed tack. We signalled, and moved slowly across the mouth of the harbour bay against the wind; past the headland and across the mouths of the dark inlets. We made our signal light again, keeping a healthy distance. At last we saw a light in reply. Someone was on the rocks at the mouth of the third inlet, sweeping a torch to and fro: *one, two*, and a pause, *one, two*, and a pause. It was the right response, agreed long ago. But who was wielding that torch? It was just light enough for us to see each other's faces. Bozic looked at me, and shrugged.

'It's the signal,' I said. 'Go in, closer.'

Kefi flung himself in the bottom of the boat, and lay there whimpering. I crouched by Andromeda, ready to duck if I heard arrows, my hand on the *harpe*. The figure on the reef had quenched his torch, and was waving something like a white flag. I saw the splashes of red, blue, yellow—

'Honest colours,' breathed Andromeda.

It was Aten, wearing his customary white kilt and nothing else in spite of the cold; and not a sleek black hair out of place. Bozic brought the caique alongside the rocks, silently. The sail lost the wind and fell loose. Andromeda stood up, and uncovered her head. 'Welcome back, Princess Andromeda,' said our imperturbable Egyptian, bowing to her gravely. 'You too, Perseus.'

'What's the news?' I demanded.

'Not good,' said Aten, folding the piece of weaving Andromeda had given to Anthe, and tucking it in his belt. 'But not bad. Is Kefi with you?'

'I'm here! I'm here!' cried the muleboy. He scrambled onto the side and leapt. Andromeda and I followed with more care: and the caique slipped backward. Its dun coloured sail and drab paintwork were soon invisible in the dawn mist.

'We have lookout points here on the headland and on West Hill,' said Aten. 'We saw you, and a runner has been sent to the boss. Everyone is in the Enclosure. I'll take you there, the men can spare me for an hour.'

'What happened to Seatown?'

'Too much for me to tell—' Aten's breath hissed, he swooped on something that Kefi had picked up: a hollow wooden tube, like a flute with no stop holes.

'I'll take that, Kefi.'

'What is it Mr Egyptian?' the mule boy asked, nervously. 'Is it magic?'

'No, it's a weapon. Don't touch the darts, they're poisoned.

197

And I wish you would remember I'm a Peruvian.'

On the headland we found Aten's lookout team, hidden among the rocks. They greeted us with joy, but Aten quickly led us onward.

'It began as soon as you were gone, Perseus,' he said. 'Trouble, just trouble at first. There were fights on the waterfront, and attacks on property: on my farm among other places. We knew what the king was up to, we handled the incidents ourselves, as quietly as possible. But the king said the boss must accept High Place troops in Seatown, because of the unrest—'

'And the boss refused.'

'Of course. Then there was the hostage raid. But you'll hear about that.'

We could see the whole of Seatown now, lying very still. It looked so small, so humble and helpless after the towers of Haifa. There was a pall of smoke over the gaps I'd noticed from the sea. Aten touched my shoulder and Andromeda's, motioning us to get below the horizon. Kefi was already crouching low—

'Be careful to stay in cover until we reach the fence. They have archers, and a big siege catapult, maybe more than one. They've been bombarding the town with Greek fire.'

'Great Mother,' whispered Andromeda. 'Are there many dead?'

Greek fire is made of oil and pitch, with some added ingredient to make it stick like glue. A bolus dunked in the stuff and set alight is deadly for the full range of a military catapult. It clings, and it burns just about anything. It is outlawed.

'Not many,' said Aten calmly. 'And he has respected the Sanctuary, so far.'

The Enclosure was right under the High Place, well protected by a shoulder of the hill: but the people were taking no chances. There was a team of men and women in all kinds of makeshift armour out with buckets, drenching the fence. The morning glory vines had withered, or been stripped clear. I looked up at the hillside, where the brambles had ripped me to bits after Polydectes' party. Everything was brown and wintery now, except for the black swathes of fire. 'I'll leave you,' said Aten. 'I have to get back. Tell Dicty all's well enough, no sign of troops moving in the east.' Kefi ran to a man in armour: hardened leather with metal plates sewn onto the breast and shoulders, shin protectors and armguards. He came hurrying over, dragging off an antique helmet with a crest of motheaten horsehair. It was Palikari.

He hugged me, and Andromeda: tears standing in his eyes. 'It's not as bad as it looks,' was the first thing he said, and then he seemed lost for words, just staring at us. 'So the monster didn't eat you, Andromeda?'

'Perseus saved me,' said Andromeda. 'We'll tell you everything, but it'll wait. What's wrong Pali? Why are you looking like that? *Where's Anthe?*'

'She's . . . she's inside. Come on.'

The Enclosure was so crowded I thought the whole town was in there. Then I realised it was mainly old people, young mothers, little children and babies. I was shocked. My heart sank, it was worse than I'd imagined. The armed camp of Seatown, which had always been there under the skin of our calm daily life, had been reduced to a last, helpless remnant—

The boss was marshalling a bucket chain. He took off his round hard cap, and beamed at us. 'My dear young people, I'm so glad to see you safe. Well done, Kefi. Now it is *not* as bad as it seems. We are the rearguard here. We're waiting to evacuate the infirm. Our neighbour islands are not taking sides, but they've agreed to give the children, the old and sick a safe passage and temporary refuge.'

'We have an army, Perseus,' broke in Palikari. 'I should have told you, first off. The villages are empty, our troops are in the hills. Some of the matriarchs have holed-up in the mountain caves, they'll be our supply posts. The rest are here.'

'Holy Mother intends to stay put,' said Dicty. 'But I think now the Greek Fire has appeared I'll have to change her mind.'

He looked sombre, despite his cheerful smile, and very weary: but he did not look beaten. I would never have imagined it, but in a strange way war-hating Papa Dicty seemed in his element. There was such a purposeful bustle going on. Every able-bodied man and woman had something to do, even the children: I saw the boss's style in that. It wasn't *all* that different from the taverna kitchen on a big night—

'Where is Anthe, Papa Dicty?' demanded Andromeda. 'Where is lady Danae?'

'They're in the hospital,' said the boss. 'Your mother's well, Perseus—'

'But *Anthe*—? Is she all right?'

There was a silence, long enough to terrify us.

'Anthe was wounded,' said Pali. 'We raided the High Place, she was part of it. But she's going to be all right.' He looked at the boss. 'Isn't she—?'

Andromeda had set off at a run for the hospital building.

'I believe so,' said the boss. 'I hope so. Let's go and see her.'

Anthe was lying at the end of the long ward, which was warm and dim after the cold morning outside. Braziers glowed at intervals, the air was full of the acrid, sickroom scent of burning herbs. My mother knelt beside the bed, her hair bound up in the Summer Queen scarf, with a bowl of water and a sponge: wiping our wildcat's face and hands. I could see bandages in the neck of Anthe's shift. Her eyes were half open, her head moved from side to side, but she didn't know me when I bent over her and said her name. Andromeda was on the other side of the bed, holding Anthe's wrist—

'The pulse is fast and broken,' she muttered. 'There's a rash and the fever's very high. Is it brain fever, my lady?'

'We think so,' said Moumi calmly. 'But she's past the worst.' Her tired face broke into a beautiful smile. 'Perseus, my son. Kore, my daughter. You came back!'

'*The little white wild convulvulous* ...' whispered Anthe, recognising no one.

The holy sisters moved about the ward, dosing patients, encouraging others, or sitting quietly by some silent body for whom all the pain and fear was over.

'We had trouble in Seatown,' said the boss, softly. 'It began soon after you left, Aten and Pali will have told you. The king offered to place armed troops in the town: I declined. He offered terms, we refused them, and held by the truce. He then decided to take his own people hostage.'

'His own people?' I repeated. 'Huh? You mean the people of Serifos?'

'No,' said Pali, without taking his eyes off Anthe. 'The dancing girls, up at the High Place. Some of the boys, too. He said they were working for the enemy. Some enemy he'd invented ... *We* all knew that it was the king's own men who'd been organising the "unrest". He was going to kill them if the boss wouldn't let the soldiers into Seatown. So we organised a raid. It was mainly the Yacht Club kids, and Aten: but I was in it, and Anthe. We had inside help. We broke into the High Place, we *almost* got the hostages out without raising the alarm. But it went wrong. Gliko was killed, Anthe took an arrow in the shoulder. It wasn't dangerous, she was fine. Then she got this fever—'

'She isn't going to die, Pali,' said my mother. 'Yesterday I wasn't sure, today I know she'll live.' She set the bowl aside and stood up. 'Well, Perseus?'

'I did it, mother—'

I didn't get any further. Holy Mother marched up with two

sisters, smacking her cane down hard at every pace. 'Ah, Perseus, here you are. What took you so long, eh? We're ready for her now, Danae.' The sisters stripped the coverlet, censed Anthe with healing smoke, and deftly moved her onto a stretcher. 'Don't *panic*, young man,' said Holy Mother to Palikari, who had gone bloodless. 'We're taking her to bathe. We're not going to make a nun of her; you'll have her back soon.'

We left the ward with Anthe, but the boss took us to another of the wattle and daub buildings, while Holy Mother led her stretcher-bearers to the bathing place. Stores of all kinds were stacked high, blocking the windows. Women of Seatown were tallying reserves of oil and grain, others were busy at a long table. I thought they were sewing. When I looked twice I saw that they were fletching arrows, which were being delivered in bundles by children—

'Welcome to my taverna,' said Dicty, dryly. 'For the moment . . . The little gods are around here somewhere, and the mules are safe too. I know you care about those mules as much as if they were human, Perseus. Are you two hungry? We'll have our welcome home meal later. I have a caramelised onion broth, braised wild rabbit, a dish of spiced eggs; herbed barley bread. Greens are unavailable, alas, but I have a gratin of root vegetables, baked with fennel seed. I can give you good watered wine now, and toasted rolls with a very nice pâte of quince and figs. The sisters make excellent preserves.'

We sat on baskets of dry goods. Papa Dicty mixed the wine, Moumi and Palikari set out the bread and pâte. We had not realised it, but we were starving.

'The raid to free the hostages was a victory to be proud of,' said the boss. 'I don't regret it. But it was a breaking point. Since the king had not committed any overtly hostile act, although we knew he was responsible for the "troubles" in

Seatown, the young people could be accused of attacking the High Place during a truce. Polydectes at once sent a herald to inform us that we were at war. But all would be well if the lady Danae agreed to become his bride. We thanked the herald and sent him on his way.

'I ordered the Yacht Club contingent off the island at that point, before the king decided to demand that I hand them over. Then the Greek Fire bombardments began, and we moved in here. There's been a lull: things were quiet for a day or two. Last night another herald arrived. The king demands that we give up Danae to him, "for her own safety", and then, or so he claims, hostilities will end.'

'And if you don't?'

'If we don't, he will come and take her.'

'You have to let me go,' cried Moumi (it sounded as if it wasn't the first time she'd tried this line). 'This time you have to!'

'My dear Achaean,' said the boss. 'We will not give you up. You are our sister and our daughter, you have lived with us for years. It would be disgraceful.'

'May I speak?' Balba the weaver stood up from the table where the munitions were being prepared, and folded her arms. 'You have nothing to say in this, Danae of Argos. Seatown will not give you up, it's a matter of self-respect. And if we did, it'd do us no good. The king has gone mad, he's going to stop at nothing.'

Papa Dicty nodded. 'Thank you, Balba. She's quite right, Perseus. We've reached the point where the only thing we can do is resist, by force of arms.' He sighed, hard. 'Cost what it may cost.'

This is why he got rid of me, I thought: so he could do this.

'What about me, and the Medusa Challenge? Does he remember sending me to fetch him a wedding present?'

'I don't know what he remembers,' said the boss, with a wry grin. 'We've heard no more about his courtship of Hippodaemia. A while ago he told us you were dead, and perhaps he believed it. But he knows you're alive now. The news that you two were on your way reached the Turning Islands days ago: the message must have been passed by faster ships than the *Panagia*. That's when we sent Kefi to Paros.'

Andromeda nodded. 'The news that we'd survived must have left Haifa before we did. But does the king know that Perseus has the Medusa Head?'

Palikari and the boss stared at me. So did my mother.

'You *have* it?' Palikari looked me up and down. 'Then where is it?'

'Right here.' I touched the *kibisis*. They peered at it, bewildered. The magic bag didn't look big enough to hold a large apple. 'I know it doesn't look like much but it's Chaldean magic, like the *harpe*. Trust me, the Snakehead is in there.'

'No,' said Papa Dicty slowly: seeing what this meant. 'I don't think he knows that you have the Head. What do you intend to do, Perseus?'

The boss and I looked at each other, and I realised that everyone in the room, down to the kids with their bundles of arrows, was holding their breath, watching us and listening with intense attention. 'I think he'll talk to me, if I offer. I think he'll let me walk in there. I plan to take him his wedding present.'

The king's brother, my good master, looked at the strange little pouch, looked at me, and nodded. 'You go with my blessing,' he said.

We got as far as the cemetery, the old boundary of the truce, before we were stopped. We wore no wreaths or garlands. We carried no green branches, or anything like a herald's staff. We had no company, it was just me, Palikari and Andromeda.

The soldiers at the boundary were common troopers, they checked us for weapons and asked no questions. They treated Andromeda with decency, I have to report; but they were thorough. Naturally, they asked me to hand over Athini's shield and the *harpe*.

'No,' I said. 'The shield is part of the gift I've brought for the king, and you can't touch the knife. It's been used in sacrifice: it's sacred.'

No one can say we didn't give Polydectes warning.

Some of the soldiers came with us. We passed through the gates, into the fortress, escorted by armed men. The High Place didn't look much different from the last time we'd seen it, on a summer evening; though there was more going on in the armoury and the forges. A fortress is a fortress, it's always a place of war. A runner had been sent ahead to tell the king that Perseus was here and wanted to parley. We waited in the grey winter noon, to find out how the king would respond.

Polydectes was at his midday meal. We were invited to join him.

We were taken to the banqueting hall where the wedding-plans feast had been held. We were not announced this time, or offered places. We were led into the centre of the room, into the hollow square between the tables. Everything looked so much smaller by daylight, and compared with the palace of Haifa. The walls were dirty yellow. Up near the rooftree I saw traces of a red and blue frieze, scallop shells and dolphins: it made me think of Popo the house-painter.

The king was alone with his commanders and chief officers. About thirty men, all told; and servants. No women. I scanned the faces, and spotted the tall old ruffian with the ponytail. The fat slob, and the scrawny young blood with the armlets and the goatee beard. The ones who had insulted my mother, last time I'd been here. It didn't mean so much as it had. But I kept faith with the big kid I had been, so short a time ago: I remembered them. And there was Polydectes looking down from the high table, the sunburst mantle cast over his armour; a bronze circlet around his brow.

He raised a finger and murmured something to the steward behind him. I remembered that smug individual too. The steward passed on the order. Our escort of troopers left the hall, as did all the servants except the steward. The king's guards then barred the doors and stood in front of them ... This is beyond reason, I thought. He thinks he's going to murder us, in cold blood, and they're all in it with him.

We'd have had to be pretty stupid not spot the barred doors as a threat. But we showed no alarm.

Polydectes leaned on one elbow, and took a draught of wine. 'Where's your mother?' he said to me. As if he was talking to a little boy.

'My mother is unwell, she send her regrets. You know how it can be when people are short of clean water, and eating poorly. Fevers spread.'

We were not short of clean water in the Enclosure. Nor of food, not at all.

'So you left her behind, in concern for my health. I'm touched. Well, what else do you have to say? What's this parley about? I'm listening.'

'I want you to leave here,' I said. 'You've gone too far. Serifos has chosen a different king. I want you to get out, right now. Take your personal goods, take your companions.' I looked around the tables. 'Soldiers or nobles, anyone who chooses to stay will face punishment. Everyone here should judge his own guilt. If you know you've done things that merit banishment or death, then leave with Polydectes.'

I cannot believe that the king had no sense of doom. He knew who I was. He'd sent me to fetch him the Medusa, assuming the quest would kill me, and I was back again, alive and well. But he laughed, as if the world was on his side.

'This is my brother's idea of a challenge! And who delivers it? An overgrown baby, a *cocktail waiter*, and—' He bared his teeth, leering at Andromeda. 'A rejected sacrifice. We won't call her by a worse name. But they do say, around the docks of the Middle Sea, that the priests discovered you and your big boyfriend had, shall we say anticipated your wedding vows? You were no longer fit for the God.'

'Ooooh!' lisped one of my pet hates, the creep with the goatee. 'Look at him snarl! We're so *fwiytened*, Perseus!'

'You and your damaged goods will stay here, boy. The cocktail waiter will have his nose and ears docked. We'll send him back to fetch the lady Danae—'

'*Go on*,' hissed Palikari. 'Before he runs out of talk. *Go for it*, our kid.'

I looked at Andromeda. Call me a coward, I needed her consent. She stared back at me, black eyes hard as the king's laughter, and her lips moved.

Do it.

'Well,' I said unslinging the shield and loosening the drawstring. 'If you won't leave, then stay. Polydectes, you sent me to fetch you the head of the Medusa. In the name of Great Athini, *here she is.*'

Andromeda and Pali dropped to the floor, burying their faces in their mantles, when they heard me call on Athini. The snakes wrapped themselves around my hand, dry and warm, welcoming my touch. I turned the shield, and held up the severed head, so that I looked at the grievous beauty of the Medusa, but the king and his chosen companions met the terror of her unreflected gaze. The king died at once: in the act of starting backward, his hands thrown up. Some of them had time to jump up from their seats or dive under the table: but the guards had no time to unbar the great doors. The king's men tried to hide their eyes, they ran around the hall screaming. But the Medusa Head compelled them, the way she'd compelled those fleeing warriors on the twilight plain in Africa. They had to look at her.

I hunted them down, until they were all stone. Not one of them escaped.

I stowed the Medusa back in the *kibisis* and sat on the floor, because my knees had given way. Everything was dark, a darkness of mind and body. You don't use a weapon like that and feel nothing. 'It's over,' I croaked. 'You can open your eyes.'

Pali and Andromeda raised their heads. We huddled together, staring at the appalling, silent carnage: unable to speak or move, as if we'd been turned to stone ourselves. 'I'm sorry, Pali,' I mumbled. 'I promised we'd both be armed when I came up here again. Not much of a scrap.'

'We aren't out of this yet,' said Pali.

'We can't arm ourselves,' Andromeda realised. 'All the weapons are stone.'

Palikari jumped to his feet.

'Come on! We're wasting time—'

When we got the doors unbarred, the soldiers were waiting on the other side. Pali and Andromeda were behind me: I had the harpe and great Athini's shield. They must have heard all the screaming. I don't know what they'd thought had been going on, but they were thrown into confusion when I leapt out. I drove them back into the corridor, out of the ante-chamber of the hall, disarming one man and slicing another's sword arm to the bone. Pali and Andromeda grabbed the weapons that those two let fall. So then it was three of us armed, in a narrow space, facing maybe twenty. They decided they were outnumbered, and fled from the king's house.

We had the man with the sliced arm: I took him to the doors of the banqueting hall, while Pali and Andromeda guarded my back. He fought like a hooked fish, but I made him take a good look . . . We burst out of the building, hauling him with us and stood in the open, backs together: me still gripping the terrified soldier.

The space around the king's house was full of the king's men. There must have been a hundred of them, fully armed; and they were still coming running, from all over the fortress. But they did nothing, they just stood and stared. I yelled as loud as I could, 'Polydectes the king is dead! Serifos has chosen another ruler! Spread the word, all of you. Those who fear punishment, get yourselves to the usurper's port at Megalivadi. Leave the island now, and you won't be harried!'

I shook our eye-witness. 'Tell them, soldier. Tell them what you saw.'

'Leave this place!' he howled. 'He has the Medusa! The king is stone. LEAVE THIS PLACE!'

I dropped him. There was panic all around. The gates were open when we reached them, we left the High Place unopposed, the crowd of soldiers parting and fleeing from us. We ran until we reached the ruins of the old shrine and the top of the white steps that led to the cemetery and Seatown. We were alone by then.

All the world felt strange. We turned and looked back. There was a tightness in the air like coming thunder; but it was the eleventh month, not summer. 'Hey,' said Palikari, slowly. 'It may be because of the Medusa, but this feels like—'

He'd hardly spoken when the first tremor struck.

There were more tremors that night, followed by a violent rainstorm. It wasn't earthquake season, maybe we'd triggered them somehow by using the Medusa Head: or maybe not. In Seatown everybody had been sure the Medusa was to blame, when the ground started shaking. But there was no damage down there, except for some mild flooding caused by the rain.

Days later, a party of us went to see what had happened to the High Place. We found it deserted. The encircling wall was down, and some of the buildings; including the king's house. There were no bodies in the open, either stone or flesh: we did not touch the rubble of the banqueting hall. We made a winter offering of wine and bread in the ruined shrine, and came away.

Andromeda and I were married at the full moon of the twelfth month. Everyone had moved out of the Enclosure by then. Papa Dicty's hidden army had come down from the hills, and the people were reclaiming Seatown; though rebuilding would have to wait until spring. Anthe was still in the hospital: but she was going to be allowed up for the ceremony. The night before the wedding the women and girls took Andromeda back to Great Mother's Enclosure, and they spent the night there: doing important, ritual things of the kind that will give you a cracking hangover—

Or so I've been told, by girls with no respect for holy secrecy.

I was up all night at Papa Dicty's. I didn't get very drunk, because I wanted to have a clear head for the wedding. I was getting scared, I thought I would not be able to face her if I wasn't in complete control. About four in the morning I sat with the boss by the hearth, a cosy refuge we were sharing with Taki the shipping magnate. Brébré was on my knee. Other members of the men's party were comatose on the benches, on the floor and in one case flat out on a table.

'D'you remember,' said my good master. 'Before you left on the Medusa Challenge, I said I wished I could be king of Serifos, and make you my heir?'

'Yes. And now you *are* the king.'

Our dining room had not recovered from the war with Polydectes. There was broken woodwork, scarred plaster. The carved beams above the bar were charred, the walls were black with smoke and daubed with stains we couldn't get out: the murals had suffered badly. Only fragments of the court ladies survived, the ghosts of a past that would not return. The boss looked at them: and smiled ruefully.

'Hm, maybe. But that's what I wanted to talk to you about, Perseus. You are the son of Zeus, your mother is the Argolide princess. And what can I say about Andromeda? A young woman of astounding worth and truly remarkable talents. You both belong in a bigger world than this little island, and the Mainland is the place to be, these days. Do you realise, you're already the heir of a kingdom up there?'

I looked into my wine, feeling torn in two. I loved Serifos. But once you've travelled, and mixed in great affairs, you change. You want to *do* something.

'Moumi would hate to go back, and I couldn't go without her.'

'I'm not sure about that. Your mother is a proud woman, and she's Achaean to the bone. Deep in her heart, I think Danae would *love* to go back to Argos in triumph. To be the one who changes the customs that allowed her to be treated that way—'

I kept on looking at my wine. I could feel him watching me, smiling; letting me go. He knew my mind, better than I knew myself. I tried to speak but I couldn't. He patted my shoulder. 'Time enough. Just think about it.'

'What about you?' I asked, glad to change the subject. 'Will you build a palace for yourself in Seatown? You can't rule Serifos *and* run a taverna.'

'Ah.' He grinned. 'Now that's another thing ... Frankly, I don't want to give up Dicty's. I've been thinking, maybe we'll do without having a king for a while. We'll need some kind of militia, but we've proved we don't need a king for that. We'll need to get together and make decisions about public affairs, but we know how to do *that* without a king—'

I'd heard about this new idea. Our matriarchs were very pleased with it. They didn't see it as having no king, however. They said, *of course when Papa Dicty is king he'll involve us in his business, as is proper.* I laughed and shook my head.

'You're going to spend your entire life in the Town Meeting, boss.'

'Well, well. We'll see.' He got to his feet, carefully: stretched his back and rearranged Taki, who was snoring alarmingly loud. The shipping magnate muttered something like *cuddle up, Rosey* ... and snuggled contentedly into his corner. 'Put the lamps out, Perseus, if there are any still alight. I'm off to bed.'

The gates of the Enclosure were decked in winter garlands: olive and bay; laurel and myrtle with their bright berries. There were flowers everywhere inside, woven into garlands, strung to and fro overhead: creamy hellebore and shell-pink daphne, hothouse violets, winter crocus, white starry spikes of asphodel. Scented braziers were doing their best to subdue the winter chill. I thought of Palikari and Anthe's wedding, which would be in the spring; but I didn't envy them. This was our day, these were our garlands, everything was right—

The men led me to the bathing place, being as cheerful and loud as their hangovers would allow; and left me at the door. Then it was Holy Mother again, with her hot oil, hot water, and the bronze scraper. It was *freezing* in that cave. I was surprised there wasn't ice on the cold douche. I stepped out, wrapped my towel around me, sat down and put my head in my hands. Andromeda ... I could hear her screaming at me, as she lay on the rock of sacrifice, her black eyes blazing. *Leave me alone! This is mine!* Her courage, her pride, her *backbone.* Great Mother help me.

'I don't think I can go through with this,' I said. 'I'm not her equal, I'm not ready. Holy Mother, what if I ever get on the wrong side of her—?'

She whipped away the towel, and tossed a long, fine linen tunic over my head. 'Stand up. We haven't time for you to sit around moping and whining.' She fussed with the shoulder brooches, tugged me about so the tunic draped right, and then produced a new belt, with the harpe and the *kibisis* strung on it. I recoiled. I'd given the Medusa Head, and the rest of the supernatural gear, to the nuns for safe keeping. The thing in that strange bag was not the same to me as the *Medusa*. It was a weapon, a horror. I'd been hoping I would never have to touch it again.

'It's my *wedding*. Do I have to carry those things? They should be locked up.'

'Don't argue. They're your honours, of course you wear them.' She handed me Athini's shield, and looked at me thoughtfully. 'Hm. I don't often do this. But just for once . . . You *won't* get on the wrong side of her, Perseus. You were not born to lose her. You're going to love that girl for ever, and she will love you too.'

'Until we die.'

'No, no, no. For ever.'

I walked out into the shadowless light of a winter morning, the weight of the shield on my shoulder. I stooped for a wreath to be put on my head, with that promise ringing through me: imagining that I'd had another kind of life. I was the prince of Serifos, about to meet the bride my family had chosen for me. Maybe we were in one of the big, beautiful rooms of my adopted grandfather's classic seaside mansion. The guests were famous heroes, princes and princesses, kings and queens: mingling with my old friends. The crowd would part and she would come towards me, this Haifan princess I had never met . . . And there she was, in her dark red dress with the flames woven on the bodice, under a delicate mantle worked

213

in purple thread. Andromeda. Her black eyes meeting mine, a shock of joy—

S'bw'r

S'bw'r

I took her hand, and everyone started cheering. We were pelted with sweets and flowers, the musicians played, the Seatown dance troupe danced around us. We were about to be led to the sanctuary, with further pelting: and then, in the middle of the uproar, the gates opened all by themselves. A young man in a cloak and hat stood there, a flower-wreathed staff in his hand. With him were a tall woman in black armour, with a white, sternly beautiful face, and an older man, tall as Athini, with a curling dark beard; who wore a sea-coloured tunic under a grey mantle flecked with white. Everyone knelt. The Supernaturals were not *themselves*, as Andromeda and I had seen them. They were cloaked in human bodies, but nobody could mistake them. They advanced on us, through the ranks of our people. Andromeda's patron set his hands on her shoulders, raised her to her feet and kissed her gently on the brow.

'My blessing on this marriage,' said the God of Making and Breaking, whom the Greeks call Poseidon. 'The art you carry in your mind, Andromeda, is the greatest power in the world. Ride the winged horse, open the springs.'

My half-sister Athini gestured briskly for me to stand up, folded her arms, and said: 'You've got something of mine, Perseus.'

Ah, well. Different strokes. I gave her the *kibisis*, with great relief.

'The *harpe* chooses to stay with you. But I'll have my shield back.'

I handed it over. The *kibisis* had vanished, somehow.

'Do you understand what you two did yet, Perseus?'

'I understand that *I don't know*,' I said, cautiously.

This seemed to be the right answer. Great Athini held up the shield. On the outer face, which had been blank metal, was an image of the Snakehead, beautiful and terrible. She showed all the crowd. 'Medusa, my emblem, is back where she belongs.'

Then Athini led me to the sanctuary: Poseidon led Andromeda. The ancient statue of Great Mother knelt on her red and black plinth. The Supernaturals bowed.

I looked at Andromeda and she looked at me, both of us were shaking.

'Are you all right, Perseus?'

'Just about,' I muttered. 'Are you?'

'*Yes.*'

All kinds of thoughts went through me, memories of the future, memories of the past: the way she said *I'll hold your tunic,* on the dock at Naxos. I was *terrified,* but I was not afraid. I knew that she was immortal, the same as I was. Our love would shine and burn, constant as the ever-living stars. The dark water would not part us, we would be together forever, in that world where truth is real.

AUTHOR'S NOTE

Snakehead is a fantasy based on the story of Perseus and Andromeda, and the Medusa Head – the most mysterious and maybe the greatest of all the Greek myths.

Although my retelling may seem very different from the well-known version (about a hero who kills a monster, and happens to rescue a princess on the way), I took a lot of my ideas from the ancient sources; and from the ancient history of the Mediterranean. It's true that alphabetic writing seems to have been brought to the Aegean, from the Phoenician city-states, around thirty centuries ago, in the eleventh century before Christ. It's true that there was a Great Disaster, which destroyed the island of Fira (now better known as Santorini), and dealt the incredible Minoan civilisation a blow from which it never recovered. It's true that the Minoans honoured women; that they had a culture of peace and plenty; and they seem to have worshipped one God.

As for the importance I've given to Andromeda and Cassiopeia, you have only to look up into the night sky to understand my reasoning. The ancient Greeks named *hundreds* of constellations after men and gods, half-gods, heroes and monsters. Only two women are honoured in the same way: the Ethiopean queen of ancient Haifa, and her daughter; whose Greek name means *great thinker, ruler of men.*